EIGHT BALL BOOGIE

A Harry Rigby Mystery

Declan Burke

LIB
ERT
IES

This book is respectfully dedicated to my parents,
Kathleen and Harry Burke

1

The doorbell rings at five in the morning, it's bad news, someone's dead or dying. Which was why Imelda got downstairs so quick, still in her nightdress, padding across the cold tiles of the porch. Flustered, thinking someone might be dying.

Which allowed the blademan to get in close, inside the elbows, driving the shank up hard under the chin. Blowing the artery, spattering the porch. Blood, glass, chrome – Christ, you could've hung it in a gallery.

These things happen, although not usually in shiny new towns on the Atlantic seaboard, and rarely to the middle-aged wife of an independent politician that's keeping the government in clover. But they happen. It's a crying shame, yeah, so have a cry, feel ashamed and get over it. The rest of the week is coming on hard and its brakes are shot to hell.

My job was to find out who and why, at twelve cent per word for the right facts in the right order. Enough facts, a decent hook, they might even add up to a front-page clipping for the dusty folder under my bed. Imelda Sheridan was dead, which was tough cookies on Imelda, but then every silver lining has its cloud.

Anyway, that was how it all started out.

*

It was early Monday, three days to Christmas, the morning not trying anything it couldn't handle itself. I stuck a pillow behind my back, rolled a one-skin, lacing it light, just to take the edge off. Sand in my eyes, a jellyfish in my gut, skull humming like a taut rope. The room stinking of stale breath, bored sex, cold cigarettes.

I sparked the jay, watched Denise sleep. Hadn't watched her sleep in a while, hadn't had the chance, on a second bite of the cherry and still trying to remember if I liked the taste of cherries. Asleep, relaxed, she looked her age, sneaking up slow on the right side of thirty. Dark hairs at the corners of her mouth, a nose that might have been too big if her ears were any smaller. The lips full, salmon pale, the hair chestnut with auburn streaks, shoulder-length. When they were open, the eyes were round and brown. She thought she could have lost half a stone around the hips but I liked the curves, liked that there was more of her rather than less.

She smelled the dope and her eyes flickered, focusing slow. She knuckled one eye, yawning. Then, sounding resigned, she muttered: 'Out.'

'No way, I saw chalk-dust.'

Buzzing on the jay, kidding her on.

'Out, Harry. Go home.'

'You know what time it is?'

'No, but I'd say it's about half past fuck off.' She smiled me a tired one that was half regret and half something I'd never seen before. 'C'mon, Harry. You know you have to go.'

'Alright. Jesus.'

I stubbed the jay, scrabbled for my tee shirt, shivering, sleet spattering the window.

'Want to join me in the shower?'

'No shower, Harry. There's no hot water.'

'Fuck's sakes, Dee.'

Officially, we were on a break. Officially, I was sleeping in the back room of my office over in the Old Quarter, the constant verbals costing a fortune in replacing Ben's toys.

Off the record, Denise was trying to work out if anyone would take her on with another man's kid in tow.

I pretended not to notice, the truth is a scab you don't want to pick at too often. Last night we'd been in the same place at the same time with the same amount of booze on board. That was all and that's never enough.

She sat up, draped a thin white cotton dressing gown around her shoulders. Said, her voice thin and tired: 'Just get dressed and go, Harry. Please?'

Then left, showing me how.

I got dressed, went downstairs. She was still standing in the hall, looking at the phone like it was primed, ticking. Ben lying on the living room floor, cartoons blaring from the TV, wearing dinosaur slippers, Action Man goggles around his neck. I was rapping about building a snowman if the snow stuck, how we could put mum's coat on it, Ben not paying attention, when she called me into the kitchen. She put the kettle on and didn't turn around.

'Gonzo left a message. Said he'd be home for Christmas.'

Sounding calm, like Gonzo rang every week, not excited and nauseous, like we hadn't heard from him in nearly four years.

'He say what Christmas?'

She turned, pulling the dressing gown tight. Her face was pale, her eyes huge, dark panda eyes.

'He is your brother, Harry.'

'Not my fault, Dee. No one's pinning that one on me.'

She shook her head, disappointed at herself for not knowing better.

'You'd better go.'

She pushed me down the hallway and stood in the doorway, shivering, not looking at me, arms folded. I stood two steps below, hanging in, postponing the moment when I'd have to admit I left the car in town.

'Ben should be dressed. He'll be late for school.'

'Christmas holidays, Harry. Kids get holidays at Christmas. Not like adults, who get holidays at Fuckallmas. It's Christmas, by the way.'

'I know it's Christmas. Jesus.' I scuffed at the doorstep, the hangover thick and dull, the dope not helping. The wind gusting sleet. She tucked a rat's tail tidy behind an ear, said: 'Harry—'

'What?'

'Don't think that what happened—'

'Don't flatter yourself.'

'No need,' she taunted, stung. 'Not after all you said last night.'

I fumbled for a comeback but she was already closing the door, not slamming it. I faced into the sleet and decided to shave at the office, dug out the smoke box and realised I was all out of skins. That was the shape of my week and it was only Monday morning, nine-thirty.

*

They reckoned the population around ninety thousand, and even if you discount all the Shinners who voted twice that's still a fair sized burg. Which was the plan. They took a town, just sitting there minding its own business, there not being too much of it to mind, and ripped out its guts. Relocated the locals to breeze-block suburbs that sprawled out both sides of the river, south behind the lake, halfway up the mountains, and they'd have poldered the bay if they'd thought anyone was dumb enough to enjoy wet sand between their toes. Threw up a new inner town, a high-rise jungle of credit finance depots, international call centres, multi-storey shopping malls, a software research plant masquerading as a university, most of which was financed by American corporates, most of which was offset by indigenous grants, lo-interest loans, repatriated profits. Midtown was all wide streets, tree-lined, Norman Rockwell's wet dream parachut-ed in to the Atlantic seaboard. It all took about five years to finish and no one laughed, not once.

My office was over in the Old Quarter, where Midtown bled into the docks, north of the river heading west. Five or six bustling blocks bisected by railway lines, pot-holed streets and alleyways that always seemed to wind back to the quays. Too noisy to be residential, the passing trade too random to make it worthwhile for shopping centre malls, the Quarter got to keep all its crumbling buildings, cracked pavements and old sewers.

The Quarter drew a volatile crew. Crusties laughed at the skate-kids, who went by sniggering. Winos, bums and buskers worked the crowds for the same chump change. College kids slumming it got a thrill rubbing shoulders with fairies, dips and wide-boys on the make.

I'd been sleeping on a couch in the back room of the office for a couple of months by then, getting used to the idea, starting to fit in with the faces on the streets. Mostly I liked them, respected their lack of ambition, their social inhibition. The kind that lived around the Quarter, they needed to know there was a pawnshop in the vicinity, an Army Surplus Store, a tattoo parlour. The bars had tinted windows, the porn shop didn't and the greasy spoon cafés should have at least thought about it. There were antique shops, a joint that sold organic Thai food and way too many second-hand bookstores. Out in the back lots that sloped down to the river, a couple of auto repair outfits kept things black and oily. The bars played jazz, trad and drum 'n' bass, and in the summer the air hummed with the thick smell of patchouli oil and melting tar. At night you could get stoned just driving around with the window down.

The Quarter was a good place to live, a good place to work, if your girlfriend was blind and your clients were even more desperate than you. Denise wasn't blind but that was only part of the problem. Denise and me, we had issues. I had only one, but Denise, she liked to share.

*

I made the office around ten, not breaking any records. Picked up the phone to order coffee from downstairs, got Herbie on voicemail. Sounding unusually vital at that early hour, as a rule Herbie was either stoned or asleep and Herbie toked himself into a stupor at least once a day.

'Harry – Harry? Fuck – Harry, get your arse up to Tony Sheridan's, up at the lake, back of the racecourse. The wife's spark out, throat slashed. The Dibble are trying to keep it quiet about the coke. Looks good, the shots are in the bag. Ring if you need directions.'

I didn't need. Everyone knew where Tony Sheridan lived, except maybe Tony on the nights he thought he lived with the brunette who ran Bojangles, an underage dive down near the river, although not so near it might get a proper flushing if the river ever flooded its banks.

I picked up a dictaphone and notepad. Thought about it, sucked air through my lower teeth, shook my head, thought it over some more – Gonzo home and a gory death all in the one morning, it might be a fluke and maybe not. I unlocked the bottom filing-cabinet drawer, pushed aside the false floor, pulled out the snub-nosed .38. Tucked it inside my belt, snug in the small of my back.

I cut down through the alley across from the coffee shop, crossed the footbridge into the car park. Wasted five minutes trying to remember where I might have left the car. Then I crossed the footbridge again, cut a right down towards the quays to the taxi rank.

The fat flushed cabbie didn't say a word, flicking glances in the rear-view mirror, chewing his bristly moustache, a smirk curling across his chops. I let it fly, no one had to tell me I looked for shit. The black two-piece was rumpled and creased because it was the only suit I owned and I wore it Monday through Friday, rotating the shirts until both went grey. The thin black tie came free with the suit and I unknotted it every New Year's Eve, for luck. The shoes were Italian and suede because women look at your eyes first, shoes second, and I had eyes that made women take a lingering look at my shoes.

In the business you need to look like shit. I work off people who like labels, who talk louder and not always on purpose when there's a shabby suit two barstools along, or in the booth behind the dusty plastic plants in the quiet corner of the restaurant. If a punter was desperate enough to come sidling through my door he had enough problems without worrying about why my threads were better than his. He wanted to see a suit and tie that matched. That was enough and not too much.

And they all sidled. Once in a while someone walked through the door, shoulders back and chin up, nothing to hide. They were the ones who wanted a missing dog tracked down.

Mostly, though, I looked like shit because I didn't care how I looked, couldn't afford to care. Down in the Old Quarter, two times out of three you flip a double-headed coin, it comes down on its edge.

Last time, it doesn't come down at all.

*

Herbie was slouched on his battered moped, elbows draped across the handlebars, the out-of-date tax disc. Bleary-eyed, shivering. A black woollen hat pulled low over his ears, a mop of red curls framing a face the colour of sour milk, chin and forehead a rash of angry pimples.

'What the fuck took you?'

'Your mother wouldn't give me my shoes back.'

'Better you than me.' He nodded up at the split-level villa. Three pillars supported the upper storey, the front of which was all glass, with a two-door garage below. He said, casual: 'They reckon she topped herself.'

'Cut her own throat?' I whistled. 'Brave girl.'

'Another theory runs like this. She opens the door and he gores her. Drags her to the living room, heels first, she's still kicking. So he works her own steak knife in the hole, over and back, sawing.'

'Who's telling you this?'

'Regan. Anyway, he puts the knife in her hand, lets the arm drop natural. Wants it to look like suicide. Chops some lines out on the coffee table, leaves it messy, rubs some into her gums, drops the wrap.'

'Any dabs?'

'Millions, and you watch too many movies. So – Regan says he takes his time after, grinds a boot into the wedding photo, giving it motive. Sparks a smoke, leaves a butt in the ashtray, stays around to make sure everything's kosher. Doesn't touch her up. Maybe he's a pro, Regan says, or maybe her pants are already piss and shit. Or maybe he gets his jollies clocking corpses draining out.'

'Always nice to have options. How long is she there?'

'No idea. They found her about two hours ago.'

'Who's on now? Regan?'

'Kilfeather.'

'Wanting his name in the paper?'

'He fucking better.'

Kilfeather waited, watching as I waved a card at the uniformed garda standing by the gate pillars, waiting until I ducked under the yellow tape and started up the tarmacadam incline. Then he waved me back. I ignored him, it was what he expected and I hate to disappoint. He watched me come, a sour twist at the corner of his mouth, saying, tasting the word: 'Rigby.'

'In all his tarnished glory. Who found her, Tom?'

Kilfeather catching fresh air was almost news on its own, especially if I could nail down the brand of dynamite they'd used to get him out from behind his desk. He leered down at me, six-two of obtuse duty, ruddy cheeks and no neck.

'No chance, Rigby.'

'Did he find her?'

'He who?'

'Tony he. Come on, Tom.'

He put his huge hands up, palms showing, miming a push.

'Back behind the line, Rigby. You know the drill.'

'You can't tell me who found her?'

'It's an ongoing investigation. I can't tell you anything.'

'Not like you to be shy, Tom.'

He didn't bite. I tried again.

'So what kind of investigation is it?'

'The strictly routine kind. And until it's over, I can't tell you anything.'

'You don't tell me what's going on, Tom, I'm going to assume the worst. With my imagination, you don't want to take that risk.'

His voice was flinty.

'I told you, it's routine.'

I kissed the dice.

'Because it's not suicide?'

'Who says it's not suicide?'

'No one. It's suicide?'

The ruddy cheeks flamed to life.

'Don't fuck with me, Rigby. Get to fuck out of my sight.'

I shook my head, patient.

'You want me here, Tom, where you can keep an eye on me, keep an ear on what I'm saying. Make like it's just the two of us, candles and wine, gypsies playing violins.'

He muttered something that didn't have any vowels. I kept my tone reasonable.

'It's only a job, Tom. You're doing yours, I'm doing mine. All I need's a couple of answers and I'm off, job done.'

He didn't answer, staring off across the racecourse to the far side of the lake, to somewhere above where the snow line might have been if it ever got around to snowing. I didn't blame him. When the sun shone, the view added an extra twenty grand that the house needed like a second swimming pool.

'How about this, Tom? I'll tell you what you already know and if I leave anything out you put me straight.'

'Why would I do that?'

'I hear things. I might know something you don't.'

'That's dangerous, Rigby. I could have you up for withholding information, obstructing the course of justice.'

'Perverting, Tom, the way I do it.'

He shot a glance over his shoulder, at the unmarked blue Mondeo parked to one side of the house, rasped: 'So what do I know?'

'She was found – by who we don't yet know – a couple of hours ago. Throat slit ear to ear, the wound so deep the spinal cord was almost severed. Her underwear was still intact. Coke on the coffee table, which may or may not be significant. Only fingerprints on the knife – steak knife, serrated edge – are hers. How'm I doing?'

He was back sucking lemons again.

'You forgot the toaster and cuddly toy.'

'No one commits suicide up at the racecourse, Tom. People go home from the racecourse and commit suicide, maybe. And who nearly severs their spinal cord cutting their throat?'

'Imelda Sheridan.'

'Bollocks. Who's the prime suspect?'

'You, now you know so much.'

'Me and half the town, Tom. Word gets around. How's the husband?'

He didn't like the implication.

'You're a sick man, Rigby.'

'It's terminal, too. Has he been questioned?'

'Why would we question him?'

'For spite. Overtime. He's a humpy cunt. Take your pick.'

'Say we did question him. What would we ask?'

'Where he was when it happened. Or would that be too personal?'

'Suicide isn't a spectator sport, Rigby.'

'You know the stats, Tom. Men top themselves, young men. She's what – early fifties? She has the big house, tennis courts out the back. Trotting around blinding us all with Prada and Louis Vuitton. Husband's best buddies with the chief whip, and if he fucks that up he can always fall back on the ambulance-chasing. If she's not in the social pages it means the NUJ's out on strike and the kids are reared, one an intern, the daughter away saving the rain forests, bless her cotton socks.' I cut to the chase. 'Why would Imelda Sheridan commit suicide?'

'Money isn't everything. She might have been depressed.'

I didn't like it, Kilfeather being so reasonable. It meant I was on the wrong track.

'And maybe she thought Santa wouldn't come. Who found her, Tom?'

'No can do, Rigby.'

'Jesus, Tom—'

The voice came from over my shoulder, gruff, a cement mixer learning German.

'Kilfeather?'

He didn't look down at me. I looked up to where a wide face was crowned with thin blonde hair. The suit was a size too small but a Big Top would have been a size too small. He had a Desperate Dan chin and you could have landed a helicopter on his chest in a gale. The smell of stale whiskey wafted across, harsh as petrol. I hoped, for his sake, he was drunk when he bought the camelhair overcoat.

Kilfeather smartened up.

'That's right, yeah. Brady, isn't it?'

'When I'm off-duty. Right now it's Detective Brady. Who's this fucker?'

'He's a local hack. Rigby they call him.'

'What's he doing here?'

'Sniffing around.'

'No shit, Holmes. How come he's here?'

Kilfeather shrugged, squared his shoulders, letting Brady know, he didn't appreciate the third degree.

'How come any of us are here? He heard about it, thought there might be something worth seeing.'

'He get it downtown?'

'Probably.'

'Who?'

Kilfeather shrugged.

'Who the fuck knows?'

'Find the fuck out or I'll cite you in the report. What'd you tell him?'

Kilfeather seethed, cheeks flaming. Dug the word out, rough. 'Nothing.'

'You took a while doing it.'

'He thinks she didn't top herself. I put him straight.'

'Straight – what's straight?'

'That it's an ongoing investigation but the signs point to suicide. That much he had already.'

Brady spat, pulled his belt up.

'Next time, send him to me. No – next time, bang him up.'

'Yessir. What charge?'

He looked at me for the first time, top to bottom in a sideways glance.

'Cheap shoes,' he sneered. 'And hey, Kilfeather?'

'What?'

'Get snotty again and I'll wipe your fucking nose.'

He went back to the Mondeo, lit a cigarette, caught Kilfeather throwing some juju eyeball. Rubbed his nose, slow and deliberate, so Kilfeather glared at me instead. I took the hint and left.

2

Herbie was still draped across his moped, shivering.

'Well?'

'It might not be suicide.'

'You got something?'

'Nothing you could quote in a family newspaper.'

'Fuck.'

He straightened up, blew on his hands, remembered he was wearing gloves. Stared out over the lake to the town sprawled across the foot of the mountain, a verruca out of control. Out across the five miles to the Atlantic, chopping up grey and white.

'Regan tell you who found her?'

'No.'

'Think he might?'

'Squeeze the sponge, Harry, it dries up.'

'Yeah, yeah.' I dug out the makings, bummed a skin, rolled a twist. 'Alright, leave it with me, I'll make some calls. It's already too late for the evening editions anyway.'

'Kilfeather's a bastard.'

'He's Dibble, Herb. That's his job. Anyway, Kilfeather isn't the problem. There's a big lad from out of town running the show.'

'You didn't get anything from him?'

'He didn't see me, I wasn't up a ladder. And a word to the wise. If he finds out Regan leaked you the story, Regan'll be springing a few leaks of his own.'

He swore, sparked up a ready-rolled from his grass-sprinkled pouch, eyeballing the garda leaning against the driveway pillar. Picked a flake of tobacco from his lower lip, flicked it in the garda's direction, leaving the middle finger extended. The garda stared back, placid. Herbie said: 'Think they're in on it?'

'Who – the Dibble?'

'Who else? Fuckers're into everything else.'

'Herb – why would the Dibble want Imelda Sheridan dead?'

'Maybe she was running a brothel, got the Inspector in a compromising position. Maybe she's plotting a coup, Tony for president, the Dibble got wind of it.' He shrugged, matter of fact. 'Could be anything.'

I didn't know whether to laugh or cry.

'Get off the weed, Herb. Seriously, man. Your head's in a jam jar.'

He started winding up, getting excited, tone urgent.

'This is front-page stuff, Harry. Banner headlines. Big fuck-off shots, see them a mile off, my name at the bottom. Mine, not those Fhotoprint fuckdogs.'

The agency took a cut of everything we cooked up, which bothered Herbie. It didn't bother me, thirty per cent of fuck all being approximately fuck all.

'Nail it down, Harry. I gave you this one on a plate. Coke,

suicide, possible murder, the fucking lot. What more do you need?'

'How about proof?'

'What're you talking about, proof?' He waggled his camera bag. 'The shots're ready to roll, beauts too, hole in her neck you could roll the black ball into. Only words these babies need are someone's name on a cheque.'

'What about some kind of idea of why? A detail or two?' I was stalling, watching the maroon Civic pulling up, the bodywork too fresh for it to be anything but a rental. 'It needs to be done right, Herb. We do it right or we don't do it at all.'

He heard the Civic, turned and looked. Shrugged, the anger evaporating too quick to be healthy.

'It'll be done alright, but not by us. Here's the fucking cavalry now.'

She was petite, five-two at most, the kind of late twenties that takes years of practice. The hair a tangerine peek-a-boo bob, the lipstick apricot. The smile friendly, chasing freckles across the bridge of a snub nose. The eyes deep enough to give me vertigo, wide enough to make me want to jump.

'Gentlemen.' Her accent had the faintest of northern drawls.

'Around here that's libel,' I said. I nodded towards the house. 'And I'd say the pedicure's been cancelled.'

'I'll take my chances.'

She ducked under the yellow tape, flashed a card at the garda, clicked away up the tarmacadam.

Herbie fired up the moped, the engine clattering, rattling, until the exhaust belched a tiny black cloud.

'Want a lift?'

'No, cheers. I'm in a hurry.'

He half-grinned, fiddling with his helmet strap.

'Anything I can be doing?'

'You could be running a check on Tony Sheridan. Background material, whatever we'll need to puff out the story.'

'Money?'

'Yeah, go the tragic route. All that cash and his wife slashed open. The punters love that shit.'

'Alright. I'll buzz you later.'

*

I was halfway to town, down around the cemetery and cursing myself for not bumming more skins from Herbie, when I finally remembered where I'd left the car. Which was when the Civic purred by, indicated left and pulled up on the gravel verge. She leaned across, unlocked the passenger door and pushed it open. She didn't speak, so I didn't spoil the moment.

She was a good driver. Her movements were easy, assured, and she didn't look at me as she drove. Up close I could see that the cream two-piece was raw silk. The tiny burn scar just above her left knee whitened every time she changed gear.

She got straight into it.

'What'd you get?'

'Nothing. But that's off the record.'

'Put your dick away, this is business.'

'I don't mix pleasure with business. And I don't do business with strangers. Especially ones who tell me to put my dick away.'

She suppressed a smile, not pulling any muscles doing it.

'Sorry, I'm Katie. Katie Donnelly.'

'And I'm Harry-Harry Rigby.'

'I know.'

I didn't know what to say to that. She said: 'Want to grab a coffee?'

'Always.'

We bypassed Midtown, crawling through the one-way system of the Old Quarter, the narrow streets looming three storeys high. Gaudy shop-fronts below, flaking paint and crumbling plaster above.

'Is the traffic always this bad?' she asked.

'It's Christmas week, the woolly-backs are in town for the annual exfoliation. The rest of us are here because we lack the imagination to realise the rest of the world isn't just another TV channel. What's your excuse?'

'I'm freelance, doing a piece on Imelda Sheridan for *Woman Now!* Full colour glossy, you know the score, she's the overachieving charity hound for the February issue. I did the interview yesterday, got shots of the house, her in the glad rags looking out over the lake, the full nine yards.' She sighed. 'And now this.'

'This didn't happen until this morning. How come you're still around?'

She nudged the car forward, knocked it out of gear. Fiddled with the thermostat, the windows misting up.

'It's a nice town,' she said. 'It's Christmas. I thought I'd stick around and pick up some local colour.'

'Try grey, we have forty shades.'

We edged around the corner and discovered the source of the traffic jam. He was short and squat, pushing seventy, the curly white hair topped by a WW1 leather flying helmet, complete with goggles. His face was full, moon-shaped and flushed. Standing in the middle of the road, windmilling arms issuing contradictory orders every time he turned around. His shabby overcoat billowed in the breeze.

'You should do a piece on him. He's local, he's colour.'

'He's not really what our focus groups tell us our demographic wants. Mind you, that changes every week. Who is he?'

'The local nutcase, Baluba Joe. They say he hasn't been sober in living memory. Directs the traffic when the mood takes him and then goes and gets rattlers when everything's snarled up. Harmless bugger, though.'

'I can see how our readers would be fascinated.'

She sounded smug. The car was too warm. I needed a smoke, coffee and fresh air, in that order.

'He's an old soldier.' She heard the edge in my voice, looked across for the first time since I'd sat into the car. 'He's mad, clinically insane. You can see it in his eyes but if you miss it he'll tell you himself. Says he spent three days wandering the Congo jungle after his platoon was wiped out in a Baluba ambush. Jungle's no place to be at the best of times, he reckons. But when you're eighteen years old, and your mates have been butchered with machetes and you're still wearing the spray, the screeching of a jungle at night is as close to hell as makes no odds.'

We inched past Joe. Froth flecked his lips. Horns tooted, engines revved. His eyes were haunted.

'Hold on a minute,' she said. 'I wasn't—'

'That was back in the sixties, so he's been forty years drinking anything that won't kill him outright and not really giving a fuck if it does. He told me, one night, that he knows everyone pities him. Asked me if I knew why.'

She parked with the minimum of fuss, turned off the engine.

'Harry—'

'They gave him a medal a couple of years back but he handed it back when the top brass wouldn't look him in the eye. Kind of took the gloss off it, he said. I told him he should have taken the medal, just to piss the brass off. Know what he said? "No one ever made officer got pissed off that easy."'

She stared straight ahead, stony-faced. I said: 'I'd never have made officer material. You didn't need that grief.'

She peeked at me from under an angled eyebrow.

'Was that an apology?'

'Women apologise. Men explain.'

'But we're finished now?'

'Yeah. Who gets to keep the Barry White CDs?'

*

The coffee shop, Early 'Til Latte, was run by a couple of gay hippies and sold more grass under the counter than coffee over it. We ducked through an archway into the tiny back room. Second-hand books lined the shelves. Posters on the wall advertised Feng Shui courses, Feiseanna, rummage sales. She sat on an old barstool with her back to the arch, crossing her legs at the knee. I squeezed behind the high, rickety table but not so far back I might need a telescope to see the pins. We looked at one another expectantly but I could tell I was the only one enjoying the view.

'So what can I get you?' I asked.

'Tony Sheridan.'

'You want cream with that?'

I ordered a couple of cappuccinos that didn't take long enough to arrive and bummed some skins from Andrea, the waitress. Katie took a sip and grimaced. I poured three sugars, made a wish and said, stirring and not looking at her: 'What makes you think I can get you Tony Sheridan?'

'Detective . . .' She dug a little black notebook out of her shoulder bag, flipped it open. 'Brady?'

'Big lad?'

'That's him.'

'He was having a laugh. Besides – what would I be getting Tony Sheridan for?'

She pushed the coffee away, lit a Silk Cut, exhaled. Crossed her legs again.

'Let's start over, Harry.'

'It's okay with you, I'd rather keep going with the legs.'

She smiled a thin one.

'Sorry, you're not my type.'

'Types are based on previous failures. You should think more about your future.'

'Look, Harry—'

'Alright, Jesus, don't get sour. If I had cleavage you'd be hearing echoes. Everyone does what they have to do.'

'My sentiments exactly.'

'And you want to do Tony Sheridan.'

'Correct.'

I let it hang, rolled a cigarette. It was her move. She pulled a manila folder from her bag, leafed through a file of newspaper cuttings, handed me a clipping. It had a modest headline: Controversial Development Officially Opened. There was a photograph of mostly men in their Sunday best, smiling their Sunday smiles, standing on the forecourt of a hotel. The dude holding the scissors was tall, well preserved and answered to Tony Sheridan if you had a homeless vote. The rest were a supporting cast of investors, councillors and the usual pick-n-mix of wives, fools, flutes and thrill-seekers, some credited, most not.

'So – what?'

'I presume you know the backdrop?'

'Sure, it's about a mile east of town, just where the river empties out of the lake. Used to get a lot of kingfishers up there. Good salmon fishing too.'

She stared. Then, patient: 'This is front page anywhere we put it. With the right spin, everywhere.'

'If, say, we turn up a steak knife in Tony's glove compartment.'

'Steak knife?'

'Forget it. I'm kidding.'

She looked over both shoulders and leaned in over the table, which caused the front of her blouse to drop a good six inches. I stayed where I was, losing my balance anyway.

'This could be big, Harry. There's a lot of typists out there calling themselves journalists, still trading on that one story, still hitting the front page, pic by-lines, the works. This is my one story, Harry.'

'Don't sell yourself short. Besides, there's other people want the story.'

'Who – pizza-face on the moped? Come on.'

'He doesn't flash me cleavage but he's a good bloke. More to the point, he has the shots.'

'So he opens a gallery, big fucking deal. The shots are useless without the story and a place to put it.'

'Say I humour you – what's the split?'

She wasted some time trying not to look shrewd.

'We take a joint credit. The money we cut fifty-fifty. You can share yours with moped boy.'

'Fair go. What do you want to know about Tony?'

'What do you know?'

I nodded at the clipping on the table.

'That hotel, it happened maybe five years ago. It was a total fucking mess.'

'Sheridan rushed the planning process through?'

'Not so fast. He turned up in the locals' corner, it's his ward and he lives up there. He made speeches about the environment, his grandchildren, endangered species. Couldn't have been greener if he was about to puke.'

'So?'

'So he got backing from the Greens up in Dublin, did a deal with some bog-trotting Independents who were looking for an abortion referendum. Went over the county manager's head, got an injunction. Happy days.'

'But the hotel was built.'

'Yeah, but two years later. Fianna Fáil were back in power, holding a majority, they didn't need Tony's vote. No one's happy up at the lake, especially Tony, his place overlooks the site. But the deal's done.'

'You said the whole thing was a mess.'

'It was. Tony wasn't happy, but if the hotel was being built he wanted his cut. So he invested, same as a lot of people around here did. Other people, people who don't usually have a hundred large lying around, were cheesed off. Tony told them there'd be jobs going, gave them the spiel about tourism potential, locally generated revenue, the works. And when the big day arrives, Tony's out front cutting the ribbon. Three months later the first salmon goes belly-up, the hotel's pumping shit into the lake, quelle fucking surprise. The way it's going, you'll be able walk

across the river in another year or two. Give it long enough and
you'll have the foundations for another bridge, and they'll probably name it after Tony.'

She waited. I drank my coffee, built another smoke.

'That's it?'

'That's it.'

'That's the dirt?'

'Who said it was dirty? You took for granted it was crooked.
All it proves is, Tony's a hypocrite.'

'He's a hypocrite. Big fucking deal.'

'It used to be.'

'Come down off the cross Harry, you'll get dizzy. Just tell me
if you have anything on Sheridan. Is he dirty? Whoring around?
Anything at all that might drive his wife to cut her own throat?
Otherwise, you're wasting my time.'

I thought it over.

'Nope, I'm just wasting your time.'

She put the notebook down.

'I'm not going to blow you, Harry, no matter how much you
wave your dick around. So get over it and do it fast. I made some
calls. This hasn't broken yet but once it gets out we're buried, it'll
roll all over us.' She checked her watch. 'Jesus, look at the time.'

'A date?'

She flicked her fringe, blew me a smacker that dripped acid.

'Split ends, Harry. A girl should always look her best.'

'In case the cameras arrive?'

'Exactly.' She packed her bag again, stood up. 'Cheers for the
coffee.'

'Huzzah.'

I watched her go, sipping the coffee, mulling over the

newspaper clipping, wondering why she had left it behind. Then I climbed the three flights of stairs to the office, hoping that somebody's dog had gone missing.

3

The hum of Thai takeaway dumped in an ashtray let me know the office door was already open. Which meant B&E, not that breaking in would have taken a mastermind, the toughest part would have been not shaking the door off its hinges in the process. A fat kid could have broken in just by leaning on the frosted glass.

He'd have to be a pretty bored fat kid. The office contained a desk, two chairs, and a filing cabinet that boasted three files, two of them containing bills, paid and unpaid, and no prizes for guessing which was the thinner. The third file, the case file, was anorexic.

The fat kid was touching forty and not liking the grain, a Turkish wrestler sucked into a rust-coloured Armani. He had bulbous lips, a thick nose. The sallow skin looked like it needed a shave once a week. He had piggy eyes, small, black and dead, and his hair was heavily gelled, slicked down.

He nodded sociably as I walked in.

'Nice place,' he rasped. The words came short, fast and from the side of his mouth, like they were cheaper that way. I nodded back, friendly as a folk mass.

'Cheers. Who the fuck are you?'

'Relax, Jesus.'

'This is as relaxed as it gets. Too much coffee, a peptic ulcer, and the speed habit in my impressionable youth doesn't help. I'd ring the Doc but he's in drying out, second time this year, the smack complicates things and there's a lot of it about recently. So – who the fuck are you?'

I knew who he was. Frank Conway, a real estate auctioneer who flogged second-hand motors on the side. A lot of people knew Frank Conway. He'd only been around town for eighteen months but he drove an '84 silver-grey convertible, a Merc SL, practically mint, the kind of motor gets you noticed. Still, we hadn't been formally introduced and the last thing I needed, the butt of the .38 digging into my spine and Gonzo due home, was more trouble. And Frank Conway was trouble. Rumour had it, Frank's cars came across the border all pilled up and ready to party.

'Only reason I ask,' I added, 'is Monday's bin day and I'd hate for someone to mistake you for trash.'

He fed me a faint smile. He nodded at the sign, stencilled on the frosted glass: Harry J. Rigby, Independent Research Bureau.

'What's the J stand for?'

'It stands for get the fuck out of my seat.'

He stood up and stretched, letting me know he was as big as he thought he was. Moved slowly around the desk, settled in the other chair. I slid in behind the desk, set my fresh coffee down, rolled a loose one. He said: 'Ever get lost in here?'

'Sorry, I don't do sarcasm before breakfast. Now – is this an interior design kick or is there something I can actually do for you?'

Usually I let the dick stuff go, but I didn't like Conway. He was too smooth, too slick and oiled, like a lazy cat's coat, and I hate cats, especially the lazy ones. He sat back, laid an ankle on a knee.

'Get much business with that attitude, Bud?'

'Tuesdays, my attitude makes me cry. Mondays I think I'm cute. Now start again and if you behave I'll let you finish because I haven't had a laugh in days.'

I was half-hoping Conway would take the hint and leave but all he did was lean forward, flick his cigarette at the ashtray, although not like he was worried about getting the scholarship. He put his elbows on the desk, cleared his throat, said: 'You're Harry Rigby?'

'Unless you're from the Revenue, yeah.'

'You're a private investigator?'

'I'm a research consultant.'

'What's that when it's not at the zoo?'

I took a deep breath and pitched the spiel.

'I research information that isn't readily available to private individuals. Running credit checks on prospective business partners, finding long lost lovers, that kind of thing. I provide covert observation for insurance companies in cases of suspected fraud. I document infidelity, or confirm that the husband's suspicions are just that, and they're usually the husband's. I assist companies with security surveillance, and sometimes I hop along behind bouncing cheques. Missing dogs and family trees are steady earners. The perks include creative tax returns, fast food, late nights and the manners of a Protestant. The ulcer I had before I took the job. The coffee's getting cold, by the way.'

He nodded, sat back. Took a deep breath, straightened his shoulders. I was guessing infidelity.

'The name's Conway. Frank Conway. And this is strictly confidential.'

'Think of me as a priest, all the women do.'

He laughed, a nasal bark.

'You should meet my wife.'

'She likes funny guys?'

'They're all hilarious, far as she's concerned.'

'Does she have a name, or is it relevant?'

'Helen.'

I dug a pad out of the top drawer, scribbled some notes.

'And has she left or is she going to?'

'Neither. I'm going to break her fucking neck.'

'And you want me for what – an alibi?'

He blew smoke rings at the ceiling.

'Most husbands,' I prodded, 'want to kill the bloke.'

'Fuck him,' Conway rasped. 'He doesn't know any better. If he did he wouldn't be screwing the bitch.'

'You know for a fact that Mrs Conway is having an affair?'

'She's screwing around. I know.'

'Worst thing you can do is jump to conclusions.' From where I was sitting, jumping to conclusions was all the exercise Conway got. 'Maybe you should consider other possibilities.'

'Like what?'

I knew, from experience, that the rational approach was pointless. When a man is so convinced his wife is screwing someone else that he can tell another man, an act of God won't change his mind. I tried anyway, needing the gig. I always needed the gig. Chasing missing dogs is no job for a grown man.

'Most dick jobs are paranoia,' I explained. 'Blokes who work so hard to compensate for the size of their dicks, they don't get to use them. It's only a matter of time before they start wondering why wifey is so happy with the situation. Sometimes the bloke is right, wifey's playing away from home, but it doesn't happen that often. And either way, a happy ending isn't on the cards.'

'What the fuck is this, The Samaritans?'

Big Frank knew and nothing else mattered. I didn't point out that maybe the fact that nothing else mattered might be the reason Helen Conway was screwing around. I said: 'She has the opportunity?'

The unholy trinity – motive, opportunity and proof. Proof was up to me, and after ten minutes with Frank Conway even I wanted to have an affair.

'I'm out of town for a night or two most weeks,' he growled. 'On business.'

'Where?'

His voice ground out a warning, harsh.

'Here and there, it changes.'

He stared. I scribbled.

'So, what? You want me to confirm she's having an affair? Breaking her neck isn't really an option until you know for sure.'

He nodded, curt.

'Alright, I'll need details – where she works, shops, gets her hair done. A recent photograph, that kind of thing.'

He dug into his inside pocket, handed me a driver's licence that should have carried a government health warning. She was the right side of forty, dark hair curling to her shoulders, head tilted back, accentuating the aquiline nose. There was mischief in the dark, almond-shaped eyes. The tiny smile was sardonic, knowing, and if the lower lip was less provocative than Ian Paisley it wasn't by more than a thumped lectern.

I'd seen her type before, mostly through binoculars, so I could understand why Conway might turn desperate if he thought she was playing away. That kind of woman comes around once in a lifetime, if you're lucky, and that kind of luck doesn't come cheap. I made a note of the details, handed back the licence. Wondering if Conway was carrying it because he'd come prepared, or in a vain attempt to stop his wife driving when he wasn't around.

'She has a bank account in her own name?'

'Accounts. I don't have the details with me.'

'One will do and I'll need it today. Hobbies?'

'Hobbies?'

'Flower-arranging, ballroom dancing, deep sea diving. Anything she does on her own, when you're not around.'

His tone was sullen.

'She plays golf.'

'At The Bridge?'

'Where else?'

At The Bridge your handicap was measured by the number of seasons your wife's little black number was out of date.

'Is she any good?'

'What's good got to do with it?'

I made more notes. Then, the biggie: 'I'll need to know about the other bloke too.'

He coughed, quick and too dry.

'Like what?'

'Like, any idea who he might be?'

He stared so long I began to suspect myself. Then, with a brief shake of his head: 'No.'

'Affairs rarely happen between strangers. They usually happen between acquaintances, social partners, workmates.'

Again with the sharp, nasal bark. He sounded like a sick seal.

'Helen doesn't work.'

'And you've no reason to suspect any of your own associates?'

'That's what I want you to find out.'

'Alright, I'll take it from here. The less you know, the better you'll sleep. If nothing turns up inside a month, six weeks, chances are there's nothing to turn up.'

'That soon?'

'Everybody's so worried that everyone's watching them, they don't notice when it's just anyone watching them. Strange but true. If anything does turn up, I'll document it and turn the file over to you, negatives included.'

'Photographs?'

'Incontrovertible evidence in a court of law. Come in handy if you want to avoid one too.'

'That's it?'

'I'll need a retainer.'

'What for?'

'Expenses. Soft drugs. Lunar real estate, maybe. Who knows?'

Another long stare. He scribbled a cheque.

'When do I hear from you?'

'When I call. You're away when?'

'Thursday usually, most of Friday. Sometimes Friday night too.'

'Next week, come back Saturday. And let Helen – Mrs Conway – know you'll be away both nights. If you can do it two weeks running, better still.'

He got up like he'd forgotten how to stand. Pawed at the creases in his trousers, turned for the door. He looked back.

'So what's the J stand for?' He seemed composed again, a man in control of his own destiny, and he looked all the more plaintive for believing it.

'It's a joke.'

'It's not funny.'

'You're not paying for funny. Funny's extra.'

He banged the door so hard my ulcer started tingling. I slipped the .38 out of my belt, put it away in the bottom drawer of the desk. Then I slugged from the bottle of Maalox I keep in the top drawer, washing down a Prothiaden, and rang downstairs for a coffee that might poison me slower.

4

I rang Herbie.

'Any joy with Sheridan?'

'Nothing yet, the server's acting up again.'

Herbie's main gig was shutterbug, although the grass he grew in his attic was a tidy nixer when things got quiet. The deal, when we hooked up, was I did the walking, asking the questions, and he handled the research, digging on the web, scanning ports, cracking passwords, finding back doors.

'So what's up?' he asked.

'Not much.' Herbie didn't need to know about Frank Conway, that was a solo gig. 'I was just wondering about Sheridan.'

'What about him?'

'Where is he? He wasn't at the house this morning, right?'

'Regan said he was in Dublin. Some business meeting.'

'Nice alibi. You up for a giggle?'

'Like what?'

'Meet me here in half-an-hour. Wear an overcoat. And look dumb.'

*

The brunette opened the door, stepped back into the narrow hallway, still groggy from sleep, winding her dressing gown tight.

'Miss Hunter?'

She nodded.

'Miss Joan Hunter?'

She nodded again, blinking.

'French,' I said, flashing her the inside of my wallet. I hooked a thumb over my shoulder at Herbie. 'Naughton. Can we come in?'

I was moving forward before she had a chance to answer and she melted back into the hallway. We filed in. It was a penthouse, one wall all window, the room spacious and bright, the décor black and minimalist. The river trudged by below and I could see the bridge in the distance. It was too warm, the heat oppressive. Orchids, thick, white and ugly, grew out of an ornate vase against the far wall. She said, suppressing a half-cough, her knuckles touched to her lips: 'Can I help you?'

I figured her for forty and looking it in the morning light. Her face was pale and drawn, dark rings under her eyes, up late last night, taking care of business in the nightclub. Herbie started in, aggressive.

'We know that every second girl in your place last night was underage,' he growled. 'Give me six hours and I'll have a statement from a minor claiming a bloke picked her up and didn't put her down, a statch rape beef. You'll beat the rap but we'll get the place closed down for two weeks, Christmas and New Year, the rags'll be all over it – kinky sex, they love it more than me. Do I have your attention?'

Her eyes blossomed and her mouth dropped open. It was her worst-case scenario realised, as delivered by a B-movie cop.

'I don't—'

'Do I have your attention?'

'Yes, yes of course. But—'

I stepped in, slipping her a break.

'Naughton is upset, Miss Hunter. We all are. There's been a particularly vicious murder and we're hoping you might be able to shed some light on the circumstances.'

'Me? But – Who? Who's been murdered?'

Herbie hurtled into the breach, harsh: 'Imelda Sheridan. Butchered this morning. You're going to need three alibis, all priests.'

Her face drained out, eyes glazed. My instinct was that she had no prior knowledge, clean as a whistle as far as Imelda Sheridan was concerned. But that wasn't why we were there.

'Miss Hunter – it's a delicate situation but you can depend on our discretion. I give you my word you will not be named in the investigation unless it is unavoidable.' I took a deep breath, for show. 'We need to ask about your relationship with Tony Sheridan.'

'Tony?'

Herbie rattled her again.

'Big Tony, yeah. You've been dancing the fandango, his wife knew. Now she's dead, stabbed to death. So – spill.'

'Tony and I . . . that's over, that's not . . . stabbed?'

I said: 'What did Imelda Sheridan think of your affair?'

'I don't know, Tony didn't say. It wasn't unusual for Tony . . .'
Her eyes started filling up. 'She was . . . I don't know, she was . . .'

I pinched my nose, tipping Herbie the sign – back off.

'Miss Hunter – can I call you Joan?'

She nodded, staring at the carpet, choking back a sob.

'Joan, from what you know of Imelda Sheridan, would she
have been likely to threaten anyone on the basis of Tony's indis-
cretions?'

She shook her head, snuffled something.

'I'm sorry – Joan? Could you repeat that?'

Then it all tumbled out in gulping sobs. We waited. When she
ran out of steam, she dabbed at her eyes and said, hiccupping
gently: 'She was the gentle type, placid . . . I don't know, mousey.
She didn't seem too worried about Tony. I thought she was glad,
it kept him out of her bed. She seemed . . . not interested.'

'Not interested?'

'Some people aren't.'

'And Tony?'

'Tony?' A hysterical giggle that snapped halfway through.
'Very interested.'

Herbie: 'Did he ever give you a dig?'

Her voice was low, husky.

'No.'

Yes. I said: 'Did he ever talk about leaving Imelda, Joan?'

'Leaving?'

'Divorce.'

This time she was emphatic, shaking her head.

'Imelda would never agree to – oh.'

'She had a strong faith? She was religious?'

'No – I don't know, maybe. But she was happy with what she had. She didn't need Tony to enjoy it.'

'She married for the money?'

She threw me a disdainful one – sure, why else?

'I'm sure I wouldn't know, detective.'

Herbie, coming in hard: 'What about drugs?'

'Drugs?'

'Imelda got an early white Christmas, a St Bernard dug her out of the drift in her living room. That kind of thing usual for Imelda?'

'Jesus, I wouldn't think so. You're sure you have the right—'

'We always have the right. You think Tony might have stabbed his wife?'

'No!' Bouncing back now. 'And I don't think—'

'That's our job,' Herbie snapped, 'the thinking. Could he have had it arranged?'

'How would I know?'

'Yes or no, here or in the station.'

'No.'

I pinched my nose again.

'Joan, we appreciate your co-operation and we realise that this must have come as a great shock.' She nodded, head down, milking it. 'Can we ask you not to leave the jurisdiction without notifying us in advance?'

She came up fast, her eyes wide.

'Am I—? Does that mean—?'

'No ma'am, but we would appreciate it if you would stay in touch.' I paused. 'Given the circumstances, we're just concerned for everyone's safety.'

She gaped, swallowed hard, and the sobs started welling up again. I made some comforting noises, patted her shoulder. We left. When the lift doors closed, Herbie glanced across, catching my eye.

'That's our job,' he drawled, 'the thinking.'

'You're a fucking ham.'

We left the apartment building foyer separately, still buzzing on the mood.

5

Back at the office I flipped through the post – all bills – binning the first-timers. Rolled a smoke, mulling over the newspaper clipping Katie had left behind, wondering again why she might have left it. Saw a face, back row, top right – black piggy eyes in a sallow face that didn't need a shave.

I got the old familiar feeling, stomach churning up concrete, hairs prickling on the back of my neck – the sensation I was being watched. I didn't go for the .38 again. I sparked the smoke instead, popped another pill and rang the morgue, wondering if I should just book a slab and be done with it. I flipped a coin. It didn't come down.

*

She was a dumb blonde, pushing fifty and pushing downhill and still dumb enough to want to be blonde. Skin the colour of vellum paper, sagging under the chin. Lips thin and just about pink, the nose narrow, the hair on her upper lip also dyed blonde. I wanted to ask how come blondes never got around to dyeing their eyebrows but her eyes were closed and the gash in her throat ran six inches east to west.

The morgue was chilly, sterile and white. Six floors of hospital hummed through to the basement but I could still hear the intern sweat. His eyes darted from Imelda Sheridan to the door, back again.

'They know who found her yet?'

He licked his lips, teeth protruding, a thin horsy face.

'How the fuck would I know?'

'You might have asked.'

'Why the fuck would I ask?'

'I don't know – job the fuck satisfaction, maybe.'

He laughed a thin, high snort, a rat with sinus trouble. Dragged the sheet back across her face.

'Rack 'em, stack 'em, pack 'em. They want more, they pay more.'

'More what – whizz?'

His face whitened, mouth slack and hanging open, lights on and nobody home.

'You need sleep,' I told him.

'What I need's a gun.'

'Careful what you wish for, Chief. Any word on the pathologist's prelim?'

'Lots of 'em. Couple of pages worth.'

'Any of them worth repeating?'

'How the fuck—'

'Would you know? I was hoping you'd learnt to read since last time.'

He rubbed a hand across his buzz cut.

'Anyone finds out I let you in here—'

'I know, I'd have to tell them you plunder the cabinet and people are dying because you've got the whizz shakes. Dry your eyes.'

I headed for the door, looking back as he slid Imelda Sheridan's slab home.

'You hear anything about the post-mortem, give me a bell.'

'How the fuck—'

I let the morgue door swish to.

*

I sipped at the coffee, thought some more about Katie. Wondering how her split ends were faring. A light bulb flared, fifteen watts. I dug out the Red Directory, thumbed through to Hairdressers and worked backwards alphabetically, on a whim.

'Hello, I'm ringing on behalf of Tony Sheridan. He'd like to cancel his wife's styling appointment . . . I can, yes . . . No? Really? I'm sorry, I must have been given the wrong number . . . Pardon? Yes, of course I'll pass that on . . . Sorry for taking up your time. Bye.'

Seven tries later, I hit pay dirt.

'Yes, well, I'm just making the arrangements, Mr Sheridan wouldn't want to put anyone out . . . Sorry? Yes, that is just like him . . . I'll certainly pass that on. You're very kind. Who am I talking to? Sandra?'

Sandra was the kind of artist, she could overpaint a Botticelli with a Barbie cartoon and throw in highlights for free. She was a walking advertisement, snipped and buffed, bleached and tucked, her skin the colour of old toffee. Her face was sharp, plastic and angular, a shoulder-mounted credit card.

'That's very kind, Sandra . . . Yes, she was. A lady, indeed . . . It was just a styling, wasn't it? You'll be compensated for the inconvenience, of course . . . Manicure too? A facial, of course . . . Yes, I understand, yes . . . Sorry? Yes, I'm sure Mr Sheridan realises that . . . Yes, of course I will. God bless. Bye.'

Tom Kilfeather wasn't a bad cop but he'd forgotten the little he knew about women the day he got married. If Imelda Sheridan had been depressed, the way Kilfeather called it, the funk hadn't been deep enough to stop her planning for the party season with a full makeover three days before Christmas. I rolled a smoke and treated myself to a stare at the far wall.

*

The big man came through the door like a rolling maul, planted his huge fists on the desk.

'If you don't knock,' I pointed out, 'it's B&E. Technically speaking.'

He grinned, wide and evil.

'Technically speaking, I could give a fuck.' He stuck his face in mine, jabbed a thumb at his chest. His breath hadn't freshened any since he ran me off Sheridan's spread, and he was sweating like an old cheese. 'Detective Brady. You, me, a little conversation.'

'By all means. It's a dying art.'

He perched on the edge of the desk, stuck out his chin. A redundant gesture, the chin was already out the window and waiting for a break in traffic.

'Impersonating a garda will get you five to ten. The broken

elbows are optional. Give me one reason why I don't run you in right now.'

'I've no idea what you're talking about.'

'Joan Hunter, Tony Sheridan's ex-tart. You braced her this morning, said you were a cop.'

'Bullshit.'

'She'll swear to it.'

'She'll perjure herself.' I nodded at the sign on the door. 'This is a research bureau. We do detective work. Not my fault if she jumped to the wrong conclusion.'

He grinned again, but not like he'd just remembered a punch line.

'Smart, eh? I like the smart ones, they don't run so fast.' He scratched his stubble. 'What'd she tell you?'

'Nothing you don't already know.'

'Tell me anyway.'

'No.'

He considered that and let it slide.

'You're the hack was up at Tony Sheridan's this morning.'

'Correct.'

'Who do you work for?'

'Not that it's any of your business, but I'm also a freelance journalist.'

'First thing, Rigby – everything is my business. Second thing – smart off at me again and they'll carry you out in three black bags. Third thing – whatever you found out this morning is null and void. The information never existed. You've already forgotten everything you saw and heard.'

'And when you click your fingers, I'll quack like a duck.'

He flexed his fingers, grinned evil again, a fox spotting a

snared rabbit. I tensed, ready to roll with it. He said: 'Ever hear of the Official Secrets Act?'

'Of course. It's right there in the book, next to Freedom of Information.'

I didn't even see it coming. One second Brady was perched on the edge of the desk, the next the world was all fist. The vast paw stopped maybe an eighth of an inch from my face, no shakes, solid as granite.

'Crack one more. Just one. I'm begging you.'

I kept schtum. The fist disappeared. Brady sat back and sparked one up.

'Okay – this is the way we're going to play it. I want to know—'

By then I was on my feet, surging forward, pushing the table up and out, Brady disappearing beneath it. He came up fast, knuckles white, face flushed. Found me scared, braced and ready. He came on, dipped a shoulder, I bought it – but he shimmied, feinted an uppercut and cracked a laugh.

'Alright, Rigby, sit down. Show's over.'

I sat back in the chair. He righted the table one-handed.

'You don't roll over, Rigby. I'll respect that. So – I want you on-side but what can we do? The information is still void, there's nowhere you can put it that won't get you ten years.'

'Why?'

'Can't say, Rigby. It's way too big. You're out of your league.'

'Sheridan's going down?'

'Sheridan who?'

We stared and smoked, Brady smirking.

'Look Brady, Tony Sheridan's place turns into an abattoir, that's big news. Plus – someone kitted her out like a suicide and threw in some coke. All the while Tony's away, presumably screwing someone else. Put all that together, it's bigger than Russia. And you want me to sit on it? That's unethical and criminally fucking stupid, and I'm not criminally fucking stupid.'

His eyes narrowed. I didn't blink.

'Okay, here's the news – fuck Russia, this is off the scale, you can't imagine. But what I'm willing to do is play it tight and keep you in touch. When it all taps out, I'll hand the lot over, reports, forensics, the works.'

'That's right, I forgot. I'm criminally fucking stupid.'

He shrugged.

'I'm a cop, yeah, but you can trust me. After I nail this one I want to see investigations, tribunals, the works.'

'You want it buried?'

He let that one slide.

'You'll get the lot, Rigby, pink frilly bows and satin fucking kisses. Scratch my back and I'll even help you put it together. Until then – it's personal.'

'Imelda Sheridan is personal?'

'Indirectly. Bear with me.'

I weighed it up, factored Herbie into the equation. The fast money said run the piece, but the story said fuck the money and I always listened to the story. Besides, Brady was holding aces and was six-four to boot. I rolled a smoke.

'I scratch your back – how?'

'Your side is I need the local dope, the inside. If you're any good, you'll hear it and keep me posted. If you're not, you won't get the gig when it's finished anyway. I want someone who'll stitch this one tight. So, you hear anything I should know, you buzz me.'

He stood up, scrawled a number on the back of a card, flipped it across the desk.

'One more thing, Rigby – no one knows I've been here. The Gardai brace you, make like I'm Lord Lucan.'

'Working a little freelance yourself, hey Brady?'

'Something like that, yeah.' He blasted me the evil grin, full wattage. 'Be seeing you, Rigby.'

He left, shoulders brushing the doorframe. I heard him again – 'I'm a cop, yeah, but you can trust me.' I laughed so hollow I heard it echo and went back to staring at the wall.

6

Conway rang as I was about to start checking out the near wall, just for a change of pace. I rang Herbie and gave him Helen Conway's details.

'Looking for anything in particular?' he asked.

'Just the usual, much as you can get.'

'Sound – when'd you want it?'

'Yesterday.'

'Alright. I'll buzz you later.'

*

I choked down the last of the coffee, thought about cleaning the office, and it was such a good idea I kept on thinking it, feet up on the desk, twitching the blinds.

It was Christmas week and the town belonged to the farmers. They lumbered up and down the streets, sailors on shore leave, grim and determined. Parcels stacked in elastic arms, necks craning around the piles. Tinny hymns drifted out of shop door-ways. High above the streets the coloured lights danced a hanged man's jig on the breeze.

I popped another pill. Three in one day was two too many but they were only twenty-five mill, summer breeze, and I need horse tranks to beat the festive funk. The light pills were another of the Doc's bright ideas, to wean me off the tranks in time for New Year, sound advice from a man whose veins had more holes than it takes to fill the Albert Hall.

I took a deep breath and slapped myself hard across the face, followed it up with a right cross that didn't quite connect. Closed my eyes, conjured up the face of a tow-headed thug, the hooded sleepy eyes, the chipped teeth, the guileless grin, the unruly mop of blonde hair. I factored in Christmas morning, a gleaming new bike and imagined the grin spreading across Ben's face to adopt his ears.

The weight evaporated from my chest. I breathed out again, locked up the office and drove the five miles out of town to The Bridge.

I talked to the barman in the Members Bar, no apostrophe, dropped a few openers about Helen Conway, but the barman stayed polite, eyes fixed on my breast pocket, where it didn't read Pringle. I sat in the bay window overlooking the eighteenth green, drinking coffee, chewing a plastic cheese-and-tomato toastie. The gale brewing up over the Atlantic was the colour of old gravy and the golfers leaned into the wind, three steps for-ward and two steps back.

Back in town I swung around by Clark's Toyshop to pick up Ben's bike. Added a couple of accessories, including a rubber bulb horn I knew he'd get a bang out of. It was almost three when I got back to the office. I stowed the bike behind the desk, checked the answering machine for the thrill of hearing my own voice and smoked for half-an-hour. Then I smoked some more and tried to make giraffes out of the cracks in the ceiling plaster. In the end I gave in, rang Conway to make an appointment.

'No can do,' he rasped. 'I'm out of the office from four on. Business that can't wait.'

'Perfect. Make sure your mobile is off too. I don't want anyone contacting you.'

Conway lived about two miles north of town, the house only three drainpipes short of a mansion. It was a square, stolid affair, in the way Edwardian Protestants built their homes to reflect their personalities, with thick ivy on the redbrick gables, a white soft-top Merc at the end of the gravelled drive and a bedroom for every night of the week. Off in the distance a stooped gardener was raking the last leaves off a vast lawn and raking fast enough to be finished in time to weed the daffodils. I parked my battered Volkswagen Golf beside the steps that swept up to the front porch and started climbing. Mulling over the new expletive I'd learned when I told Conway I'd be calling on his beautiful wife.

His beautiful daughter opened the door. She was wearing a white-and-blue striped sweater and the baffling expression all seventeen-year-old girls wear, the one that suggests they're simultaneously highly strung and bored to constipation. Her blonde hair was tied up in a ponytail and she had her mother's nose, down which she looked at me, and her father's manners.

'Yes?'

'Mrs Conway?'

She had her father's laugh, too.

'Mrs Conway is my mother. What do you want?'

'I've an appointment to see Mr Conway.'

'And who might you be?'

'I might be Calvin Klein but then I might just be wearing his Y-fronts. Get your mother.'

She chewed the inside of her lip, taken aback. I had to admit, she didn't look the kind of girl who had to ask a question twice, if she ever had to ask a question at all. Seventeen-year-old blondes with wide blue eyes and hips unworthy of the name have all the answers already, cursed with intuition. She called back down the hallway, over her shoulder.

'Mother, there's a gentleman at the door.'

Her timing was off but the punch line was good. Then Helen Conway pulled the door open wide and her daughter ceased to exist. Devoid of makeup, the soft lines either side of her eyes put me in mind of quotation marks. The simple black dress would have been appropriate at a millionaire's wake. The thin string of pearls designed to enhance the gentle curves of her throat should have retired gracefully and long ago. Her hair was jet black, and if it was a dye-job her stylist was wasted, he should have been in Rome retouching the Sistine Chapel.

'Yes?'

Polite, frosty.

'How do you do?' I slipped her an ingratiating smile. 'I have an appointment to see Mr Conway?'

'Mr Conway isn't at home right now. Can I help you?'

'I do hope you can. My name is Bob Delaney.' I flourished a card that read Robert L. Delaney, Sales Representative, First Option Life Assurance.

'There must be some kind of mistake.'

She handed the card back. I waved it away, still smiling.

'Not at all. I spoke with Mr Conway yesterday, on the phone. He was very interested in discussing the possibility of realigning your current life assurance commitments owing to the significant cost reduction strategy we employ at First Option.'

'Is that a fact?' She sounded faintly bemused. The delightful Miss Conway snorted, turned on her heel, pounded up the stairs. I heard the muffled sound of a slammed door.

'Indeed it is.'

I was getting a pain in my face from all the smiling, and if you're not inside the door within sixty seconds of hitting the step, chances are you're not going to make it at all.

'Well, as I say, Mr Conway isn't at home at the—'

'I don't mind waiting.' I dropped her the shoulder, swerved into the hallway, smiled again. 'I make it a habit to be early for my appointments.'

'Well, if you're sure . . .'

She recovered quickly, ushered me down the hallway. I wanted to call a cab halfway along but we got there in the end. The kitchen was all shining chrome, polished pine and terracotta tiles, and the Rovers could have kicked around a five-a-side without unduly disturbing the chef, who had probably got lost on his way back from the mezzanine level.

'Nice,' I said, nodding approval. 'Airy.'

'Can I get you something to drink, Mr –?'

'Delaney. But call me Bob, please. And I'd love a cup of coffee, if it isn't too much trouble.'

'No trouble at all, Mr Delaney. Cappuccino? Espresso?'

'Just black, please.'

The kitchen was bright. Patio doors reached from ceiling to floor, revealing no swimming pool in the back yard, which surprised me, but the sea was only a back-flip dismount away, grey and sullen and a wave-break from anger. Beyond, the Donegal mountains were snow-capped, the kind of view you can't buy for love or money, although the combination might get you a down payment. She poured something black and sludgy from the pot bubbling on the Aga.

'Sugar?'

'No thanks, I'm watching my figure.'

She smiled, distant, a woman who'd heard all the lines so many times she'd forgotten her cue. She put the coffee down, nothing for herself, lit a cigarette without offering me one.

'If you'll excuse me for one moment, Mr Delaney . . .'

I rolled a twist while I waited for her to come back from ringing her husband, who was out of the office with his mobile turned off, per instructions, or else I was in deep schtuck, as was he. When she returned, she lit another cigarette and sat down, composed. I tried another of my asinine smiles, nodded in the direction of the patio doors.

'Let's hope the rain keeps off.'

'Naturally.' Her voice was dry frost, as befitted an Ice Queen, and I half-expected her words to drift across the tabletop and gas me. 'You said you were speaking with Francis?'

I thought, Francis?

'That's right, yesterday afternoon.'

'And he wants to change our insurance policy?'

'Most people do when they discover how favourably First Option compares with our competitors.'

She wrinkled her nose, like she'd smelt something sickly-sweet. Most people turn rabid when you say you can save them money, foaming at the mouth to find out more. The Ice Queen hadn't even raised an eyebrow. I figured that Frank Conway had hit the jackpot when he'd married the beautiful Helen, felt the urge to check their marriage licence against their delightful daughter's birth cert, just for the hell of it.

'What time did you say your appointment was for, Mr Delaney?' Still suspicious, still polite.

'I didn't, but it's for four o'clock. Mr Conway assured me he'd be here.'

'If he said he'd be here, he'll be here. He's usually punctual.'

Punctual means predictable and predictable means having a schedule to work around.

'It's not essential that Mr Conway is here, actually. Perhaps you could help me out with a few details before he arrives? It'll save time and time is money.'

'Details?'

'Oh, simple stuff.' I opened the battered briefcase, took out a sheaf of brochures and forms. I didn't know what half of them said, and I was pretty sure she wouldn't be interested, but I pushed them across the table for show. 'How much your premium is, what the return adds up to, how it affects your tax allowance. The kind of settlement in place in the case of divorce. That kind of thing.'

'Divorce?'

She was still a long way off interested but I thought I heard a note of surprise.

'It's sad, Mrs Conway, but true. All life assurance policies taken out by married couples with First Option have a divorce clause inserted these days. It's standard practice.'

She laughed, delighted at the vulgarity of it all. My stomach somersaulted.

'I'm sure we don't have a divorce clause, Mr Delaney.' Twisting her wedding ring absent-mindedly, the light snagging in the rocks and screaming for mercy. 'Francis and I were married long before that kind of thing became necessary. As you know very well.'

She smiled, coy. My stomach sprinted across the hurdles and took a flyer at the pole vault.

'I can't imagine why Mr Conway would even contemplate divorce.' If Helen Conway was fishing she could count on reeling me in. 'It's just a standard question we ask at First Trust as part of our comprehensive customer package.'

Her eyebrows flickered under a brittle frown.

'You mean First Option.'

I grinned, tried to look embarrassed.

'First Option, of course. I'm not that long with the company . . .'

'Yes, well, I'm sure I'm just wasting your time, Mr Delaney. Francis handles our finances and you really should be talking to him.' She checked her watch, a tiny gold number. 'And I don't want to be rude, but I am expecting some company . . .'

'Of course, of course. I'm sorry for holding you up.'

'I really can't understand why Francis is late. He's usually so punctual. He hates it if someone keeps him waiting.'

'Well, maybe something came up. I'll ring him and make another appointment. At his office, perhaps.'

'That might be for the best.' She stood up slowly, but not so slow that I wouldn't get the hint. 'I'm sorry you've had a wasted trip . . .'

'Not at all. It was a fine cup of coffee.'

She chuckled a fluttery one out of politeness and my stomach took off, looking for a high building to bound over. I stuffed the brochures into my briefcase. She showed me to the door and shook hands. Her grip was dry and strong.

'Goodbye, Mr Delaney.'

'Bob.'

'Of course.'

*

She was waiting at the bottom of the drive, hidden from the house by the high shrubbery. Arms folded, shivering in the biting wind, smoking. She had closed the gates and made no effort to open them. I got out of the car.

'An insurance man.'

If you're going to sneer, throw in a pout, it takes the sting out of it. I slipped her the patter.

'I sell ah-ssurance – there's a difference. Insurance suggests a guarantee. I make the inevitable financially soluble.'

'Bullshit.'

I didn't take it personally. When you're seventeen, everything is bullshit, especially the bullshit. I opened the gates, got back in the car. She came and stood beside it, giving it the once-over. I wound down the window. The sneer was toxic.

'Nice car. I like old cars.'

'I collect antiques.'

'You collect antiques selling insurance?'

'The money isn't great,' I admitted, flashing her a leer, 'but I know a bargain when I see one.'

She tossed her ponytail. The big blue eyes flashed and her face hardened.

'You're a cheap bastard,' she spat.

'Oh do stop flirting,' I told her, grinding the gears. 'I'll get a nosebleed.'

*

I pulled into a lay-bye half a mile from town, changed the false number plates. I was getting back into the car when a white soft-top Merc purred by. The Ice Queen was driving, and if her company had turned up they were all midgets or else they were riding in the trunk.

I caught her at the lights on the new bridge, three cars back, staying that way as the traffic snaked through town. She turned into the car park off Francis Street, behind the bank, parked facing out across the river. I slipped into a gap on the far side of the car park.

She sat for twenty minutes, checking the fishing maybe. Then she got out, beeped the alarm, strolled towards the footbridge. I slipped out of the Golf but I didn't make five yards before she opened the door of a Volvo Estate and sat into the passenger seat. The Volvo's engine was already running. It took off with a throaty roar.

There was no sign of the Volvo by the time I cut out into the rush hour traffic. I took a gamble, cut east along the river on the far side of the bridge, gunning the Golf south towards the Holy Well, where big houses meant lots of space and not so many people. Across the lake Foynes Hill lurched off towards Leitrim, to the left the fields fell away to the river. The lake beyond was a drop of mercury, silver, static and dull. In town it was murky, the dark clouds jumbling overhead. On Foynes Hill the sun was still shining, weak as orange squash. On Foynes Hill the sun always shone, winter or summer, night or day.

I caught them, the big Volvo neutered on the tortuous bends. Staying well back as they motored past the Holy Well, following the lakeshore and turning into the picnic site at Hughes Point. I turned into the next picnic site, maybe half a mile away through the winding tunnel of pines. I dug Herbie's digital camera out of the glove compartment, jogged back through the trees.

Dusk was coming down, sleet sifting through the gloom. The picnic site was bounded on three sides by thick pines, on its fourth by the road. I could make out two picnic tables, an over-flowing rubbish bin and the Volvo parked on the other side of the clearing, and that was about as idyllic as I can ever handle. Three paths cut through the trees, curving up and away towards the Point, which faced north across the lake towards the town.

I skulked back in the trees, took a couple of shots of the car, considered wandering up one of the paths, just to see if my luck would hold. I'd decided not to push it when I heard footsteps crunching on the gravel path behind me, the Ice Queen, wearing a mauve silk scarf to keep her hair in place. The man was wear-ing a heavy tweed overcoat and olive-green Wellington boots, holding a golf umbrella in front of them to deflect the sleet. I hunkered down behind a massive pine, aimed the camera along the path, getting a couple of shots off.

They passed by about twenty yards away, the breeze carrying their conversation towards the road. I made out a pair of red jowls, a skiff of grey hair under the flat cap. He could have been anyone, including the Pope or a drag queen who didn't get the joke.

They made straight across the picnic area for the Volvo. Its lights arced around, illuminating the pine I was hiding behind. Then it was gone. I sprinted back through the pines to the Golf, only tripping face-first into trees a couple of times, but even so there was no sign of the Volvo or the soft-top Merc when I finally made it back to the car park behind the bank.

It was a bust, the latest in the endless list of thrilling coups perpetrated by Harry J. Rigby, Research Consultant.

7

I strolled across the footbridge, crossed the street to the office, checked the answering machine. The metallic voice whined: 'You have reached the offices of First Option Life Assurance. Our representatives are currently unavailable but we do value your call. If you leave your name, number and the nature of your request, one of our representatives will contact you as soon as possible. Thank for you calling. Please speak after the tone. Goodbye.'

Beeep.

'Harry? It's Dutch. Give us a buzz. Cheers.'

Beeep.

Dutchie didn't like answering machines, said they reminded him of when he was a kid, making his Holy Communion, all that praying and half-afraid no one was getting the message. I changed the tape, rang Denise to tell her about Ben's bike – with Gonzo back in town I was staying close to them both – but there was no answer. I left a message of my own, short and sweet, short because I knew Denise wouldn't listen to it all and sweet because

I didn't know any other way to be. Then I closed up shop for the day, sidled back across the street to The Cellars.

I claimed a stool at the bar, beside the arch, where the pub sloped down to a bottleneck. Through the arch was a snug. Beyond, a narrow passageway led outside to the toilets. Opposite the toilet door was another door, a door Dutchie kept locked because Dutchie was particular about who played his pool table.

The bar itself was rough oak, two foot thick, broad. It faced four booths, in which all the tables had beer mats stuffed under their legs. The benches were upholstered in worn red velvet. The carpet was pocked with tiny scorch marks. The low ceiling was tuberculosis brown.

Dutchie ambled down the bar, dressed all in black, as always. Black denim shirt, black moleskin trousers, black motorcycle boots that buckled to the side and came with steel toecaps as an optional extra. The way he was built, Dutchie was never going to make a good accountant and his head was shaved to the skull.

'Alright?' he drawled.

'Dutch.'

'What'll it be?'

'Cappuccino.'

'Fuck's sakes.'

Dutchie ran a clean shop. That meant no drugs, no knackers and no ties. The pub was quiet when you needed it to be and busy enough from its regular trade for Dutchie not to have to entertain undesirables, which in Dutchie's book meant anyone who asked for mineral water, Cappuccinos or Irish coffees. I ignored his dispirited search among the sachets stuffed under the bar, nodding at Baluba Joe, sitting at far end of the bar, the pint in front of him standing sentry over a half one, the flying helmet placed to one side. Over his head, pinned to the bar, was the yellowing newspaper cutting that announced Joe and his mates were to be awarded their medals for not dying in the Congo.

'Alright Joe?'

'Fuggoff.'

'Sound.'

Dutchie came back with the Cappuccino. He sat up on the dishwasher behind the bar, sipping from a bottle of orange juice. I nodded at Joe.

'Thought he was inside?'

'He went in Saturday.' Joe checked himself in every Christmas for the week that was in it. 'Came back out today, said he didn't want to peak too soon.'

'Fair enough. So what's up?'

'Nothing much. Just wondering if you and Dee are on for a meal out tomorrow night. Michelle is booking a Chinkers.'

'One step at a time, Dutch.'

'It being Christmas and all . . .'

I filled him in on the morning's events.

'So she threw you out. How many times is that?'

'Seven.'

'Seven?'

'I only count the times she's sober.'

'Smart.'

He chugged some orange juice. I changed the subject.

'Know a Frank Conway?'

He choked on the juice, wiped a dribble from his chin with the back of his hand. Then he hopped down from the bar, dragged a tray of steaming glasses out of the dishwasher. He left them over the sink to drain dry, wiped his hands on a cloth.

'Conway the auctioneer? Slimy bastard, drives a big dick substitute. Runs a sideline importing second-hand cars across the border. Thinks his wife is too good for him. She thinks she's too good for everyone else.'

'Someone has to be. Anything else?'

'Why, what's up?'

I sketched the outline of Frank Conway's visit.

'So why are you digging on him? Shouldn't you be digging on her?'

'I am.' I told him about my trip to Hughes Point. His mouth turned down at the corners.

'So who's the bloke?'

'Fuck knows.'

'Dirty bitch.'

'That's as may be. All this afternoon told me was, Helen Conway went for a walk at Hughes Point with some bloke drives a Volvo. He could be her father for all I know.' I took a deep breath, swallowed the Cappuccino in one gulp, wiped the froth from my lip. 'But even if she is carrying on, Conway still isn't kosher.'

'Like how?'

'Like he comes to me saying his wife is knocking out tricks, but kicks for touch anytime I try to get around the back of it. Gets agitated, knows more than he's saying.'

'If he knows so much why'd he come to you?'

'I don't know. Maybe Frank's not worried about his wife screwing someone else. Maybe Frank's worried about her screwing him, making off with the family jewels.'

He shook his head.

'Conway might have problems. Cash isn't one of them.'

'What do you hear?'

'You know there's E in the motors, when they come across the border?'

'Yeah. What else?'

'There's whispers about a knocking shop, on that new estate out the back of the college. Curtains are never open, there's blokes coming and going all hours of the night. Sounds to me like a student nurse flop, but you never know.'

'Anything legal?'

'Last I heard he was involved in that development that went up out at Manor Grange. Bought the land for a hundred twenty, put forty houses on it at a hundred and eighty grand a pop. There's another one planned for down at the river, opposite the new hotel. Apartments, state of the art, they look like something off a Polish industrial estate. The site cost him a hundred fifty, there's seven pre-booked at one-sixty each and they won't be ready to go for another six months.'

'So maybe it isn't real estate. Maybe he fancies the ponies, or the stocks.'

Dutchie took a long swig of orange juice, dropped the bottle in the bin.

'If he does I haven't heard. But I'll ask around.'

'Cheers.'

He moved away up the bar, the early evening trade filtering in. I dug out the paper, gave myself a migraine trying to work out the Simplex crossword. I was rolling my last smoke when someone tapped me on the shoulder, Katie, nodding at the Cappuccino.

'You drink too much coffee.' She seemed relaxed, far too cheerful, which meant she knew something I didn't.

'Sorry, I can't afford medical advice. I like your hair, by the way.'

'Thanks. I had to cancel my appointment, by the way.'

'Yeah, I like the fact that you left it alone.'

She smiled. I thought of a second-hand car with 'Wash Me' scrawled on a dusty back window.

'Ever drink anything stronger?' she asked, sitting up on the stool beside me.

'Sometimes I leave the sugar out.'

'Maybe I should introduce you to alcohol.'

'We've met. Town wasn't big enough for both of us.'

Dutchie wandered back down the bar. I introduced them, ordered a round. Katie swirled the ice around her G&T, downed the lot in one swallow.

'Tough day?'

'First anniversary.'

'Of what?'

'Learning to mind my own business.'

'Not so long ago when you were interested in my business.'

'That was just business. You're being personal.'

'And I thought we were friends.'

'You know what thought did?'

'What's that?'

'Pissed the bed and thought he was sweating.'

'I remember that now.'

We chatted for a while, talking about everything and saying nothing, and the while nuzzled up to a couple of hours and started whispering sweet nothings. She was good company, sharp with it, and she liked to talk. I liked listening, liked her frank opinions and the way her smile caused her nose to wrinkle. Liked that she took the time out to flirt without really meaning it, the way that, five or six pints later, she was still tossing her hair and laughing at my jokes. By then I had the idea that she reckoned I was a challenge, and I didn't have the heart to pretend otherwise.

'Messing aside,' I said, 'the first anniversary of what?'

She stared into her drink, stirring it with the pink swizzle stick that was Dutchie's idea of a gag.

'I was getting married.' Her fringe fell forward, hiding her eyes. She shook it back, straightened her shoulders. 'Then I wasn't getting married.'

'He broke it off?'

'Three weeks from the big day out, his brother's family home from South Africa, the works. We were going out for a year, engaged for eighteen months. Next thing he turns around and says he can't go through with it, he doesn't love me anymore. What the fuck love had to do with it in the first place. He was good in the nest, took regular showers, paid his share of the bills. That was about the height of it.'

The pub had filled up, the babble of conversation loud enough for us to talk without being overheard. It was pleasant sensation, like we were trapped in a bubble.

'There's worse reasons for getting married.'

'Ach – I was just fed up with the job, doing the same thing every week. The wedding was just an excuse, something other than the pub on a Friday night, curry chip for a treat. Biggest favour anyone did me, him walking out.'

'Sounds like a bit of a prick if you ask me.'

'I'm not asking. You're as big a prick as he was, Harry, most blokes are. That's your job. A woman's job is to change you from being pricks to something better. I wasn't good enough at the job, that's all. End of story.'

It was getting on for eleven o'clock, as good a time to change the subject as any.

'Seeing anyone now?'

She looked up from her drink, nose wrinkling.

'That's the best offer I've had in weeks. So you can imagine how pathetic the others were.'

'I didn't mean . . .'

She laughed.

'So say something you do mean.' Her voice soft and warm again. Eyes locked on mine, gaze steady. Fear churned through the anticipation, and a warm tingle ran up my spine. My throat went dry. It was the old familiar feeling, the kind of old and familiar that needs carbon dating. Besides, there was already plenty of space for a wedge to be driven between Denise and me, and with Gonzo back in town I wouldn't need to buy a new mallet. I took refuge in my pint. She laughed, frustrated.

'You play this hard to get with every woman who buys you a pint?'

'I'm not hard to get. That's my jokes.'

'True enough.' She sipped her drink, considered me across the rim of the glass. 'So what are you, queer?'

'It's worse. I'm married.'

'I don't see any ring.'

'We call him Ben. He's four years old.'

'Nice name.'

'I couldn't spell anything more complicated.'

'I can sympathise.' The wide-eyed gaze dared me to look away. I took the dare. She stubbed her cigarette out and said, just loud enough for me to hear: 'I'm not that fussed on complications myself.'

She dug a pen from her handbag, scrawled a number on a beer mat. Then, without saying another word, she got up and left. I watched her go and then tore the number off the beer mat. I looked at it for a long time, knowing what I should do. Then I put the scrap of paper in my wallet where I knew Denise would never find it, behind the condom.

Dutchie leaned across the bar as I put my jacket on.

'Are you driving?'

'Don't be daft. Alfred's waiting with the limo.'

'Don't take the bridge. The Dibble were pulling there earlier on.'

'Cheers.'

I downed the last of the pint, which put me at least five full pints over the limit, but I'd never thought with such clarity before. My reactions were sharp, vision twenty-twenty. I hadn't had a woman come on to me like that in years, not even Denise, especially not Denise. I felt buoyant, untouchable. Bulletproof.

Of course, that was before all the shooting started.

8

If you're going to get kicked senseless it's best to take certain precautions. Getting drunk is one. That way you go with the flow and don't resist, which is how bones get broken, especially when there's three of them and one is wielding an empty beer keg like it's a beach ball.

I didn't even see them coming. One moment I was drunk and warm, thinking about Katie and feeling pretty damn good about myself. The next I was rolling in the gutter, ducking flailing boots and what felt like a length of thick chain. I locked my hands around my head, curled into a ball and tried to scream.

They were quiet, efficient and deadly. The only sounds were hollow thuds, squishy splats. They booted my kidneys, chain-whipped my legs, pounded my stomach. One of them rabbit-punched my shoulders, fist wrapped in a knuckle-duster. I drifted into semi-consciousness, feeling the blows but not the pain. And then something heavy bounced off my shoulder and clanged away across the cobblestones, jerking me back to reality. It was the beer keg and they had stopped.

I heard a voice close to my ear, straining to catch its breath, a voice with a northern twang.

'Stay away from her, big man. Ye hear?'

I didn't answer. I wasn't able to breathe, the gorge in my chest rising into my throat. I managed a nod, a snuffle that sent something thick and slimy down the back of my throat. The voice came again.

'Else it'll be the wee man getting it. Ben, ye call him?'

He ruffled my hair and then I heard footsteps, quick but not hurried as they strolled away down the alley. Leaving me to snuffle some more snot and blood, face down in my own vomit. I tried to move. Bolts of pain shot through me, tripped the circuits. The world went black except for a dull red glow right in the middle of the nothingness. When it started to fade I followed it down.

*

I couldn't have been lying there long. Dutchie said, after, that a bloke angling for a sneaky piss behind the beer kegs spotted me, rapped on the pub door while Dutchie was still clearing up. They carried me inside and Dutchie propped me up in one of the cubicles. Once we figured out nothing was actually broken, he went for tissues, hot water and Dettol.

'Fail the breathalyser?' he asked.

I groaned. I was wedged in an oil drum that some maniac was attacking with a Kango hammer. Except it wasn't noise that brutalised every synapse, it was pain. Searing here, vicious there, throbbing everywhere. Funny was the last thing I needed. What

I needed was a syringe full of the purest smack to wrap me in a cotton-wool cocoon.

Dutchie dabbed at the open cuts and grazes with the Dettol-soaked tissues. Compared to what the rest of my body was feeling, the stings were fluttering kisses. When he was finished he collected the tissues, dumped them in the bin. He came back with a bottle of brandy, poured a couple of large ones.

'Get that into you. Any time you've brandy inside you, things could be a lot worse.'

I hate brandy but the double went down the hatch like it was suicidal. Dutchie poured another, kept pouring, and after I'd lost count of exactly how many brandies I hated, the pain started to subside. Dutchie watched me drink, sipping his own. Eventually he said, in a neutral tone: 'You were lucky, Harry.'

'I'd come out of a barrel of tits sucking my thumb. Luck had nothing to do with it. They knew exactly what they were doing.' I grimaced, shook my head, which only caused me to grimace some more. 'Bastards,' I whispered. 'Fucking bastards.'

'Without doubt. Any fatherless fuckers in particular?'

I shook my head again, gently this time.

'One of them sounded northern.'

'Those fuckers never need an excuse.'

'They had one.'

'You got verbal with northern cunts?' He pursed his lips. 'Not like you, Harry.'

'I never said a fucking word. They jumped me from behind. Never even seen them coming.'

'So why?'

I drank the rest of the brandy, pushed the glass forward for a refill.

'He told me to stay away from her.'

'Her? Who her?'

'He didn't say. All he said was, stay away from her. Otherwise it'll be Ben next time.'

'Scumbag.' He drained the dregs of the bottle into his own glass and said: 'Katie?'

'I doubt it. She used to be engaged, some bloke who did a runner. He's hardly following her around, knocking lumps out of every bloke she meets in a pub.'

'So – who her?'

'Who else? Helen fucking Conway.'

'You were seen? Today?'

'Maybe I'm not as smart as I think I am.'

'No one's that smart, Harry. Think it was the bloke or her that sent the lads?'

'Does it matter?'

'Depends on whether you're taking it any further.'

'With the Dibble?'

'It's what any law-abiding citizen would do.'

'That'd be right, give the boys on the nightshift a laugh.'

'Give them something to do, at any rate.'

I shook my head, the brandy kicking in nicely. I was tired, sick and sore. Tired, mostly. No, sore mostly, and tired. And sick. I thought of the backroom in the office, dark, cold and empty. It made me want to puke.

'Drive me out home, Dutch. I'll sort you with a cab when we get there.'

'You're going to Dee's?'

'I'm paying for the place, Dutch. Since when is it Dee's?'

'Since she keeps chucking you out if it.'

I shrugged. It was too late to get into it about Gonzo. He said: 'If you want to stay here, Michelle won't mind. The bed's made up in the spare room. Don't worry about the kids, a bomb wouldn't wake them.'

'Cheers, Dutch, but no. I want to die in my own bed, boots off.'

I was lying, naturally. I didn't want to die in my own bed, boots on or off, or in any other bed for that matter. I didn't want to die, period, but even then I didn't know how fragile life can be, and how permanent death is. How squalid and black and final death really is.

*

Dutchie rang for a cab to meet us back at the house. I limped down the alleyway at his shoulder, the side he was carrying the baseball bat. He poured me into the car and we drove for home.

'What are you going to tell Conway?' We were passing the hospital.

'That a bottle of brandy is going on the expenses.'

'You're keeping the case? What are you, fucking insane?'

'Only now and again. You'd go mad otherwise.'

'Cop on, Harry. What about Ben?'

'Ben'll be okay. I'll look after Ben.'

'You'll look after Ben? Check the mirror, Harry, you've got mail.'

'No fucker'll touch Ben when I'm around, Dutch. I'll be cute.'

'You look cute. Cute like Quasimodo. And what happens to Ben if you're not around?'

'I don't know, Dutch. Give me a clue.'

'Jesus, Harry. It's loonyfuckingtoons.'

I don't like agreeing with people, it gives them the confidence to contradict you next time out, so I left that one hanging. The cab was waiting when we arrived. Dutchie turned as he was about to get in. I waited on the doorstep, not wanting to hear what he had to say.

'Let it go, Harry. It was only a hammering. Don't take it personal.'

'I hear you.'

'Yeah, that'd be a first.'

'Take care, Dutch. And cheers.'

I should have listened to Dutchie and not taken it personal. Maybe that way I wouldn't have ended up at the bottom of the river, a bullet under my ribs. Then again, maybe I'd have ended up there anyway, things have a way of working themselves out. Look at the platypus.

9

The lights were on in the sitting room, and I could hear the low murmur of the TV. I padded upstairs to the bathroom. Hoping the mirror would hold, because I still had three of seven left to serve on my current run of bad luck.

I'd got off light. The only visible damage was a bruised nose, a cut above my right eye. I mopped up with a handful of toilet paper, stuck a Band-Aid on the cut, went back downstairs.

Denise was curled up on the couch, a duvet tucked around her legs, smoking a joint, a fire dying in the grate. She didn't offer the jay so I slumped into the armchair, wincing at the dull bolts of pain, and looked at the TV too.

She looked lifeless, sprawled out on the couch, worn, tired. Denise could sparkle when she scrubbed up but when she wasn't interested she really let things slide. Shrouding her body under baggy jumpers, hiding behind a stony mask that emphasised the lines around her eyes. Laughter lines, she called them once, but nothing's that funny. Nothing had been that funny since Ben was born, anyway. That day, Denise retreated behind a wall there was no climbing over, no going around and no tunnelling under. A damsel in distress, waiting in her tower for a handsome prince to saunter by, or maybe just a different frog.

It wasn't post-natal stress either. Denise loved Ben right from day one and without reservation. Denise just hated Ben's father, hated herself for succumbing to his soft-chat. I didn't blame her. I didn't much like Ben's father myself, and I liked him less with each day that passed.

There was a movie on, based on a true story, Denise loved true stories, they made her feel that her own life wasn't as bad as she thought, or maybe they just distracted her from how bad it actually was. We sat in silence for about ten minutes until the ad break kicked in. When she spoke her tone was flat.

'I presume you've a good reason for being here.'

'I lost my keys to the office.'

'Well, I hope you're here to pick up spares.'

I sidestepped it.

'I thought Gonzo might have arrived.'

'You couldn't ring to find out?'

'I did ring. You weren't home.'

'You couldn't ring again?'

I shrugged. She tried another tack.

'You drove in that condition?'

'Dutch drove. He wasn't drinking.'

'And what happened your face?'

'I slipped in the alley. That's where I must've lost the keys. It looks worse than it is.'

'Pity.'

'Jesus, Dee.'

She whirled, face flushed.

'Don't Jesus me, Harry! Coming in here half-pissed, giving me grief.'

'I'm giving you grief? You need to get out more.'

The words were out before I realised what I'd said.

'Think I don't know that? Think I like sitting at home on my own while you're out gallivanting? Think I prefer sitting in this . . . this fucking hole while you're out enjoying yourself?'

'You're the one chucked me out, remember? And all I had was a couple of pints in Dutchie's.'

'Really? And how is Dutchie? I haven't seen him in months. Oh that's right, I haven't been out in months.'

Part of the problem was that Denise didn't have many friends. Some of them had moved away from town, some married, most of them wanted to talk about something other than their kids when they went out for a night on the tiles. There were times when Denise bordered on the obsessive when it came to Ben. It was probably because he was an only child, but the time had never seemed right for us to have another kid. The fact that we'd had sex maybe five or six times since Ben was born didn't help.

'Give it up, Dee. I was always asking you to go out.'

'To the pub. That's not going out, it's a life sentence.'

She shook her head, disgusted, and then realised the ad break was over. We sat in silence for the rest of the movie. When it was over, and Sally Field had finished crying and kissing the lawyer who'd vanquished the fiendish Iraqis, Denise got up. She emptied the ashtray, stood on a stool to put the joint makings on top of the bookcase, picked up the duvet.

'By the way,' she said, the door half-open, 'Gonzo left another message. Said he has a couple of things to do tomorrow but he'll meet you in Dutchie's, after ten.'

She closed the door. I stayed sitting in the armchair, feeling like someone had just kicked me in the gut, how I'd puke if I tried to get up. Then I remembered that someone had already kicked themselves happy on my gut, how there was nothing left that nature hadn't screwed down tight. I went out to the kitchen, made a sandwich, washed it down with a pint of milk. Then I went back to the sitting room and put on some mellow trip-hop, the volume low because Denise hated trip-hop and pretty much everything else I liked to listen to. I rolled a joint, for medicinal purposes only.

Gonzo, the Eight Ball Gonzo, was coming home. I sparked the jay, waited for the lightning to crack, the earth to erupt beneath my feet.

10

Dutchie had a theory about Gonzo. He reckoned Gonzo wasn't a bad bloke as such, it was just that the universe was too small to cope.

Halfway down the jay I took Gonzo's photograph down from the mantelpiece. I'd have binned it years before but Denise had insisted on keeping it, Dutchie playing shutterbug the night Ben was born, Gonzo flat on his back, panned out on Dutchie's pool table. Long and skinny, shoulders hunched, like he was always waiting for someone to sandbag him from behind. Laughing up at the camera, face flushed and eyes small, a jay smouldering between the fingers of his right hand, the black ball in his left.

Gonzo cut to the chase, reckoned that pool was a simple game. People complicated things, trying to play shots you'd need a degree in quantum physics to understand. He reckoned the only eight ball worth worrying about was a gram of crystal meth, which he claimed was just about enough to keep you wired for the weekend. For Gonzo, playing pool was all about getting the black ball into a certain position and letting gravity do the rest. Which was why, in the photo, his left hand was hovering over the centre pocket of the pool table, ready to drop the black. It was the only trick shot he ever learned, the only angle he ever worked out. He called it the Eight Ball Boogie.

We'd been close for brothers, close enough to want to kill one another and too close to actually follow through, although he'd tried it on one night, out back of Dutchie's place. Late enough to be getting early, a lock-in in full swing, the doors bolted. A couple of jays doing the rounds, a game of cards on the pool table, stud poker, two cards down, a three-card flop showing. I was sitting on a pair of tens, a king showing in the flop. We were the only two left in the pot, and it was all paper but not so much you could have dressed a skinny stripper. Gonzo wasn't too flush, and he needed the pot to stay in touch. He dug in the watch pocket of his jeans, dropped a wrap of silver foil into the pile.

'That's an eighth,' he said. 'I'll make it fifteen. Seeing as how I know you.'

'You're a sweetheart.' He could have been bluffing, or he could have pulled a second king. It wasn't likely, I'd pulled one myself, but I didn't have anything to back up the tens. And he could have just been having a laugh, knowing we'd end up smoking the dope anyway. It was hard to tell what he was thinking from the wrong side of his shades. He was sitting back, relaxed, like he was waiting to thumb a lift on the next glacier passing through.

'He's spoofing, Harry.' Celine, head on my shoulder, eyes closed. Not needing to look to guess that Gonzo was on a bluff.

'No speech play,' Gonzo intoned, mechanical. He grinned at me. 'Fifteen to you, Harry – time for steel balls.'

'Let Celine have her say.' The pot wasn't worth throwing

fifteen quid away, but I wanted him to think I was tempted, make him sweat for it. Besides, I liked to hear Celine talk, liked it so much I'd asked her if she was interested in talking at the top of an aisle. She said she'd talk about if we talked about getting a place together. Once we moved in we talked about everything except getting married, but we were getting around to it, and sooner rather than later.

'Sting the fucker,' she murmured.

Dutchie and Chizzer took a bet on whether Gonzo was bluffing. Michelle started shuffling the cards, impatient.

'C'mon, Harry,' Gonzo said. 'Call it, or I'll be showing Celine my balls of steel.'

That she didn't like, an edge in her voice.

'Take him to the cleaners, Harry. Teach him some manners.'

He just laughed at that. Michelle pppffffed, threw the cards on the table, climbed down off her barstool.

'Anybody for a fresh one?'

'I'll have a cider,' I said, throwing the cards on the table. 'All yours, Gonz. Take it home.'

Gonzo flipped the shades up, cackled harsh, turned over his cards, no king. Celine shook her head, disgusted. Chizzer took Dutchie's fiver. I watched Gonzo's eyes, dead and shiny, a double eclipse.

'Play the player, Harry, not the cards.' He raked in the cash, jabbed a forefinger in my direction. 'Lesson number one.'

'Send me the bill.' He was about to kick off, you could always tell with Gonzo. I needed to get away from the table. 'Deal me out, I'm giving Michelle a hand with the beers.'

'Work away.' He nodded at Celine. 'I'll show blondie some real stud while you're gone.'

'Asshole.'

She sounded tense.

'Change the record, Gonz,' I said, but he left the needle in the groove. I took off to the bar, he followed, one thing led to another and from nowhere Gonzo swung his bottle. It broke my arm, but only because I had my arm up to protect my face. When I fell back against the bar he freaked, coming at me with the broken neck of the bottle. I grabbed for his wrist and he battered me with his free fist until Dutchie and Chizzer jumped him.

It took both of them to hold him down. Michelle and Celine bundled me into the car, drove to Casualty. It took three or four hours to see a doctor, another couple for them to X-Ray my arm, set it in plaster. By then Gonzo had calmed down, which was just as well, he was the only one waiting when I came out of the cubicle. We sat in the car, smoking, burning off the hospital smell.

'Something I want to say,' he muttered.

I was touched by his penitent tone and then it all kicked in, the dope, the broken arm, the early hour. I realised that it couldn't have been easy for him, my moving in with Celine. Gonzo and I had been living together for nearly twenty years, wards of the state after a drunk driver orphaned us. All our lives we'd been shunted from one institution to another, being fucked over by staff, or bigger kids, or teachers who knew they could vent their frustrations because no one gave a fuck about us back home.

We'd grown up and grown hard, fighting the odds and always losing, but one thing we never did, we never took it lying down. An allergy to penicillin was about all we had in common, but he was my kid brother and all through the bad years, even during the hassle from the Dibble, the Provo threats when Gonzo started dealing, nothing had prised us apart. But even that doesn't tell you how close we were.

'I wanted to tell you,' he said, 'that I fucked Celine.'

I didn't kill him. That's how close we were.

The worst thing was the way he smiled when he said those words. It was a canine smile, dead and dry. I sat there, dumb, the cigarette smouldering as I read the No Smoking sign on the glove compartment over and over again. Not knowing if I should laugh or cry or kick someone's head in. Celine's, preferably, but Gonzo's would have to do because you don't hit a woman. Not even if she's dug her talons in deep, ripped your guts out, so you don't have to go to the bother of puking them up whole.

After that night I knew only two things for sure. One, you play the player, not the cards. Two, I would never, in my entire life, be as happy again as I was before Gonzo said those three simple words, 'I fucked Celine'.

*

It took me a while to realise that Gonzo smiled that way because he was relieved I finally knew. Not about Celine, that was the first and last time Gonzo and Celine got it together, although it was the kind of once that tends to last. Gonzo wanted me to know what he was really like, what he was capable of, who he really was. I'd always known he was erratic, even begun to suspect that he was actually a sociopath, gone so far as to get a book out of the library and check off the symptoms. But I'd never thought there was a vacuum at his core.

When he smiled that night though, I knew there was no line he wouldn't cross. Gonzo had screwed Celine simply because he knew Celine was the only woman I had ever considered living with, having kids with, getting old with. Maybe even being happy with.

Celine cried for a week solid but I hung tough, moved out of the apartment, sleeping on Chizzer's couch for a couple of weeks until I found a bed-sit down near the docks. It was just about big enough to let me exhale all the way out but I didn't mind, I wasn't planning any dinner parties.

After a month or so Gonzo called around and after a couple of false starts we kissed and made up over a bottle of Southern Comfort, Ritz mixer, because, come hell or high hippies, Gonzo was my brother and we had no one else. All the while I knew that screwing Celine was only part of it, that Gonzo needed my feedback to fully enjoy his sick kicks. I ignored the self-loathing by hating Celine. Not blaming her, just hating. Sometimes you just need to hate.

It would have been neat and tidy if I'd met Denise on the rebound but it was nearly a year later when I walked into the bank, got skewered by a bold gaze, big brown eyes. The smile was the clincher. It was wide and warm, and when she turned up the wattage it warned off shipping.

One night I bumped into her in Bojangle's and told her, flushed with maybe three pints too many, that she was the kind of beautiful that would finally persuade the UFOs to land. She liked that, said it was the first compliment she'd been paid since she'd arrived in town. One thing led to another, and another led to the other.

She was bubbly and fun, exactly what I was looking for, because I'd been looking for nothing at all. The sex was good, so good it was practically all we did. It wasn't inevitable that she'd wind up pregnant but she did, nearly five months later. All the morning-after pill did was make her sick, although not nearly as sick as the news that it hadn't worked. She told me the night before I was due to go on holiday with the lads. I didn't enjoy the holiday much, but I wouldn't have enjoyed being at home much more. I was gone three months too, which didn't help, but that's a whole different story.

We argued about abortion but kept flipping sides. I was more practical in the morning, when she was going through a nurturing phase. That changed in the evening, when maudlin self-pity kicked in after she'd had a few defiant pints, a guilty cigarette. She told me it was none of my business anyway, it was a woman's right to choose. I asked her if she thought the baby might be a girl, who would grow up to be a woman, with the right to choose. One evening I arrived at her flat to find her sobbing. She eventually gulped it out, she'd once helped a friend get to Liverpool and that no matter what her nightmares were about the soundtrack was always the wailing of babies.

I was more chilled at night. Mellow after a couple of joints, thinking about playing Mozart to her belly, how I'd be able to teach him Pelé's body-swerve. In the morning I'd wake up in a cold sweat, unable to breathe, the weight of the day, and the rest of my days, a slab on my chest.

One morning I woke to find her sitting on a chair, holding an unlit cigarette, watching me. She told me she was having the baby, that it would be a boy, and that his name would be Ben. I liked the name.

I asked her to marry me. I thought it was the right thing to do.

'Two wrongs don't make a right, Harry. The only good reason

for getting married is that you don't have to go home for Christmas dinner.'

It was a difficult pregnancy. The night we finally told her parents, three months down the line, I had my own parentage questioned. Maura cried and Brendan threatened me with physical force before chucking me out of the house. Denise moved into my poky bed-sit, so I couldn't breathe out all the way anymore, and we started making plans, none of them together. Her hormones ran riot and she developed cravings for garlic bread, mint ice cream. Her weight shot up by nearly two stone, not counting the burgeoning Ben. She became addicted to talk shows, toy advertisements. I tried to ignore the macabre cabaret in my head, the rhythm section distorted by a feedback screech of panic.

Dutchie offered me a couple of nights working behind the bar. I took them, as much to get out of the flat as for the extra money. Once I had a few quid stashed we moved out to Duncashlin, opposite the big American medical supply complex, a once-plush estate that had been allowed run to seed. The rent was cheap because the back walls were damp but it had two bedrooms. Once we moved in Denise spent all her free time converting one of the bedrooms into a nursery.

I worked back a lot on the job, weekends too, and not only because Denise and I were arguing over the remote control, matte or emulsion, Nescafé or Bewley's. Eventually she started sleeping in the nursery, complaining that I wasn't taking her need for extra space in bed into consideration. I knew my elbows weren't the problem but I didn't mind. I'd been thinking of sleeping in the nursery myself but I can't stand the smell of new paint.

In total, before and after Ben was born, we went without sex for just over fourteen months. It took Denise a fortnight to tell me sex was the only thing we had in common.

Ben was born on a Tuesday, three days late, seven pounds three ounces. Once the formalities had been observed, Gonzo took me out on the kind of tear that could have toppled an ancient civilisation. We ended up back in Dutchie's, yet another lock-in, which was when the photograph of Gonzo panned out on the pool table was taken. The christening was held two months later, and everything went according to plan bar the god-father not turning up. There was no excuse and no apology, not even a card for Ben. Radio silence, for nearly four years, and it wasn't his going away that finally killed me, it was that I knew he could never come back.

But he'd come back anyway. I knew why, and I knew I had to stop him, and I knew that I wasn't the only one who couldn't afford for me to die trying.

*

I looked in on Ben on the way to bed. Found myself, as usual, looking down at a tiny bottom cocked in the air. I dredged him up from the depths of the quilt, settled his head on the pillow, sat on the edge of his bed. Watching him breathe, light and shallow.

He was a good kid, but the only way Ben would ever win a Bonny Baby contest was if he set about the other kids with the nearest blunt object. Which, knowing Ben for the tow-headed thug he was, wasn't beyond the realms of possibility. He was a brute of a four-year-old, strong for his age, with a prominent brow and hooded, sleepy eyes, his father's eyes. He had a guileless face and his mother's smile, although his chipped teeth were a mess. Ben never walked anywhere he could run, was still naïve enough to believe that the world should open up before him the way he wanted to find it. He was a good kid, affectionate and open, and if he could have done with a sister or a brother to knock some corners off, he wasn't doing too badly in the circumstances.

A spectre – three spectres, knocking corners off me – loomed large. I kissed him on the forehead, went to bed, hoping I'd wake up the next morning to find that Gonzo's homecoming was just another nightmare.

*

Denise was still awake. I sensed it without turning on the light. A hunched lump on the other side of the bed, against the wall, like she was trying to get into the bedroom next door by a process of osmosis. I had no right to be there, but there were only two bedrooms and Ben's bed was a single. I had no intention of sleeping on the couch, either, already starting to stiffen up. Besides, I was paying the mortgage.

I lit a smoke when I was under the covers, waited for the inquisition. She didn't disappoint.

'Who is she?' she asked.

'Who's who?'

'She. Her. The one you were with.'

'I told you. I was on my tod.'

'All night? Until now?'

She tugged at the quilt, to remind me that she already had about ninety per cent of it tucked under her chin. Breathing through her nose, heavy.

'What's up, Dee?'

She didn't answer, didn't move, until I stubbed the cigarette and lay down. Turning towards her but not so near she might have to move away, because she had nowhere to go.

'We should be in Dallas, Harry. You know we should be there. Everyone else is there. I'm sick and tired of not being able to do the things we want to do.'

The things *she* wanted to do, the reason for the last chucking out. The last place on earth I wanted to be was in Dallas, with her parents, to celebrate her sister's fifth wedding anniversary.

'Look, Dee—'

'No Harry, you look. Look at yourself. Look at our lives. When was the last time we had a holiday?'

'We went to Wicklow, last year.'

'That was two years ago, Harry. And Wicklow isn't a holiday, it's an assault course. Marian and Jeff went to Barbados last September. Barbados is a holiday.'

'Marian and Jeff don't have responsibilities.' What they did have was over a quarter of a million dollars in the bank, courtesy of Jeff's software rewrites on Tenga Warriors III: Apocalypse Hence. I knew it was a quarter of a million because Jeff was coy like a kid with a new dirty word. 'They can up sticks and go wherever they want, whenever they want. We can't. It's as simple as that.'

'You think I don't know that?'

'So what's the problem?'

'*That's* the fucking problem.'

'I'm the problem.' Staying calm. 'My job is the problem.'

If Denise wanted a fight she was in the wrong building. I'd gone fifteen rounds already, been knocked down in every one. I turned away from her, tried to make myself comfortable. I was nearly asleep when she spoke.

'Harry?'

'What?'

She turned towards me, cuddling close, her voice different, coquettish. Denise knew every game in the book, knew them so well they bored her. Which was why she didn't bother to play by the rules anymore.

'What would you do if *I* had an affair?'

My guts churned, third time that night. Denise knew all about Gonzo and Celine, it was her last resort. I took a deep breath.

'You have to be married to have an affair, Dee. We're not even seeing each other anymore.'

'Okay then. What would you do if I fucked someone else?'

'Have you?'

She laughed, delighted at my sullen tone.

'Of course I haven't. Don't be daft.'

She kissed my cheek, the touch no more than a breath. I closed my eyes, balled my fists, tried to breathe. I wanted to leave the room, the house, to emigrate – whatever it took to slough off the sick emotional seesaw. But I didn't move, knowing that I had nowhere to go that I wouldn't want to kill myself for leaving behind the tow-headed thug in the next room. Seething at the power she possessed, the ability to reduce my entire existence to gut instinct. And if she didn't know it for fact she sensed it, teasing: 'It's just a question, Harry.'

'Just a question?'

'You know what I mean. A rhetorical question.'

'You're not supposed to answer rhetorical questions.'

'It was in a questionnaire.' She was flirting by now. 'It's a questionnaire question.'

'Know your problem, Dee?'

'I only have one?'

'Too much *Cosmo* and not enough *Viz*. Those magazines are fucking with your head.'

'Maybe. But better that than no fucking at all.'

And she began stroking the inside of my thigh, her palm cool and soft. I closed my eyes. Too weak to stop her, not wanting to anyway, half afraid it was another wind-up and too desperate to believe that it wasn't.

'You still didn't answer my question,' she murmured. Brushing my erection, holding off, teasing. I turned until my mouth was at her ear.

'If you fucked anyone else, I'd kill him and cripple you.'

There was dead silence. Then she eased herself slowly on top of me, sending bolts of pain ricocheting through my body. Somehow it didn't seem to matter.

'Mmmmmm,' she said, slipping me inside her. 'Right answer.'

Afterwards she slept sound. I cuddled behind her, spooning, my elbow resting on her hip, my hand flat against the ribcage under her breast. Feeling her heartbeat rumble through my palm, up my arm. I drifted off trying to work it out, knowing that if I never slept again I still wouldn't understand her.

11

I crawled out of bed just before noon, drank a pot of coffee. Smoked a couple of twists, coughed up everything that wasn't nailed down. Then I smoked some more, read the note on the kitchen table that said Denise was gone shopping, be back before Christmas, but didn't specify what year. I stood under the shower until the water ran cold, drank some more coffee, went outside to find the car not there. The walk into town finally sobered me up.

The sleet was coming down again, soft, not sticking, the day mild. I took the long way into town, left Herbie's number on redial, getting an engaged tone. Dropped a padded envelope through his letterbox, not knocking him up, I had reeled Herbie in from cyberspace once before and it wasn't a pretty sight.

I made the office by one, ignoring the navy Mondeo parked across the street, the two blokes looking bored and doing it in all directions. When I got upstairs I rang down for coffee. Then I started counting to ten. They kicked the door in on twelve.

Brady accounted for two-thirds of the boarding party. The small guy was dapper in a charcoal-grey three-piece, patent leather shoes. The tie had a Windsor knot and his skull was shaved close to the bone. He had big, round eyes, narrow cheekbones, and the lips were no thinner than a paper-cut. He was a fruit, a banana, bent for sure but so yellow about it people didn't really notice. Pushing sixty, looking at retirement and liking the view.

'Let me guess,' I said, eyeballing Brady. 'You're the bad cop, right?'

'See, they told us about the bullshit,' Brady rasped. 'Okay? So you don't have to be cute. We're already impressed.'

I looked at the Fruit.

'Get to the punch-line. I'm busy.'

The Fruit sighed, sat down, rearranged his face into what he probably thought was beatific tolerance. From where I was sitting, it looked like he was having a stroke.

'Let's start again,' the Fruit said. His tone was neutral, dry. 'I'm Detective-Inspector Senan Galway.' He jerked a thumb over his shoulder. 'This is Detective-Sergeant Ronan Brady.' He crossed his legs, clasped his hands around a knee. 'Do you have ID?'

'Loads, as it happens. For who, exactly?'

Galway sighed again. Brady flexed his fingers, balling his hands into fists. He looked like he was expecting trouble, which made me nervous, the Dibble expecting trouble is a self-fulfilling prophecy.

'For Harry Rigby. He's a . . .' He spoke over his shoulder. 'What is he?'

Brady, rolling back and forth on the balls of his feet, snickered.

'A research consultant.'

'Right,' Galway confirmed. 'Harry Rigby. The research consultant.'

'That's me.'

'I know it's you. I still need ID. It's procedure.'

'It's procedure to know whose rights you're abusing?'

'Don't be cute,' Brady growled. 'Show him the ID.'

'Fair enough.'

I dug the driving licence from my wallet, held it out. When Galway reached I flipped the licence back, said: 'Do you?'

'What?'

'Have ID?'

Brady darted forward, nimble as Nijinsky. Placed his fists on the desk, weight on his knuckles, leaning forward until his face was about six inches from mine. It looked pretty, a kaleidoscope of purples and reds, even a tinge of yellow in the whites of his eyes, which were bulging like they were about to pop out and squelch in my face. The smell of stale whiskey could have cleaned drains. He enunciated each syllable, slow and distinct.

'Give. Him. The. Fuck. En. Eye. Dee.'

'You should floss,' I told him and then he was around the desk, barging me face-first against the filing cabinet, pounding a huge fist into my kidneys. One punch was enough, from Brady a dirty look would have been enough. He let go. I slumped to the ground, coughing up a kidney.

Brady snapped the driving licence out of my hand, handed it over. Galway gave it a cursory glance, put it back on the desk, nodded. Brady backed off, careful, like he'd never done it before. I dragged myself back onto the seat. Galway took a little box from the inside pocket of his jacket, popped a mint. Not wanting to be there, finding the rough stuff distasteful. My heart went out to him. My other kidney stayed where it was, in a coma.

'Now,' Galway said quietly, 'tell me about Conway.'

I sounded like a gut-shot accordion.

'Who's Conway?'

We stared. Galway didn't blink. I couldn't remember him blinking since he'd entered the office, although it was possible he had sneaked one in while Brady was using my face to sand down the filing cabinet.

'Francis Conway,' Galway intoned, bored as granite, 'auction-eer. He was here yesterday morning, in this office, for almost an hour. What did you talk about?'

There was a knock on the door. Andrea walked in with the coffee. Her smile froze halfway to the desk. I winked as she set the coffee down, letting her know everything was okay. Brady watched her go. Galway stared at me. When the door closed he said: 'Last chance.'

'Very generous. I don't know any Conway.'

He waved a careless hand. Brady moved around the desk, started tugging at the top drawer of the filing cabinet.

'It's locked,' I told him. 'In case some lowlife wants to see what I keep in there.'

'Give me the key,' he rasped, flexing his fingers. I gave him the key. He yanked the drawer open, pulled out the files, flittered them across the floor. He did the same with the second drawer, and the third. I rolled a twist and looked at Galway. Galway stared back, unblinking.

'This is procedure?' I asked.

'I'd have thought you'd be well acquainted with procedure by now.'

'I am. I thought this might be a new Interpol directive the locals haven't tumbled to yet.'

Brady rammed the filing cabinet doors home.

'Nothing,' he growled.

'Try the desk,' I said. 'That's not even locked.'

He muttered something coarse, pulled the top drawer open. The notepad and chequebook went the same way as the cabinet files. Then he paused, picked up the newspaper clipping Katie had left behind. He handed it to Galway. Galway looked it over, shot me a look of cool appraisal. It made my flesh crawl, like he had finally decided how much I was worth. He tapped the clipping.

'What's this?'

'They call them newspapers. People read them. You could always look at the pictures.'

'What's it doing in your desk?'

'Somersaults, mainly. But I'm teaching it to miaow.'

The mint swapped cheeks. Galway nodded again. Brady opened the bottom drawer. I heard a sharp intake of breath, and then my neck was seized in an iron grip. Brady hooked the gun by the trigger guard and placed it on the desk in front of Galway. The fingers were talons. Bolts of pain shot through my shoulders, doing wonders for my posture.

Galway wasn't looking at me. Galway was looking at the .38, resplendent in all its short, stubby glory. It didn't look too impressive lying there, but Galway knew as well as I did that a Special can stop a charging Rhino if you pick the right spot. He looked at me, a gleam in his eye.

'I hope you've a licence for that. Because if you have it's a fake and I'll peg you to the wall and not charge for the nails.'

I gurgled, Brady's huge vice still folded around my throat. Galway motioned with his hand. Brady relaxed his grip, took one step back to the window, the better to block out the light. I gasped, whooped in a couple of deep breaths that caught fire on the way down. Galway nodded at the gun.

'Have you?'

'Have I what?' I snapped, rolling my head from side to side. Galway frowned at the surly tone but too many people were taking advantage of my sunny disposition for me to care. Hospitality is one thing, taking liberties is another. Galway pointed at the gun.

'Have you a licence for that?'

'Where would I get a licence for that?'

For a second I thought Galway was going to spontaneously combust.

'You wouldn't,' he smirked. 'Like I said, it'd be a fake.'

'Exactly. Like the gun.'

'Say again?'

'Like the gun. It's a replica. I bought it from a barman on Ibiza, an English bloke called Winston, if you can believe that. Got special permission from Spanish customs to bring it on the plane, too. Nice blokes, Spanish customs. They ask first, strangle later.'

Galway studied my face. Then he nodded at Brady. Brady picked up the gun, snapped it open. Threw it back on the desk.

'Replica,' he said, disgusted. Galway's lips disappeared.

'What do you need a replica gun for?'

'We get a lot of Dibble around the Quarter. You can't be too careful.'

His eyelids flickered. Red spots appeared below his cheekbones. I wondered if I hadn't pushed him too far, let stubbornness cloud what little judgement I have. Brady seemed to be of the same opinion. He shuffled from foot to foot. Finally he came around the desk, stood behind Galway. Galway came to a decision.

'Alright, picnic's over. Let's talk Conway. We can talk here or we can talk in the cells. Personally,' he added, popping another mint into his mouth, 'I'd rather talk in the cells, where we can have a little privacy. But that's up to you.'

I nodded. Then I sparked the twist, exhaled at the ceiling, picked a stray flake of tobacco from my lower lip.

'First off, we'll do this here because unless you want to arrest me you have no legal basis to take me anywhere. Second, I'm telling you nothing about Conway because the only reason I might know a Conway was if he was a client of mine and it'd be unethical to breach client confidentiality. Third, I'm letting fuck-wit there off with the Tyson bullshit but only because he's a repressed homosexual and I'm blaming his parents.'

Brady tensed but didn't move. It was just as well. I was in no shape for jumping through the window.

'Fourth, if he so much looks crooked at me again I'm taking him, you and the whole fucking Dibble to the cleaners, because I'm your worst nightmare, a sucker who knows his rights. Fifth, both of you can fuck off out of my face because my coffee's getting cold and if there's one thing I hate more than Dibble who've watched too much Kojak it's cold coffee. Any questions?'

Galway worked up a glum expression.

'Don't make me get a search warrant.'

'What are you going to do?' I asked, nodding at the mess on the floor. 'Spray some graffiti?'

'If I have to get a search warrant I can't guarantee the safety of anything in this office.'

Brady was quick on the uptake. Picked my mobile phone off the desk, dropped it on the ground. Then he tipped the filing cabinet over, waited for the crunch, laid the mangled phone on the desk again, leaving the filing cabinet horizontal. Galway shrugged, an exaggerated gesture.

'Accidents have a way of happening.'

'Speak up, Chief. The tape doesn't pick up whispers.'

Brady glared. If looks could kill, I'd have been cremated on the spot.

'It's illegal to record conversations without mutual consent.'

'So sue me. It'll go all the way to The Hague and I haven't been abroad in years.'

'Alright, alright. Jesus.' Galway held up his hand. He sounded tired. He stood up. 'We could have done this the easy way.'

'There's an easy way now?'

'I'll be seeing you again, Rigby.'

'Maybe, I spend a lot of time in public toilets. And watch out for the first landing on the way down. It doesn't squeak when you stand on it.'

Brady stayed behind when Galway left. Rubbing his nose, and there was a lot of it to rub. I waited.

'You don't know Frank Conway,' he said.

'I don't get out so much these days.'

'I know Frank Conway. He's scum, a real lowlife. He'd have his grandmother re-zoned for the tax relief.'

I waited again.

'You keeping anything from me, Rigby?'

'Same as before. Nothing you don't already know.'

'Want some advice?'

'No.'

'You're smart enough to play dumb. Don't be dumb enough to play it smart. Conway's a dangerous bastard.'

'He hasn't seen my big brother.'

He nodded again, made for the door.

'Galway wants Conway,' he warned, a parting shot. 'And what Galway wants, Galway gets.'

'Galway wants your ass. Is he getting that?'

He stared, stony-faced. Then he grinned, eyes crinkling. For a moment he was a different man, friendly and almost human.

'He's getting it, alright. Back of the fucking head he's getting it.'

He left. When I was sure they weren't coming back I slumped in the chair, hands shaking, breath coming too fast. I couldn't work out which was the new bruise when I checked my back in the bathroom mirror, but when it finally arrived my piss was a pale shade of pink.

I put the gun away, limped across to The Cellars. Needing a drink like a hole in the head and finding some comfort in the prospect of both.

12

Dutchie took me into the pool-room, coffee for him, Red Bull-vodka for me, ham-and-cheese toasties all round. He stirred his coffee, chewed his gum and didn't interrupt while I told him about the heavy gang. When I was finished he said: 'Want my advice?'

'No.'

Everyone wanted to give me advice. All I wanted was peace and quiet, maybe an Audi with go-fast stripes.

'Drop Conway. He's bad news.'

'That's what sells, Dutch. Why?'

'His motors? The second-hand ones?'

'They're ringers?'

'More than likely. Anyway, you know Tommy Armstrong?'

'Stretch Armstrong? Gangly fucker, talks like he's chewing hot spuds?'

Dutchie nodded, sipped some coffee.

'He drives for Conway. Picks up the cars in Belfast, takes them across the border.'

'Nice work if you can get it.'

'Stretch picks them up at the port, coming off the ferry.'

'They're coming *through* Belfast? From where?'

'Amsterdam, via Liverpool.'

'Makes sense. There's good E in Amsterdam.'

Dutchie sniffed.

'Fuckers around here wouldn't know a good E from a blue Smartie. That Belfast shite is muck. Cheap speed, a dab of trips, that's your bag.'

'Belfast shite?'

'That's where all the trade's coming in from. Churning it out like Polo mints, they are. Two cheers for the peace process.'

'East or west?' I asked.

'Does it matter?'

'It might, if my client's trying to fuck them over.'

'East.'

'Nasty.'

'No nastier than West. Want a laugh?'

'Did it this morning, got it over with.'

'Just as well. According to Stretch, Conway's planning something big.'

'A new town hall?'

'Bigger. Stretch didn't say, but at a guess I'd say Conway's bypassing East Belfast, not paying his dues. Branching out on his tod.'

'Christ on a landmine. How smart is that?'

'You tell me. Those fuckers aren't happy since Blair cut them off at the knees. They're itching so bad they don't need an excuse to scratch.'

I thought it through. Conway trafficking E explained Galway

and Brady, but it didn't explain why Conway might think his wife was screwing around. Or why he might want me to think she was. But there had to be a connection. It was too much of a coincidence otherwise.

'This is kosher?' I asked.

'Like a plague of frogs. Stretch doesn't have the imagination to make it up.'

'True enough. Then there's this.'

I handed him Katie's newspaper clipping. He scanned through it.

'Sheridan? What's he to do with anything?'

'That girl Katie, who was in last night? She gave me that, yesterday. When Abbott and Costello were in this morning they found it in my desk. It got their attention.'

'So?'

'So they were asking about Frank Conway, auctioneer. The real-estate slimebag who happens to be up to his arse in illicit loot. Tony Sheridan's a politician.'

Dutchie nodded.

'So we just drop the real estate bit.'

'Correct.' I pointed out Frank Conway, top corner of the photograph. 'That apartment complex he's building on the river, where the shoeboxes are going for one-sixty a throw. Remind me about the environmental bullshit that went with that.'

'You're talking brown envelopes.' He shook his head. 'So what? They need somewhere to put all the punters they're decentralising from Dublin. Re-zoning scam or no re-zoning scam, those apartments were always going to be built.'

'Maybe, maybe not. But that photograph puts Conway and Sheridan together in the same picture.'

'That's a big picture, Harry. There's a lot of people in it.'

He was right in a way, but he was wrong too. It was a big picture, the kind with a real big frame.

I was wrong too, but I was right in a way. The one time I got it right, I didn't even know it.

*

I finished the drink and we went through to the bar. Dutchie plunged the glass and plate into the soapy water in the sink, nodded at the sticking plaster above my eye.

'What did you tell Dee about the hammering?'

'That I fell in the alleyway. By the way—'

'What?'

'Gonzo rang.'

He stopped plunging. His eyebrows nearly disappeared into his crew cut, which is no mean feat.

'Gonzo?'

'The one and only, thank fuck.'

'Jesus. Fuck.' He beamed. 'Fucking hell, Harry! What'd he say?'

'He left a message, said he'd be home for Christmas. He'll be in here tonight.'

He laughed out loud. It sounded forced, too much, not Dutch. I let it slide. I wasn't feeling much like myself either.

'Tonight? Typical fucking Gonz. How long's it been?'

'Four years, near enough.'

'Too long.'

'Not nearly long enough, Dutch. See you later.'

'Yeah. And Harry? We already know you're a miserable bastard. You've nothing left to prove.'

'Fuck you.'

'I'll have to clear it with Michelle first.'

'No hurry. What time tonight?'

'Here for eight?'

'Sound.'

*

I went back across the road to the office. There was a message on the machine, Herbie with news, call. I called.

'Alright Harry?' Herbie sounded fresh and vital again, he'd obviously gone for snow for his Christmas treat. 'I got that Helen Conway stuff for you. Got a pen handy?'

'Shoot.'

He reeled off a list of figures. Taking dictation from a coke-fuelled stoner can take a while when you don't have shorthand but in the end I knew more about Helen Conway's bank accounts than she needed to know herself. There was also information on insurance policies, health plans and membership of various clubs and organisations. Political donations, a trust fund, two company directorships, one of which was a subsidiary of her husband's real estate company. When Herbie got himself motivated, he was rapacious.

'Busy girl,' I commented. The bank accounts alone were impressive, nearly three hundred grand spread across five different banks at home. There were also the kind of accounts where you get a tan making a deposit, one in the Seychelles, another in Barbados, and she also had the obligatory Swiss deposit box, although that was probably for show. 'Nice work, Herb. Give me the same on Frank Conway, yeah?'

'Who he?'

I counted to five.

'He'll be Helen Conway's husband, Herb.'

'Oh, yeah – right.'

'Get a chance to download those pictures yet?'

'What pictures?'

'From the camera. I dropped it around this morning.'

There was a brief pause. I could imagine him panicking, trying to recall what he'd been doing earlier. Herbie, who was hard put to remember his real name most of the time. When he spoke again he sounded cautious.

'You were here this morning?'

'Not *there* there.' It would have been too easy to wind him up. 'I slipped the camera through your letterbox. In a padded envelope.'

The sigh of relief was audible.

'I haven't been downstairs yet. Hold on.' I heard him pounding down the stairs. Moments later he was back. 'Alright, I have it. Give me an hour and I'll see what I can do.'

'Sound. I'll be in the office until five.'

'Hey, Harry?'

'What?'

I knew what was coming.

'Anything moving on Imelda Sheridan?'

'Nothing, no. Hear anything more from Regan?'

'He's not taking my calls. You didn't get anyone to talk?'

'No go, Herb.'

'Fucking seen it on TV last night, Harry. They were all over it.'

I realised I hadn't heard the news, or seen a newspaper, in nearly two days.

'They talk to anyone?'

'No. It was a short report, long-range shots of the house, the usual shite.'

'So what are you complaining about?'

'It'll be dead in the water if we don't do something, that's what. Yesterday's fucking news, Harry.'

'I know, Herb. But I can't sell the story unless there's an angle, something to hang it on. They'll laugh me off the phone otherwise.'

'What are you talking about, angle? Sell them the facts. Just type it up, fuck the poetry. Tell it like it happened.'

'We don't know what happened. Besides, the Sundays pay better, and they love the kinky stuff. I say we stick it out, stay awake, hit one of the Sundays for a spread. Do the shots some justice.'

It was a curve ball, appealing to his vanity. He didn't even swing.

'Something you're not telling me, Harry?'

I didn't answer. He'd have thought I was insane if I told him that I didn't want to dig too deep around Imelda Sheridan because, no matter how ludicrous it sounded, gut instinct told me Gonzo was involved. But then Herbie was one of the lucky ones, Herbie had never met Gonzo.

Plus, I didn't know how Frank Conway and Tony Sheridan fitted together, or how close, or what kind of cesspit might turn up if I dug in the wrong place.

Plus, I was stiff, sore and tired, in no mood to answer to anyone, least of all Herbie.

'Harry?'

'I got laid last night, Herb. Which makes two nights in a row, first time in about five years. That's what I wasn't telling you. Happy now?'

'Harry—'

'I'll buzz you later, Herb. Sit tight.'

I smoked a couple of cigarettes, sifted through the events of the last twenty-four hours. Brady and Galway, Conway and Sheridan, the Three Stooges – they loomed large, shadows up a wall. I closed my eyes, bumped them around, trying to get them to fit. It didn't work, mainly because Helen Conway kept distracting me, svelte for her age in something black and silk with a suicidal neckline. The dodgems kept on bumping until Brady took offence at Conway digging him the elbow and a bare-knuckle brawl broke out.

I left them to it, wondered how much Helen Conway knew about her husband's sideline in narcotics. The bank accounts suggested she was up to speed, but that kind of evidence is circumstantial at best and slander at worst. Besides, Helen Conway didn't come across as the kind of woman who had recently discovered the high life. Helen Conway had been born in the stratosphere, six miles clear and rising.

There was a knock on the door some time around three. Katie poked her head in. When she saw I was alone she came all the way. She was holding two Styrofoam cups.

'Coffee? My treat?'

'Sure. Pull up a pew.'

She sat down, lit a cigarette. Fiddled with her lighter while I rolled a twist.

'What happened your face?'

'I fell leaving the pub. Sobered me up enough to get Dutchie to drive.'

'Tell me about it,' she said, a rueful tone. I got the impression she had something to say, that she was embarrassed about having to say it. I also got the impression that Katie wasn't used to being embarrassed. Hence the fidgeting, the faint puce tinge at her cheekbones. She spoke quickly.

'What I said last night . . .' The puce deepened to a rosy pink. 'I was drunk. That's not my style.'

I shrugged, magnanimous as all hell.

'Don't beat yourself up. Women find me irresistible. Desperate ones, mainly.'

'Thanks a lot. Now I'm desperate?'

'Desperate enough to give me your phone number.'

'That's desperate.'

'Thanks yourself.'

She smiled, and the embarrassment seeped away. The storm struck again, fast enough to leave us becalmed in its eye.

'So how is . . . Bren?' she asked. Her stare was bold, slightly mocking.

'Ben. He's fine, no deterioration in the last twenty-four hours.'

She got into it.

'Did you remember anything about Tony Sheridan you'd for-gotten yesterday?'

'Not a thing.'

'Hear any more about Imelda?'

I shook my head. She bristled.

'Is this the tough-guy routine again, Harry? Because if it is—'

'No kidding, something else came up, something that's more likely to pay the bills. The story's all yours, knock yourself out. If you pull something out of the bag I'll put you in touch with Herbie, with the shots. I won't even charge consultancy.'

'Can you give me some names? People I could talk to?'

'I'll give you the names of people I don't mind pissing off. Some of them might even know what they're talking about. You want to check anything they say, get back to me. Again, no fee.'

'This other job,' she said, as I jotted down some names and numbers. 'It must be paying well when you're throwing freebies around.'

'It's the festive spirit. Stick around, you might even get a compliment.'

'I'd prefer hard information. No offence.'

'None taken.'

She took the list of names and numbers, stubbed her cigarette, checked her watch. She got up, shouldered her bag and stretched, stifling a yawn. Her blouse tightened in all the right places.

'I'd better be getting on. Any plans for later?'

'Just the one – to stay away from flirty brunettes with cleavage to spare.'

Her eyes narrowed, mock serious.

'That was a compliment, right?'

'That was hard information. No offence.'

'None taken. See you around.'

'Take care, Katie.'

She left, but not like she had a train to catch. Five o'clock came and went. I rang Herbie.

'Harry!' He'd been into the coke again. 'What're you up to?'

'Just winding up now. Any word?'

'The whole fucking dictionary. Can you get over here?'

'Why, what's up?'

'Surf's up, Harry. We hit the jackpot.'

'Nice one, Herb. I'll be over in about ten minutes.'

*

I was halfway to the car park when I remembered Denise had the car. Then I remembered I hadn't told Denise about the Chinese dinner Dutchie and Michelle had planned. Fumbled in my inside pocket for the mobile, then trudged back to the office, cursing Brady every step of the way.

Denise wasn't home so I left a message on the machine, be ready for eight, and headed for Herbie's. Flurries of sleet were coming down with the dusk, quick gusts that caused the orange streetlights to flicker and dull. The streets were wet so it wasn't sticking, which was a shame, I'd promised Ben a snowman for Christmas. But then, even kids stop keeping count after the first broken promise.

Herbie's house was sauna warm, almost humid. It was always the same, winter or summer, the heating on full blast to nurture the crop in the attic. Herbie wandered around the house barefoot, in T-shirt and cut-off jeans, a stranded beach bum who hadn't been on a beach in maybe five years. There was no one around to cop him on, either. Herbie lived on his own, early twenties with no visible source of income, holding down a three-bedroom house just off Fortfield, Upmarketsville. No one asked where he got the money to live like that. No one cared, either. So long as Herbie could pay his own way no one gave a damn where the money came from. In one way, that was a good thing. In lots of other ways, it didn't bode at all well.

He answered the door wearing shades, a spliff smouldering. Better still, his death metal T-shirt had 'First Served, First Cum' scrawled across the chest.

'Classy stuff, Herb.'

'Whatever.' There was something on his mind. 'That camera, Harry?'

'What about it?'

'That my camera?'

'I know you wouldn't trust it with anyone else.'

'Fucking wondering where that got to. State of the art, that camera.'

He handed me a cold beer, took me upstairs to his computer room. The camera was sitting on the desk, so I slipped it into my pocket while he printed out Frank Conway's file. I figured I was doing him a favour, both of us using it. I like to see people get value for money.

He handed me a sheaf of papers, Frank Conway's details. A quick scan revealed nothing of note. His finances weren't as healthy as I'd presumed they'd be, providing Dutchie's information on Conway's real estate ventures was on the ball, but they weren't so sick they needed therapy either. There was a blip of about a year-and-a-half, where nothing showed up, which suggested Frank Conway had gone to ground, but so far they haven't decided that that's against the law.

'So, what?'

He sat down at the computer, clicked the mouse. A murky image came up on screen, two people walking through a wood, obscured by a huge golf umbrella. It was the Ice Queen and her beau at Hughes Point, although I'd never have known if I hadn't been the one behind the lens. The fact that I hadn't been able to use the flash didn't help.

'That,' he said, 'is about as useful as a blind hippy.'

'No argument.'

'But this,' he said, clicking the mouse again, 'was a little more interesting.' Another image came up on screen. It was the picnic area, deserted except for the big Volvo on the other side of the clearing. The picture was dark, the evening a lot gloomier than I remembered.

'I know they were driving a Volvo, Herb.'

He used the mouse to square off the Volvo. Another click doubled the squared-off image in size, maintaining the clarity of the original. Another couple of clicks and I was able to tell that the Volvo was navy blue, there was a dent in the front bumper, the seat covers were composed of tightly strung wooden beads and the driver liked wine gums. All we were missing was the chassis number.

'I ran a check on the registration,' he said, smug.

'Really?' I patted him on the shoulder. 'I'd have tried tracing the seat covers myself.'

He rose above it, on a roll.

'The car is registered to one Della McGowan. Address: The Priory, Foynes Hill.'

I stared at him. I was getting a bad feeling.

'Herb – who's Della McGowan?'

'McGowan was her maiden name.'

'And now it's . . . ?'

'Sheridan.'

'Della Sheridan? *Imelda* Sheridan? The car is Imelda fucking Sheridan's?'

'Was,' he corrected.

'You're winding me up.'

This time he shook his head.

'Jesus, Herb. Tony Sheridan's banging Helen Conway?'

'Unless the car was stolen. By the way.'

'What?'

'Who's this Helen Conway?'

'You don't want to know. Trust me. Anyway, Tony Sheridan is enough.'

'Isn't he, though?'

Herbie knew as well as I did that Tony Sheridan was in the social pages more often than he was in the Dáil. Which was ironic, considering that he was one of three independent TDs the government was relying on to maintain its narrow majority. If Frank Conway sued for divorce and named Tony as the respondent, the story would make the Six-One News and the front page of every paper in the country, *The Catholic Herald* included. And it wasn't inconceivable that his resignation – which would be inevitable given Tony's corn-pone pronouncements on the moral integrity of the family unit – could help to bring down the government.

A sweat broke out on my back that had nothing to do with Herbie's attic crop. Suddenly the hammering I'd been given didn't seem as excessive as it had the night before.

'Wipe the file.'

'What?'

'Wipe it, Herb. Hit delete. Everything you've given me, lose it.'

'But this is the angle, the hook. The fucking *spread*, Harry!'

'Trust me, Herb.'

I told him about the beating, pulled up my shirt.

'Fucking hell.'

'That was when they thought I was just sniffing around. If they get a whiff that you can hook Helen Conway to Tony Sheridan, they'll be around quick smart. Wipe it.'

'You're going to bury it?'

'You'd rather we buried Ben?'

He wiped it.

'So what happens now?'

'What happens now is you get paid. Then we keep our mouths shut and hope we don't find anything else.'

'Sounds like a plan.'

We went back downstairs. I put my jacket back on, tucking the print-outs into my inside pocket.

'Fancy a quick toke?'

'Christ, no. My head's fucked up enough as it is.'

'I can imagine.'

He didn't know the half of it. Death threats, police intimidation, the break-up with Denise, maybe losing Ben – I'd been through it all before, naturally, although I was pretty sure that all four had never collided at the same time. And then there was Gonzo, staring me down, sawn-off and double-barrelled, locked, breeched and both hammers cocked.

It was going to be a long and lousy night.

13

I walked back into town, hailed a cab. The sleet was coming down hard, the flurries a little thicker. It still wasn't sticking, though, the streets wet and shiny under the orange streetlights. Ben was in the living room, sitting in front of a blazing fire, Pokémon cards scattered on the rug.

'Hey, Ben.'

He was absorbed in a cartoon, Johnny Dangerfield. I barely registered.

'There'll be snow tomorrow,' I told him. 'Then we'll build the biggest snowman ever.'

I waited for a response, decided to buy myself a Johnny Dangerfield mask, went through to the kitchen. Bracing myself, but either Gonzo hadn't arrived or Denise was hiding him under the stairs. She was sitting at the table, a coffee at her elbow, leafing through a magazine. Pots bubbled on the cooker. The windows were steamed up.

'You're cooking dinner?'

'Dinner cooks itself, Harry. It's a woman's secret. Don't tell the lads.'

'You didn't get my message?'

'I got your message.'

'I thought you wanted to go out?'

'Not if it's where you're going. Besides, where do you think we'd get a babysitter at that short notice? It's the day before Christmas Eve. People are out enjoying themselves, having a good time.' She went back to the magazine. 'Some people, anyway.'

It was pointless trying to argue and I didn't even want to. I went upstairs, had a shower, lay down for a quick nap. Ben shook me awake about three seconds later.

'Dinner's ready, Dad.'

'Alright, son. I'll be down in a minute.'

We ate in silence. Ben and I watched *Willy Wonka* until it was time for him to go to bed. I watched as he brushed his teeth, getting more paste on his chin than his teeth, brought him downstairs to Denise, head buried in my shoulder.

'Want to put him to bed?'

'You're doing a great job,' she said. 'For someone who's had so little practice.'

'Cheers.'

I tucked him in, gave him a kiss.

'Be a good boy for your mum, okay?'

'Okay,' he muttered, already dozing off. I said: 'Who's coming tomorrow night?'

'Santa.'

'That's right.'

'And Eddie.'

'Eddie? Who told you that?'

He turned, settled. His eyes were closed.

'Mum said Eddie's coming tomorrow.'

Eddie. I hadn't heard Gonzo called by his Christian name in maybe ten years.

'Who's Eddie?' I asked, brushing his cow's lick off his forehead.

'Dunno.'

He didn't know. I didn't know who Eddie was either, not now, not after four years away. Ben's mouth was gaping open, which suggested that we both cared about the same. I watched him until I was sure he was asleep, went downstairs. Denise was flicking through the TV channels. I called a cab.

'You're going out?'

'No, I'm just teasing the cabbie.'

'You don't think you'll be a gooseberry?'

'If Dutchie and Michelle wanted privacy, they'd stay home. They don't, they want to meet people. I'm people.'

'Just about.'

*

The cab dropped me at the office. I went upstairs, pulled Ben's bike out from under the desk. Opened the bottom drawer of the filing cabinet, took out the gun, stuck it in my belt, invisible under my jacket. Then I dug a padded envelope out of the top drawer of the desk. I scribbled the office address on the front, stuck a stamp on it, slipped Herbie's camera inside. Left the office, Ben's bike under one arm, and posted the envelope in the tiny branch office at the end of the street. Then I headed across the road to The Cellars.

Dutchie was already at the bar, a pint and a short in front of him. He looked at the bike.

'Traffic that bad?'

'Ben's Christmas present. Mind if I stash it out back, pick it up tomorrow?'

He led the way out to the storeroom. I put the bike in behind the beer kegs. Then I pulled the gun out of my belt. He didn't look as surprised as he should have.

'The Dibble were around this morning,' I reminded him. 'If they turn the place over, plant a real gun, they have me by the curlies. If there's no fake to replace, they can't put in a plant.'

Dutchie laughed, short and hard.

'Wise up, Harry. Those boys'd plant cabbage in concrete if they thought it'd get them a free Danish with their coffee.'

The gun went in under one of the Guinness kegs. Marie, the girl who helped out whenever Dutchie was busy or unavailable or just plain lazy, pulled us a couple of pints.

'So where's Michelle?'

'Meeting some of the girls from work. She'll be in later. We knocked the Chinkers on the head.'

'Suits me. Dee isn't coming.'

'Couldn't get a babysitter?'

'Or wouldn't. Does it matter?'

'Not to me. Try a short?'

We were comfortably drunk by the time Michelle got in, maybe an hour later. She wasn't the most conventionally attractive of women, her hair a frizzy blonde job that would never go out of fashion because it had never really been in style. Her nose was a little too pointed, her chin sloped away like it was ashamed of itself, but she was sexy in the way she carried herself, confident of who she was and what she could do. She leaned in, kissed me on the cheek while Dutchie organised a stool. She sat up at the bar between us, looked me over.

'Fighting, Harry?' She tut-tutted. 'And where's Dee?'

'The negotiations are still at a delicate phase.'

'You're still out?'

'Mostly.'

'It's a start.'

'Keep the jump leads handy.'

Gonzo arrived just after ten. I had my back to the bar, clocked him straight away. He pushed through the crowd, grinning a tentative one. Stood in front of me, hands jammed into the pockets of his frayed denims, shoulders hunched.

'Harry,' he drawled. 'Long time no see.'

'Gonz.'

I gave him the once over. Taking in the dirty blonde dreads, the faded Levis stuffed into a pair of heavy-duty biker's boots. The shoulders that had straightened, broadened, giving him a couple of extra inches up and out. He was bulky but carried it easy. It was just as well. Another couple of pounds and the bright orange Puffa bomber jacket he was wearing would have made him look like the Michelin Man.

'Nice jacket, Gonz,' Dutchie said, reaching out to shake Gonzo's hand, making a production number of it. 'No danger of being knocked down wearing that.' He winked, nodded at me. 'If you're wondering about the smell, it's the whiff of burning martyr.'

Gonzo laughed. My guts curdled.

'Alright, Dutch? How's tricks?' He looked at Michelle. 'How're you keeping, Chuck? You're looking well.'

'Good to see you, Gonzo.' She kissed him on the cheek, barely making contact. That didn't stop him grinning, wolfish, rubbing his cheek to erase an imaginary lipstick mark.

'Hmmm,' he said. 'Maybe I should come home more often.'

I let that one slide. I remembered that smile. It burned, an acid sloshing around with the porter and whiskey. I let it.

'Pint, Gonz?' Dutch asked.

'Stout.'

Dutchie and Michelle made small talk while Gonzo and I stared one another out, neither of us wanting to make the first move. The arrangement suited me. The way I felt about it, the less I heard from Gonzo the longer I'd live, longer and happier. He blinked first.

'How've you been, Harry?'

'Fine. Up times, down times. You know the drill.'

'Yeah.'

He drank deep from his pint, downing half of it in two gulps. Wiped his mouth on the back of his hand, which left some of the creamy head stuck to his upper lip. That irritated me. I let it.

'I was out at the house,' he said then. He smiled, slow and lazy. 'I looked in on Ben. He's a cute kid.'

I wanted to punch him there and then, get it over with.

'Yeah. He got his mother's nose.'

'She's looking well, too.' The corner of his mouth twitched. 'I didn't see a wedding ring, though.'

'That's because we're not married, Gonz.'

'How come?'

'I was afraid you'd turn up.' I'd had enough of the small talk. 'How long are you staying, Gonz?'

He shrugged, taken aback.

'I don't know. Couple of days, maybe a couple of weeks. I told Denise I'd do B&B but she said I was being daft. She made up a bed in Ben's room.'

'For who, me?'

'Harry!' Michelle's tone was stern, letting me know I'd overstepped the mark. I waved her away. I hadn't even started my run up.

'If it's a problem—'

'Of course it's a problem, Gonz. All I want to know is how long it's going to *be* a problem.'

'I'm not sure,' he said, picking his words with care. 'I'll be taking a look around, see if there's anything happening. If there isn't, I'll be off again.'

'Anything like what?'

'Anything like anything. Bar work, maybe. I did some sign painting on the islands, when I was out in Greece. I've a few quid put away, enough for a second-hand van. Maybe there's some courier work going. Know of anything?'

'No. Dutchie's the man to ask.'

'Yeah, okay. I'll ask Dutch.'

He looked hurt, wounded. I put him out of his misery.

'The way it is, Gonz, you can stay as long as you don't get in the way, and I'm only saying that because I'm expecting you to take off first chance you get. But don't look for something that's not there anymore. Alright?'

'Jesus, Harry . . .'

Maybe it was his reasonable tone. Maybe I thought I'd never get the chance to say it again. Maybe it was the beer, the bile. But it was coming and coming hard. I let it go.

'Fuck you and your 'Jesus Harry'. Everyone thought I was a

soft prick and fuck me if you didn't prove them right.'

'Come on, Harry.' Now it was Dutchie's turn, laying a hand on my shoulder.

'Back off, Dutch.' I looked at Gonzo. 'You fucked the woman I was going to marry. I should have kicked you into the middle of next week, and don't think I didn't consider it. But what I did was ask you to be my child's godfather.'

'Follow Brando and De Niro? You're kidding.'

'What's that, funny?'

'C'mon, Harry—'

'Denise used to say it was like something out of *The Omen*. That was funny. For the first two months, it was funny. After that, it wasn't funny anymore. After that I was wondering if something had happened, something serious. Wondering if maybe you were dead. Four years, not knowing. All it needed was a phone-call or a postcard, a fucking message on the fucking answering machine.'

Dutchie touched me on the shoulder.

'Harry,' he urged, wary. 'It's Christmas.'

'It was Christmas last year too, Dutch, and the year before that. It was Christmas for the last four fucking years, Dutch.' I looked back at Gonzo. 'Just for the record, how come you left so quick?'

'Just had to get away, Harry. When you have to go, you go.'

'You couldn't wait one more fucking night?'

'I didn't realise it meant that much.'

'Ben being christened? Didn't mean that much?' I didn't know whether to laugh or cry. 'Tell you what, Gonz. Just forget it, all of it. Let's pretend we don't even know each other.'

'People change, Harry.'

'You're changed?'

'Yeah.'

'I'm not. Now rev up and fuck off.'

He thought that over. Then he hauled off and drove a punch at my head like he was grabbing for fresh air the far side. I went down like I'd been torpedoed. Dutchie was between us by the time I got up, stunned, shaking my head.

'Enough,' he said, terse. 'Any more and you're both out. Hear that? Harry?'

There was blood on the back of my hand. I'd bounced my head off the bar on the way down and my eyes were watering. It was a good buzz, though. Gonzo's fists were still clenched, waiting for it to kick off. The old Gonzo, unrepentant, the thin veneer of contrition scraped bare and ugly in the slipstream of one vicious swing. I patted Dutchie on the back, dabbed at my bloody nose with the tissue he gave me. I'd got what I wanted.

'Second time today,' I told Gonzo. 'First one hurt.'

'Thought you might laugh if I tickled. You being such a grumpy cunt and all.'

Dutchie manoeuvred his stool between us, put up another round. Then Gonzo got one in, and after that we started to lose count. We talked at right angles for a while, slow to start, faster as the beer paid off. He told us about Greece and Spain. I told him about Denise and Ben, Ben mostly, but I didn't say anything he couldn't have guessed anyway.

Closing time came and went. Dutchie suggested a few late ones. The idea of a club, all noise and desperation, was appealing for once. When we got inside, we settled ourselves in the darkest corner we could find. We shouted at one another across the table until we realised we weren't saying anything worth hearing. Dutchie went to the bar. Gonzo shifted around to sit on the stool beside me, nudging me in the ribs.

'Who's the bird?' he shouted.

'What bird?'

'That bird, on the edge of the floor. She's been clocking you since we came in.'

She looked away when I glanced over my shoulder but there was no mistaking the delightful Miss Conway's pout. She was standing on the edge of the dance floor, grinding a hip against the big bloke beside her, hips kinking in time to the rhythm. She was wearing a cropped belly top that showed most of her flat stomach and all of her cleavage, which was also flat.

'Never seen her before.'

'Sweet.'

'The way cyanide smells.'

Dutchie came back with the drinks. He had just settled into his seat again when Michelle came back from the toilet and dragged him, protesting, onto the dance floor. Gonzo shouted: 'Fancy a buzz?'

'No.'

He slipped the corner of a plastic wrap out of his shirt pocket, twitched it. Then he squeezed two pills from the wrap, holding them in his palm under the table. They looked like Paracetamol except for the grooved line running across the circumference.

'C'mon, Harry. You know you want to.'

I knew he wouldn't give up until he got his way. I knew, from bitter experience, that it was easier to agree, to succumb. Maybe that way, when I woke up in the morning, Gonzo would be gone again, taking the car with him, maybe, and it'd be worth it just to see him gone.

Then I met his eye. He was the old Gonzo again, the one-man party who didn't give a shit and took even less, the five-year-old trapped in the body of a sociopath.

'No chance, Gonz. Forget it.'

He shrugged.

'Maybe you're right,' he said, popping both pills. 'These fuckers haven't paid off all night. That's four and five right there.'

'Five?'

'Nothing's happening. You get a quick buzz like you're about to come up and that's your lot.'

'Maybe the pills aren't the problem.'

'There was a time you weren't such a pious bastard.'

'And there was a time you weren't a total cunt.'

He sipped his pint, chewed the inside of his lip.

'Fuck sakes. How many times do I have to say I'm sorry?'

'Once'd be a start. Wouldn't mean a fucking thing, but it'd be nice to know you can say it all the same.'

'Jesus. Okay, Harry, I'm sorry. I'm sorry I fucked Celine. I'm sorry I didn't come to Ben's christening. I'm sorry I didn't ring. I'm sorry your life is a pile of shite, that you're a miserable fucker.' He sparked a smoke. 'Let me know if I'm leaving anything out, yeah?'

'How about being sorry for coming back, for lying through your teeth?'

'What are you talking about? I told you, I'm looking to get started—'

'Yeah, I know. Sign-painting and a second-hand Hi-Ace. Give it a rest, Gonz. It's so tired it's yawning.'

He looked at me, shrewd.

'Never could keep anything from you, Harry. Never was able to kid you.'

'Save the nostalgia for when you retire, Gonz. What are you trying to do, make me feel good about myself?' I laughed, bitter. 'I don't need you to tell me I'm smart, I know I'm a fuckwit, otherwise I wouldn't be sitting here talking to you. So cut to the chase. Give me some of that old eight ball boogie.'

He stared, squinting, like he wasn't sure I was really me. It was an old trick he had, letting the other person think he was taking them seriously, gaining time while he thought up another lie. I was pretty sure he was about to start spoofing again. He didn't. He told me the truth. It wasn't the whole truth, I found out later, but at least he wasn't lying.

'Ever get bored, Harry? So bored your brain shuts down because it has nothing to do?'

'You were bored, so you decided to come home and fuck us all up again. Is that it?'

'There's only one place you get that bored. I was there eighteen months, kept my head down, got out eight months early.'

'Boo-fucking-hoo.'

He ignored me.

'Stir isn't as bad as people make out. You need to fuck some fairy early, so no one tries to fuck you, but you're fed and watered, everything's taken care of. Anything you want you can get, providing you can pay for it.' He shrugged. 'Seven fucking tabs got me twenty-six months. There's paedophiles walking the streets, sticky-fingered fuckers running the country, I'm banged up for a few party favours. The big laugh inside was when they started letting the Provies out. Funny, that was.

Fucking hilarious. Worse than psychos, we were.'

'I've heard sadder on *The Waltons*. So, what?'

'When you're bored, Harry, you talk. You'll talk to anyone, even the screws. You'll talk to yourself. Then you get really bored and you start listening, just for a change of pace. And you hear all sorts of mad shit on the inside. Most of what's said is crap. Wasters pumping themselves up, throwing their weight around, hoping someone'll catch it. Anything anyone tells you when you're inside, it's cell-talk, bullshit.' He jabbed the air with his cigarette for emphasis. 'Unless they're selling it.'

'It isn't bullshit because they're selling it? Tell it to Ronald McDonald.'

'You get to know the score. What's what and who's who. Punters who say fuck all are the ones in the know. When they say something, it's worth hearing. Worth paying to hear, too.'

'And you heard what?'

The wolfish grin flashed.

'What I heard isn't the point. What I didn't *say* is the point. And what I had to say was worth hearing, only I didn't say anything. So, I'm owed.'

'Owed?'

'Owed. And I'm collecting.'

'You're putting the bounce on?'

'You watch too many movies.'

'Blackmail has a new name now? They call it something different inside?'

'It's an investment, Harry. Like with houses. You don't sell it now because it'll be worth more next year.'

'Get away from me, Gonz. You might be contagious.'

'Relax, Harry. A couple of days, I'll be gone again.'

'You think I'm having you around Ben when you're fucking around like this? Think again, Gonz. Tomorrow morning you're gone, and if I never see you again it'll be too soon.'

'You're in for a cut. I owe you that much.'

'You owe me nothing. Because that's all you've ever given me. Nothing.'

Dutchie and Michelle arrived back at the table, laughing, faces flushed. I went to the bar. When I got back I slipped in beside Michelle, as far away from Gonzo as possible. The lights came up soon afterwards and we finished our drinks, shivering when the bouncers opened the front door to allow the night filter through the club. Dutchie dug some tickets out of his back pocket.

'Do us a favour, Gonz.' Gonzo was sitting closest to the coat-check cubicle. 'Get the jackets, big man.'

'Sound. Someone ring a taxi. It's fucking freezing out there.'

'The phone's out by the cubicle,' Michelle told him.

Gonzo took out his mobile phone, tossed it at me.

'You know all the numbers.'

Gave me his own number, in case the cabbie needed to ring back. Fat chance. I tried about six numbers, no joy.

'Bad as the fucking Blue,' Dutchie said. 'Never around when you need one.'

Gonzo came back excited, wearing my jacket. He handed me the bright orange Puffa.

'You can bury me in that if you want,' I told him. 'Otherwise, no chance.'

'I met two birds checking the coats. They're off for a kebab and I'm buying.'

'Classy stuff, Gonz. What's that got to do with my jacket?'

'They were laughing at mine, the tarts. Come on, just until we leave the kebab house. I'll pay for your grub. If I haven't pulled by the time we leave you can have it back.'

I shrugged. The choice was to let Gonzo wear my jacket or try to rip it off his back, and I was tired. Gonzo started jogging on the spot, his dreads bouncing on his shoulders.

'Yeah yeah yeah.'

We left, pausing on the steps outside to watch the entertainment. A girl, puce with embarrassment or rage or a combination of both, was screaming abuse at an older man who was dragging her into a silver-grey Merc SL. It took me a couple of seconds to realise the older guy was Conway. His face was flushed, jabbing a finger at the big bloke who'd been with his daughter inside the club. The big bloke was standing on the steps, hands on hips, like he'd reached the end of a catwalk.

'I'm not telling you again!' Conway's voice was a strangled snarl. 'Next time it'll be you in the back of the car! Fucking pervert.'

He looked around, trying to work out exactly where the catcalls, the jeering, was coming from. His eyes caught mine. He looked away, came back to check out Gonzo and Dutchie, and got in the car, which roared away down the street.

'What was that all about?' Michelle wanted to know.

'Jail-bait,' I said. 'Still at school, I'd say.'

Gonzo clicked his tongue.

'Shame.'

The sleet had stopped. The temperature had plummeted. Stars glittered against a clear black sky. Gonzo spotted the girls from the coat check, one wearing thigh-length PVC boots, the other chewing gum and looking bored. He sallied forth.

We piled into a booth in the kebab house and chewed on the

plastic food while Gonzo tried to impress the two girls. Their ages combined would hardly have made up his, and they spent the best part of an hour giggling at his efforts. Then, without any visible sign of communication, they stood up and left. Gonzo stared after them, nonplussed.

'Are we right so?' Dutchie asked. Michelle was snuggled against him, head on his shoulder, eyes closed.

'Yeah,' Gonzo said. 'I'll be back in a minute.' He winked and tapped his breast pocket. 'Just taking a whizz.'

He disappeared in the direction of the toilets. Dutchie looked at me.

'He on something?' he asked.

'You sit where you are,' Michelle ordered without opening her eyes. Dutchie grinned, started reminiscing about chemically inspired mayhem. Twenty minutes passed. Eventually Dutchie did the decent thing and went after Gonzo. Thirty seconds later he sprinted back around the corner, face drained.

'Harry!' He sounded choked, breath coming short. My first instinct was that Dutchie had got into a row, that a fight was brewing. Then I caught something in Dutchie's eye that told me there was no fight, that whatever was wrong was very, very wrong. I bolted out of my seat.

The urinals were empty, the stench of ammonia blinding. Dutchie pulled me down the line of cubicles, pushed in the door of the last but one. Gonzo was slumped between bowl and wall, jammed into the narrow space. Shaking hard, head back, face bathed in sweat. A thin line of blood trickled from one nostril. Concrete settled in my stomach. I pushed past Dutchie into the cubicle, tugging at Gonzo's arm.

'Get up, you fucker!' He was heavy, way too heavy, and it took a huge effort to dislodge him. When I finally pulled him loose he flopped forward onto the floor, face down in the piss, the sodden toilet paper. The blood mingled with the piss. A pink stain ebbed from his face.

'Is he . . . ?'

'How the fuck would *I* know?'

'Take his pulse.'

'Where the fuck is his *pulse*?'

'His wrist!'

'I know it's his fucking wrist! *Where* on his wrist?'

'How the fuck would *I* know?'

'Jesus!' I groped at Gonzo's wrist but I hadn't the faintest idea of what I was looking for. 'Christ sakes, Dutch. Ring a fucking ambulance!'

I sat on the floor, pulled Gonzo's head onto my midriff, cradling his head. His face was contorted into a rictus, the skin fiery to the touch. I bent my face to his but I couldn't tell whether he was breathing or not. When I slipped my hand inside his shirt to feel for his heartbeat, his chest was clammy with sweat. The heartbeat was there but the party was winding down.

'Alright, Gonz,' I whispered. 'It's going to be alright. Just hold on.'

I didn't believe a word of it but I thought I should say something and I couldn't remember any prayers.

14

Brady came through the door like it was last orders on Sunday night. If I hadn't had other things on my mind, I might have wondered why it was Brady coming through the toilet door. I might have been surprised that the cavalry turned up so soon, too, and I might have thought it odd that Brady was still on duty. But I had other things on my mind.

The kebab house manager was standing in the doorway, rubbing his hands in a sweaty fret. Brady shouldered him to one side, shoved past Dutchie, got down on one knee. Feeling the side of Gonzo's neck, staring into my eyes, waiting for a pulse. Then he stood up, surveyed the cubicle, not noticing that one knee of his pants was a sodden stain. He rasped: 'What're you on, Rigby?'

'Nothing.' I pulled Gonzo tight. 'Where the fuck's the ambulance?'

He didn't answer. He hunkered down, rifled through Gonzo's pockets. It didn't take him long to find the plastic wrap. He opened it, tipped a tablet out onto his palm, grimaced.

'How many?'

'I don't fucking know.'

'If he dies – and he's dying – your name's first on the report, in red fucking marker. Last time. How many?'

'He said five. Said he wasn't getting a buzz.'

Brady looked around as Galway pushed past Dutchie, picking his way between the puddles of urine, deft as a poodle.

'OD,' Brady reported. 'E, looks like Flats. He's still breathing. Pulse faint. No blockage.'

Galway said, like he had a razor under his tongue: 'And there was me thinking you were kidding about public toilets.' Then, to Brady: 'Get him to casualty.'

Brady did a double take.

'Me?'

'You. And do it quick-like. I don't want any fucker dying on my watch.'

'What about the medics? The ambulance?'

'No ambulance, they're both out at a pile-up on the motorway. Some prick jumped the reservation, ploughed into a Renault coming on. A kid went through the prick's windscreen, still in his safety seat. What the fuck a kid is doing up at this hour.'

Brady still looked dubious.

'You want me to take him? In the squad?'

'Do it fast or there'll be no point doing it at all.'

Brady squared his shoulders.

'I'm taking no fucker to Casualty in the squad. What if he kicks it?'

'Christ.' Galway looked down at Gonzo, sour. 'Alright, put him in the car. I'll take him.' He nodded at me. 'You take that fucker down the station. Book him on suspicion, possession, resisting arrest, whatever takes your fancy. Just don't let him out of your sight until I get back.'

'Fuck you,' I said, clutching Gonzo tight. I was feeling a pull, a bond, that I wasn't even sure had anything to do with Gonzo. 'I'm going to the hospital.'

Galway poked Gonzo's leg with the toe of his hi-shine shoe. He popped a mint under his tongue, worked it around his cheek.

'One more word, you'll be going to the hospital and know fuck all about it.'

Dutchie spoke up.

'I'll follow on to the hospital, Harry. Alright?'

Galway turned for the door, saying: 'Let the cunt die in his piss, I give a fuck.'

Michelle was standing outside on the street, hugging herself, as Brady half-carried, half-dragged Gonzo to the blue Mondeo. Dutchie told her that Gonzo was fine, kissed her on the side of the head, but she stayed rigid, staring. I could read her mind. 'Dutchie,' she was thinking. 'There but for the grace of God. Oh my God, Dutchie.'

I didn't blame her. I was thinking it too.

The Mondeo pulled off, Gonzo lolling in the passenger seat, Dutchie in the back trying to support Gonzo's head. I watched it go until Brady clamped a hand on my shoulder, directed me towards a squad car. He pushed me into the back seat, sat in beside me.

'Sit still,' he said. 'Don't do anything stupid.'

From the depths of my torpor I heard someone say: 'Put your safety-belt on. I'd hate to see you fined.'

He looked across, laughed a reedy laugh, turned away again. Then he straight-armed me flush on the ear with a punch of pure napalm. The side of my face blazed into flame. My head pitched back, clipping the reinforced glass window. Stupefied, screaming a sound I'd never heard before, I balled a fist on the recoil, putting every last atom of my existence into a punch that was four years brewing.

I was still swinging when Brady's second caught me full on the bridge of the nose. I saw something flash, bright and impossibly white, and then the light dulled to something red and warm. I dove into the embers, found myself a convenient black hole.

*

I was lying on a thin, grimy mattress, a couple of migraines playing charades inside my head. Wrists handcuffed somewhere down around my kidneys. My head was an over-ripe melon, big, soft, raw and pulpy. My nose was blocked. When I snuffled, my ears nearly exploded. My shirt was covered in snot and puke. That made two nights running. I was on a roll.

I put the erection down to the handcuffs. When it finally went away, I started kicking at the cell door. Brady unlocked the handcuffs, marched me down to the end of a long, narrow hallway. The room was big, bright. Apart from the chair Brady pushed me into, there was a table with a scuffed Formica top and a blackened foil ashtray, for show. The carpet was threadbare and snot-green. The walls were a dirty-brown colour, the paint streaky, like someone had been left there long enough for a dirty protest to get out of hand.

Brady sat on a corner of the table, one leg dangling, placed Gonzo's plastic wrap on the table. He looked comfortable, assured, on his own turf, or maybe he was just more relaxed when he didn't have to impress the boss. He dug a packet of cigarettes out of his coat pocket, offered me one. I could barely hold it, my hands were shaking so hard. Brady lit the smoke, cocked his head to one side.

'You carrying anything, Rigby?'

'Could be.'

'Could be?'

'The jacket's his. He wanted to wear mine. There could be something in the pockets.'

He held out a hand, snapped his fingers. I unzipped, handed the jacket across. He made a cursory search of the pockets, inside and out, ran his hand down the lining. Then he handed it back. I put the Puffa back on. It might have looked ridiculous but it was warm, quilted on the inside and worth every penny Gonzo had paid for it. Providing, I acknowledged, he had actually paid for it.

'Alright. Now, at the risk of repeating myself, tell me about Frank Conway.'

'First off – am I under arrest?'

'Not yet, no. That's up to Galway, when he gets back.' He leered. 'He might want to frisk you himself, by the way.'

'I'm all a-tremble. Why haven't you arrested me?'

'You want me to?'

'I'll try anything once. Besides, you'd be surprised how much false arrest is worth these days.'

'I wouldn't. And who says it'd be false arrest?'

I stubbed the cigarette.

'Come on, Brady. Even I'm not thick enough to walk into a bacon factory with gear on me, and you have nothing that says I've ever taken anything stronger than Solpadeine. So what's the drill?'

'You're here because Galway wants you here.'

'You're pimping for Galway?'

'He calls the shots.' He scratched at an ear. 'Still, while you're here, no reason we can't be chatting.'

'I'll wait for the coffee morning. Cheers all the same.'

He drummed a tattoo on the tabletop, came to a decision.

'You like Frank Conway, Rigby?' He waved a dismissive hand before I had a chance to answer. 'And save the routine, I might start heckling.'

'I like everyone, Brady. Even you.'

'Okay, let's do it this way. Your brother, Eddie?'

'We call him Gonzo.'

'Gonzo. Jesus.' The grim smile belonged in a morgue. 'That's not what he called himself when we knew him. He called himself Robbie back then, Robbie Callaghan. Passport to prove it, too, with an address in Shepherds Bush. Clocked up some serious air miles, did our Robbie. Amsterdam, Hamburg, you name it. Fascinated by real estate, too. Which was why he dropped in on Frank Conway every time he was home.' He dropped the jovial tone. 'Gonzo we know,' he growled. 'Gonzo's a good mate of ours. We had him over for tea and biscuits one day, he liked the place so much he stayed eighteen months. We had to take his medication off him on the way in, but he didn't seem to mind.'

'Gonzo'd be too polite to say.'

'I can imagine. Anyway, Conway's scum. Cheap with it, too. He jumped when the shit hit the fan and didn't bounce until he hit Torremolinos. And there he stayed, until one fine day he upped sticks and disappeared. Six months ago we tracked him down here. We can't make anything stick, because all along Robbie keeps schtum. Same old story, it even has a happy ending, Conway's back in business. This time we think the gear's coming in through Belfast. Stop me when I tell you something you don't know already.'

'Go on. I like the sound of your voice.'

'Jesus, Rigby. You're a – What do you call it? A research consultant?' He laughed, harsh. 'I'd get a new job, Rigby. One where you don't need to put one and one together.'

I let that one float.

'Okay, here's what we reckon is going on. Eddie – Gonzo, Robbie, whatever the fuck he calls himself – does eighteen months. It should be two years, but who the fuck does a full stretch these days and he was a good boy. He gets back here last week, scouting Conway. Once he's sussed what's going on, he tells Conway he's looking for sick pay. Conway makes with the fatted calf, tells Eddie he'll look after him. Gives him a little something, just to show willing. Maybe it's a lot of something, and Eddie's back on commission. Except maybe there's something more in the little something. Something that shouldn't be there.'

'No chance. Gonzo knows his drugs.'

'Gonzo knows fuck all, panned out on a gurney with his face inside out. It makes me want to cry, but it'll keep, until we've nailed Conway.'

'Why don't you nail him now?'

Brady sniffed, thumbed his nose. Offered me another cigarette. I turned it down, started rolling a twist. The shakes had subsided. I was already sober, the hangover kicking in. Brady said: 'Four-MTA.'

'Say again?'

'Four-MTA. Four-methylthioamphetamine, if you prefer. It's what the Dutch boys started on, when the authorities put the boot into PMA.'

'PMA?'

Brady looked like he was enjoying himself.

'PMA is a primer for MDMA. Ecstasy, like. When the punters started dropping like flies a couple of years back, the vice boys in Holland tried to stamp PMA out. The lads making E just switched to Four-MTA, came up with Flatliners. It's supposed to be a super-E but it's more of a super-Prozac. Gets your serotonin off the charts but doesn't reabsorb it back into the brain. Worse, Flats take about two hours to kick in. Some punter thinks he has strong E that isn't going off, he drops another. Half an hour later another one goes down the neck. By the time the first one starts coming off, there's four or five down the hatch and ready to dance.'

I said, dull: 'Gonzo had five tabs tonight.'

'That'd be right. And once you peak on Flats it levels out. There's no up and down, like E. Once you're up there you think you're coming down again. So you pop another one. And so on. The heart develops arrhythmia trying to keep up and the other organs start to overcompensate. Everything heats up. Meanwhile, the brain is drowning in serotonin. You're dying but you've never felt better in your life.'

'Sounds like a good way to go.'

'If you want to go. Anyway, we think Conway has diversified into Flats but we can't nail him until we catch him red-handed. No one says fuck all about a new drug. Dope, E, smack, coke – every fucker's talking about those. But a new buzz, people keep it under the duvet.' He tapped the plastic wrap. 'Eddie was lucky,' he said. 'Don't let Conway get lucky too.'

There was a knock on the door. A garda stuck her head into the room. She jerked her head at Brady.

'Phone.'

Brady got up, stubbed his smoke.

'Think it over, Rigby. Think about what you owe Frank Conway.'

He left. I thought it over. Gonzo was back in town to put the bounce on Conway, that much I knew. Which was why Conway had been checking me out, trying to work out if I was in cahoots with Gonzo. All that added up.

Gonzo falling for dodgy E didn't make sense, though. Gonzo knew his Class A inside out, although it was possible Flatliners had passed him by while he was on the inside. But even if everything Brady said fell into place, there was still the matter of Helen Conway and Tony Sheridan. The last thing Frank Conway had expected me to find was the first thing I'd tripped over. No one gets that lucky first try. I never got that lucky, period.

I rubbed at my temples, the side of my head a fire of dying embers. Stifled a yawn, too tired to think. I had the feeling of watching a car pull away from me, late at night, its tail-lights fading, watching it go with nothing left under the bonnet.

Brady came back into the room. He said, soft: 'Rigby.'

His tone told me everything I needed to know but I lumbered down the corridor to the phone anyway. Dutchie was on the line. He had something wedged sideways in his throat.

'Harry?'

'It's me, Dutch.'

'Jesus, Harry.' He choked. 'Jesus.'

I was aware that Brady was watching me. I focused on the poster thumb-tacked to the wall above the phone. Four tacks: three red, one blue. The blurb on the poster wanted information on criminal activity, had a free-phone number in bold red numerals underneath with a guarantee of anonymity for the caller in the small print. I wondered who the poster was supposed to target, stuck away in the back of the bacon factory. My voice wandered in from somewhere out over the Aran Islands.

'What happened, Dutch?'

'Don't know, Harry. I don't fucking know. They were pumping him out, no worries, and he just took a fit. Started thrashing around on the table, foaming at the mouth. They fucked me out, and then this Paki came and asked if I was family. I said yeah, he's my brother, he said Gonzo had gone into arrest and he was sorry, he'd done everything he could.'

'They give him penicillin?'

'Jesus, I don't—'

'He's allergic, Dutch. We're both allergic.' I thought, briefly, how an hour ago was the time to lay that one on Dutchie. 'He wasn't wearing tags?'

'I don't know, Harry. I wasn't—'

There was no reason why Dutchie would have been wearing tags. I didn't wear tags. It was just one of those things you never get around to doing, like buying limescale tablets for the kettle. I bit my lower lip, and maybe that was why my eyes started to water.

'He's dead?'

'I'm sorry, Harry.'

'Dutch? He's dead?'

'He's dead, Harry.'

I pursed my lips, sucked at my cheeks. My eyes prickled. Someone had let a bear into the building and he had my ribs in a hug, crushing my chest so I couldn't breathe.

'Alright, Dutch. Hold on there, I'll be about twenty minutes.'

'You're coming here? Why?'

I didn't know. It just seemed the right thing to do.

'Don't they need someone to identify the body?'

'They will, yeah, but tomorrow morning's plenty of time. You okay?'

'Never better, Dutch.'

'Yeah, stupid fucking question. I'm not thinking straight. I'll meet you back at the pub, I need a drink.'

'Not for me, Dutch.' My voice sounded hollow, but it might just have been a bad connection. 'I'm getting home. Dee should know.'

'Yeah, yeah, of course. Jesus.' Dutchie choked up again. I tried not to notice the tremble in his voice. Dutchie and Gonzo had been good mates once, a long time ago, but mates are mates. Time and distance don't change that kind of thing.

'I'm sorry, Harry.'

'Wasn't your fault, Dutch.'

I hung up. I felt limp, battered and bruised, body and soul. My knees trembled. I didn't know where to look, what to do. Brady was still watching me.

'No luck, Rigby,' he said, quiet.

'Fuck you, Brady.'

'Rigby—'

I turned to face him. Arms out wide, palms up, daring him to come on. I wanted to hit something, anything at all, and Brady looked softer than the wall. Not by much, but enough.

'Step up or step back, Brady. Come on.'

He didn't move. He didn't even blink. He said, harsh: 'Don't get tough, Rigby. You might get to like it.'

'It suits me just fine. And I'm walking out of here right now.

You want me to stay for breakfast, do something about it. And bring your mates.'

I brushed by him, digging an elbow into his chest. He let it skip, followed me down the corridor into the reception area. The garda behind the desk looked up from his newspaper, looked away again.

'I'm letting you go, Rigby, because Galway said so. But don't go taking holidays. Galway'll be looking for you.'

'I'll be found.'

Brady called something out as I pushed through the door but I didn't hear it. I was too busy listening to the bells of The Friary tolling four o'clock and realising it was Christmas Eve.

15

The night was cold, clean, fresh. I walked quickly through town, breathing hard in short, white plumes. My fists were balled, cached in the pockets of the Puffa. Shaking, but not from the cold. Trembling with fear, anticipation, the adrenaline rush. I detoured past the kebab house, feeling evil.

The street was deserted. The shutters of the kebab house were down, the neon signs dead. Through the shutters I could make out someone sweeping the floor. I punched the metal grille. She looked up, brushed the back of a hand across her forehead, started sweeping again.

I shuffled through the slushy streets towards the taxi rank. Head down, hoping to be jostled, ears pricked for a cat-call. No one spoke. No one looked in my direction. I was drifting.

When I got to the top of the street I hesitated, listening to a perverse instinct that wanted to see Gonzo, maybe touch his cold body. I made about a hundred yards up the Mall towards the hospital before turning back. There was no chance of seeing Gonzo, the body would already be in the morgue. Besides, the truth was that I didn't want to see Gonzo, it was just that I should have wanted to see him. Gonzo was dead, end of story. I was alive, living happily ever after.

I trekked back down the Mall, headed for the quays. The taxi rank looked like every taxi rank looks at four in the morning, cold, empty and mocking. I stood around for twenty minutes or so, kidding myself, stamping numb feet. Then I struck for home, crunching through the discarded chip wrappers, heading out across the new bridge.

I jumped the wall on the far side, making for the wooden bench, the frosted grass crackling like Krispies. Looking back out over the bridge to the bay beyond, next stop Iceland. I rolled a twist, not caring about the wet soaking through, staring out across the sheer drop of sixty or seventy feet. It was quiet as a new hearse, only the litter moved. The lights changed from green to amber, to red and then back to green, for an encore. I sparked the twist and tried to remember why I should care that Gonzo was dead.

The cigarette was half-smoked when I heard the car, not really paying attention. Then I realised it was coming up fast behind me, roaring out of town along the river. It screeched to a halt. I stood up to get a better look and the passenger door flew open. Everything slowed, the last few seconds before the kettle finally boils.

The first thing I noticed, he was wearing a scarf across his face, a baseball cap with the brim pulled low. The second thing was, he was cradling what looked like a sub-machine gun. The third thing was, he was unslinging what looked like a sub-machine gun, kneeling down and taking aim.

The sheer drop into the river was right behind me, but I took the step backwards anyway, stomach churning. I laughed a dry, brittle cough that got stuck halfway out, put my hands out, palms up, to ward the gunnie off. Still not convinced it wasn't all some kind of sick joke. And then a tiny voice in the back of my head confirmed it – yes, it is a joke – but the tiny voice didn't laugh. Or maybe it did, and the clock-click of what looked like a sub-machine gun being cocked drowned it out.

I had one place to go and I couldn't swim but if I didn't learn fast I wasn't going to learn at all. I threw myself backwards and heard two flat cracks, nails being punched into a biscuit tin. Then I was looking down at the oily-black surface of the river, wondering how I'd been spun around. Then I felt the branding iron in my gut.

The somersault crashed me feet-first into the river. I went deep and touched bottom, felt the mud give, sucking me down. I struggled, knowing I should, but I didn't have much air in my lungs when I jumped and taking the bullet on board hadn't helped. Hitting the water squeezed out the last of the cool, pure oxygen. My lungs burned hot and raw, began to melt.

The last thing I thought was, 'O Jesus, this is it.' Then my heart blew and a million needles shot into my brain. The blackness came down, and there in the shadows I saw a couple of friends I hadn't seen in a long time, a lifetime. My father was there too.

All told, it wasn't such a bad deal.

16

How you drown is, you're underwater, not breathing. You lose consciousness. Carbon dioxide overwhelms the oxygen in the blood. The brain sends out a message that oxygen is required. You breathe. Water floods your lungs. You drown. It's not pretty.

Not everyone drowns that way. Sometimes the involuntary breath causes a laryngospasm. The flood of water touches the vocal cords, triggers a reflex action. The throat seizes up. Nothing gets by the blockage. You suffocate. That's no prettier.

That's how people drown. But I'd been shot, too.

The branding iron in my side dragged me back to consciousness. I might have been down there five seconds or five minutes, ankle-deep in the mud, when I finally realised I wasn't dead. If I'd been dead, I wouldn't have known I had a branding iron melting my flesh. I wouldn't have been able to wish I was dead, either.

Breaking point arrived. My brain shut down all auxiliary functions, focused on kicking my left foot free of the sucking mud. The mud gave. The Puffa did the rest.

I broke the surface like a porpoise in heat, felt the air on my face, body convulsing, coughing up a lungful of river. I was deaf and blind, the whole world pitch black. When I finally grasped that I was under the bridge, the current sweeping off the bend, carrying me across the river rather than out to sea, the panic subsided. That gave me a chance to think, to come up with a plan that might keep me alive.

The moment passed. I started panicking again.

I paddled for the far quay, frantic, battling the current to stay under the bridge, the Puffa buoying me up at the waist. Thinking that, whoever they were, they were pros. There were no shouts, no wasted bullets fired at imaginary targets, nothing to let me know where they were, what they were doing. Which was just as well, there wasn't a damn thing I could have done to stop them and I had other things to worry about. Like, if I didn't get out of the water quick smart, the cold was going to kill me quicker than any gunnies.

It took twenty minutes to reach the far quay, three yards forward and two yards back, every second a bullet in the back of the head. When I finally got there the stone was smooth, slimy. I let myself be carried downstream, buffeted by the swell between the dock and the huge coal freighter moored just beyond the bridge.

The rusty ladder embedded in the quay came at me fast. I bobbed by, reaching. I didn't make the same mistake the second time, crashing in on the ladder with a sodden clang. I clung to the rungs for a minute or two, until the branding iron seared into my side, and then I let go again. I passed the next six ladders. By the time I got to the seventh I was down at the deepwater, two hundred yards from open sea, and fainting. My fingers were numb, the ladder rungs icing over. Twice I fell back into the water. On the third attempt I hauled myself out onto the dock, giddy with achievement.

I limped across the quay on jelly legs, crawled into the doorway of an abandoned warehouse. Unzipped the Puffa, pulled my shirt up, stared at the second belly button that had appeared just above my right hip. Felt for the exit wound, praying there was one, walked my fingers around it, right leg kicking uncontrollably. Ducked under my elbow to find a raw hole the size of a squash ball where I had always thought my kidneys were supposed to be. The blood was thin and black against the blueish, goose-bumped flesh.

I dug my keys out of the Puffa's pocket, unhooked the leather keyholder. Folded it over, bit down hard. Then I balled my handkerchief, twisted it into a knot, took a deep breath and poked it into the hole. An electric shock shot down through my leg and bounced back up to fry my brain. I gagged on something hot and sour, collapsed back into the doorway, waiting for sirens to sound on the clear night air.

Noises wafted past the outer limit of my consciousness, strange noises, sounds I had never heard before. I realised I was talking to myself in a guttural tone, the words chopped up, blocky. My eyes blurred and cleared, blurred again. Sweat poured down my face, soaked my back, warm against the chill. I wondered, idly, if I was shaking from cold, or shock, or septicaemia.

I imagined a blazing log fire, a mute television screening *Willy Wonka*, a Christmas tree blinking in the corner. Ben a warm lump sprawled across my chest. A black hole in the corner of the room that seemed to be oscillating, expanding and contracting, enticing me to investigate further; warmth came in waves from its core. The temptation was too much. I put Ben to one side, carefully, so he wouldn't wake. Got off the couch, struggling towards the darkness, feeling my body starting to thaw. Something nagging at the back of my mind, something important, something I couldn't afford not to remember . . .

Ben.

And then it was dark and cold again, and I was jammed in the doorway of a deserted warehouse. Dying, shivering so hard parts of my body were splintering, I could hear them shatter. Slowly, precisely, I started putting the pieces back together again. There were some parts left over when I was finished so I just left them out, pretending not to notice.

I sat up, eased my shirt back into my jeans, zipped up the Puffa, hands trembling. Peered around the corner of the warehouse. Four hundred yards away, the bridge was deserted under the orange streetlights.

I knew there were at least two of them and that they were pros. I knew they had a sub-machine gun and that they wanted me dead. That was all I knew but that was plenty to be getting on with, if they were still around I didn't need the news to get any worse. All I had going for me was that they couldn't be certain I'd made it out of the river, which meant they'd have to split up to search both shores. It wasn't much, but I was alive, which just about gave me bragging rights over Gonzo.

A shiver passed through me, top to bottom, that had nothing to do with my sopping clothes, the biting wind. I didn't indulge it, I had Ben and Denise to make safe. I was guessing that, if the pros knew I'd be crossing the bridge, they'd know that the bridge was taking me home.

There was a public phone-box in the industrial estate, on the far side of the docks, which gave me a simple choice. Cutting through the docklands would get me to the phone quicker, but also increased the chances of bumping into the pros again, and I was pretty sure I'd already used up all my nine lives. Avoiding the pros meant going all the way down to the end of the deepwater quay, away from the bridge, doubling back up the far side, coming into the industrial estate from the rear. Which was twenty minutes in a flat-out sprint, and I wasn't even sure I could walk straight.

I thought of Ben, asleep in bed, his behind sticking up in the air. When I had him fixed in my mind I pushed myself up out of the doorway, took off at full tilt.

I was doused in sweat after fifty yards. After five hundred, my lungs were on fire again, the branding iron wiggling around in my side, legs useless stumps of marble. It was maybe five hundred yards more before I remembered Gonzo's mobile, when it started ringing deep in the inside pocket of the Puffa.

I swore at my stupidity, slipped my hand inside the jacket, folded my hand around the phone to muffle the sound. It was a smart move. At that hour, down at the docks with no traffic, no one around, the chirping would have sounded like a twenty-one gun salute.

I didn't take the call. I'd had enough bad news to do me for the rest of my life, and the call meant bad news. Whoever the pros were, they knew Gonzo – had known Gonzo – well enough to know his mobile number. When the phone stopped ringing I dialled a number, the phone buried deep inside the jacket. It took her maybe ten or twelve rings to answer.

'Dee?'

'Who's this?'

Her voice thick with sleep, sounding nervous.

'It's me. Harry.'

'Harry? What's wrong?' She paused. Then, coming back stronger, accusation in her voice: 'What's wrong, Harry?'

'I'll tell you everything later. Right now you have to get dressed, pack a bag, get Ben out of the house.'

Silence.

'Dee?'

A deep sigh, then: 'Harry, I don't know how long—'

'Just take the car and get out of town. It doesn't matter where.' A light bulb popped – Brendan and Maura had a holiday home about an hour north of town. 'The bungalow,' I told her.

'Stop it, Harry. You're scaring me. What's going on?'

'I'll explain it all later, Dee. Okay? Right now I need you to pack a bag and get out of the house. It'll be alright tomorrow, I swear.'

'What will?'

'Jesus fucking *Christ*, Dee! Get Ben out of the fucking house now! Fucking *now*!'

'Okay. Jesus.' She sounded sullen. 'Where'll I go?'

'I told you, the holiday home. Tell Brendan our place flooded, that I'm staying behind to keep an eye on the place until it gets sorted.'

'They're away for Christmas, you know that. They're gone to Dallas, to Marian and Jeff.'

'Fuck.' I'd forgotten they were away. 'Okay, that's even better. You have a key, don't you?'

'Yeah, but—'

'But nothing. I'll come and pick you up tomorrow. Alright?'

'What about the presents?'

'What presents?'

'Ben's presents, Harry. Jesus.'

'Fuck the *presents*, Dee! Just get out of the fucking house!'

'It's Christmas, Harry!'

'Jesus H.' I took a deep breath. 'Alright, grab something small and get out. I'll bring the rest.'

'Okay, okay. Harry?'

'What?'

'Where's Gonzo?'

'I'll tell you everything tomorrow. Okay?' I gave her the mobile number. 'Ring as soon as you get there. And go now.'

She hung up. My knees buckled and I keeled over against the wall. Rolled a smoke, the tobacco still dry, buried deep in the Puffa's pocket beside the mobile. Considered my next move. If I stayed out all night in my condition, hypothermia was the best I could hope for. And if the pros knew where I lived, chances were they knew where I drank, which ruled out Dutchie's place. The office was a non-starter, if the Dibble could find me there anyone could.

When I finished the smoke I dug out my wallet, checked behind the condom. Dialled the number, and either the phone was in the bedroom or Katie was a late-night kind of girl. She answered on the third ring, cautious.

'Who's this?'

'It's Harry. Harry Rigby?'

'Jesus, Harry. You frightened the life out of me. What time is it?'

'About three. Listen, Katie, I need a big favour.'

'How big?'

'Huge. Can you put me up for the night?'

'Yeah, yeah. Sure.' She hesitated. 'Why, what's wrong?'

'I'll explain when I get there.'

'Alright.' She laughed, sounding nervous. 'You haven't killed anyone, have you?'

'Not yet, no.'

'Alright then.'

She gave me the address, an avenue off Northlands Estate, a plush neighbourhood on the far side of town with a commanding view of town and bay.

'Okay, I'll be there in a while. And Katie?'

'What?'

'Thanks.'

'De nada.'

*

The door opened a crack. Haunted eyes peered through the gap. I was shivering hard, slumped against the wall. It had taken fifteen minutes to wake him up, get him to the front door.

'Who's there?' he whispered. He probably intended it to sound fierce but his voice was cracked, brittle.

'It's me, Joe. Harry Rigby. From the pub?'

The crack widened.

'Harry who?'

'Harry Rigby, Joe. Can you let me in? I need—'

Somehow I couldn't finish it, couldn't say the word out loud, but maybe he saw something in my eyes he saw every day in the mirror. Or maybe nobody had asked him for help in a long, long time. And maybe he was always disposed to being a Good Samaritan and no one ever took the time to find out. Whatever it was, he opened the door, gave the street outside a quick scan, dragged me inside.

It was no warmer in the hallway. The house, three stories of faux-Georgian craft, had been condemned ten years previously, still standing only because the rear of the train station didn't exactly inspire the Celtic cubs with notions of urban chic. Joe was the sole occupant, a squatter who'd never need to assert his rights unless rats ever became a must-have townhouse accessory.

He was wearing the same overcoat and soiled pants from the day before. Hair rumpled, eyes raw, bloodshot. His bristles rasped as he rubbed his chin, none too sure of the next step in the hospitality game. The smell of cheap cider breath was foul.

The hallway was high, long and dank. Mould oozed up the walls. The stench of cat piss seeped into my pores. A battered black pay phone was bolted to the wall, one of the ancient ones that had a Button A, Button B and a barbell receiver. There was a scorch mark just inside the door, but apart from that the carpet had no discernible pattern. He noticed me staring.

'Lighter fluid,' he said. His voice was gruff now, no self-pity. 'Couple of years ago, at Halloween. The kind of thing they do nowadays.'

A bare bulb hung low over the kitchen table, at which a single chair sat guarding an empty bottle of stout. A line of washing – a pair of faded pink long johns, two shirts with yellowing armpits – stretched from over the cracked porcelain sink to the glowing Sacred Heart on the far wall. Other than that, the kitchen was as neat as it was empty. He looked at me and frowned, bushy brows knitting.

'Christ, son. What happened to you?'

I sat, gingerly, on the chair, tugged my shirt out of my jeans. His eyes widened and he disappeared back into the hallway. When he returned he had a grimy sheet that he'd torn into strips and a tub of foul-smelling orange cream that I didn't ask too many questions about. He sat on an upturned wooden box, cleaned the wound, applied the grimy bandages. His hands shook but his movements were deft, his touch sure. When he was finished he sat back and lit the butt of a cigarette.

'You were lucky, son. It was a big one but it went through clean. If it had hit anything it'd have blown your back out.'

'Felt like an electric shock when it hit. Thought I'd been fried.'

'Seen it happen. He went berserk, charged off into the jungle on his own, just screaming.' He stubbed the butt, looked away. 'None of my business, son, so you tell me what you like. But I never put you down for running with a bad crowd.'

I kept it short. When I was finished he shook his head but didn't start any sermons.

'You keep your head down, son. If it comes looking for you, kick it in the balls. But don't go looking for it.'

It was good advice, the sage words of an old man, the kind I particularly hate passing up.

'Thanks for everything, Joe. I really appreciate it. No kidding, I thought I was dying out there. But I have to shoot through.'

'Want to kip here? There's plenty of room.'

'Cheers, Joe, but no. I don't want to put you out anymore than I already have.'

Mischief blazed in his eyes.

'A night like this, and you with holes back and front? She must be some woman.'

'Aren't they all, Joe?'

'True as God, son. True as God.'

He stood up and left. When he returned he was carrying an oil-soaked rag, carrying it careful in the crook of one arm. He sat down, put the rag on the table. Looked at me, folded back the rag. An old cowboy's gun sat there, a Colt Peacemaker .45, a six-shooter, oiled and gleaming. The barrel wasn't quite long as a piece of string.

'Mad what you find in the jungle,' he said. 'There's three bullets to go with it. If you're interested.'

I was tempted, I really was, but Prothiaden and guns are a bad combination. Anyway, I wasn't sure I had the strength to point it anywhere but the floor.

'I've never used a gun in my life, Joe. Wouldn't know where to start.'

'It's knowing where to finish, son. Starting's the easy bit. You just make sure the safety's off and let your mind go blank.'

I shook my head again. He didn't push it.

'You need anything again, son, you don't worry about putting me out. I'll be here, or you'll know where to find me.' He gave me the number of the pay phone in the hall. 'I think it still works,' he said, his tone matter-of-fact. 'Haven't heard it ring in years.'

He didn't have to tell me, he'd never had any reason to make a call himself. I slipped the number into my wallet and left.

*

It was an hour to Katie's, giving the centre of town a wide berth, and uphill all the way. She answered the door in her dressing gown, a short cream kimono belted at the waist. As far as I could make out she wasn't wearing anything underneath, but I was too shattered to investigate properly. Besides, I had one or two things on my mind. She toasted me with the glass of wine in her hand.

'Come on in,' she said, breezy, flirting. Then, when I stepped in under the hall light: 'Jesus Christ, Harry! What . . . Jesus!'

I could see myself in the mirror at the end of the hall. Hunched over, sopping wet, the side of my face bruised and swollen, hair plastered tight to the skull. It wasn't a pretty sight and I was no oil painting to start with, unless Bosch had turned his hand to portraits. I tugged at my jeans.

'Can I change out of these?'

'Of course. Upstairs. March.'

She gave me a T-shirt and her biggest sweater, a pair of pow-der-blue tracksuit bottoms. I stood outside the shower, poking one limb inside at a time, trying to keep Joe's bandages dry, but I hadn't even started to thaw out by the time I crawled back downstairs again.

She had made a pot of coffee, a bottle of Jameson and a pack-et of painkillers sitting beside it on the low table between the plush armchairs. I sat down, poured a third of the bottle into the coffee pot, gulped down a mug and then looked at her. I hadn't wanted to before. Katie was something of a distraction at the best of times, and the loose kimono was destroying what little concen-tration I had left.

Tiny worry lines creased her forehead. I didn't blame her. If someone I barely knew turned up at my front door at five in the morning, I'd have been worried too. Worried he might freeze to death in the cold outside, because the only way he'd have got in was on the other end of a battering ram.

'Bren okay?'

'Ben. He's fine.' Rather, I hoped Ben was fine, hoped with

every fibre of my being that Ben was just fine and dandy-o. A little tired, maybe, but still in possession of all his limbs and his endearing innocence. I acknowledged that Katie was due an explanation of sorts. I poured another mug of coffee, popped three painkillers and gave her one, of sorts. I told her what I thought she needed to know, leaving out the bit about Gonzo screwing Celine all those years ago, not because I respected Gonzo's memory, but just because. She didn't reach for a notepad and pen but her eyes sparkled all the same.

She was cool. Once I'd reassured her that the pros wouldn't be kicking her door down, she accepted the situation, started dealing with it.

'He's dead?'

'Him, O'Leary and romantic Ireland.'

I was trying to be cool myself. I knew I was teetering on the abyss, that I'd tip over into the maw if I tried to make sense of it all. I'd hated Gonzo, my own brother, hated what he was, who he was and what he represented. That didn't minimise the shock of his death. Whatever he was, or became, Gonzo was my brother. My only brother. My only family.

'And then someone tried to kill you?'

'The fucker was maybe ten yards away when he fired. Pointing at me. Even I can work that one out.'

'What about the Guards?'

'What about them?'

'You have to tell them.'

'Of course. Once I know it wasn't them doing the shooting.'

'The Guards?'

'This isn't South Central, Katie. The only punters use machine guns around here are Provies and Special Branch.'

'The Provies?'

'Yeah. Dissidents, call them whatever.' I shrugged the possibility off. Things were bad enough without dealing with the prospect of Provies chasing me down. 'I've done nothing to piss them off, though. Far as I know.'

'But the Guards?'

'Branch. Thing is, I had that chat with Galway and Brady this morning, about Frank Conway. Except nothing got said, because Conway is a client of mine who happens to be involved in some very dodgy dealings. Maybe the Dibble aren't getting their cut, maybe they think I'm in on it and taking me out was supposed to be some kind of warning to anyone who was thinking of doing the same. And maybe not. All I know is, they let me go quick smart after Gonzo died. They didn't even search me properly. Either way, if the shooters were Dibble I won't have to go to them. They'll come looking for me.'

She sipped her wine, peeking out from behind the bob, which had fallen in front of her face. Sitting forward, chewing the inside of her lip. She looked vulnerable, tender and intensely desirable. I marvelled at the mind's ability to create diversions in order to stave off self-destruction. To distract myself, I dug out the mobile and punched in a number. She answered on the second ring.

'Dee?'

'Harry?'

'Yeah. You okay?'

'Okay?' There was a short pause. Then: 'You got me out of bed to drive eighty miles in the middle of the night, Ben developing pneumonia the whole way, and you won't tell me why. Would you be okay, Harry?'

'Maybe not. But you sound fine. You're there already?'

'No traffic. Why would there be? Any normal person would be tucked up in bed, asleep.'

'You're different, Dee. You're special. How's Ben?'

'He's asleep. What's going on?'

'I'll tell you everything tomorrow, I swear. When I get there. Don't leave the house, keep the doors locked, curtains pulled. Okay?'

'No it's not ofuckingkay. Harry—'

'Have to go, Dee. Chat to you in the morning.'

I hung up, heaved a sigh of relief, switched the mobile off. A huge weight lifted off my shoulders. Then the weight changed its mind and sandbagged me across the back of the head. I slumped back into the armchair.

'You okay?' she asked. Again with the lip chewing and the peeking out from behind the bob.

'I'm grand. Really. I'm just too tired to deal with it now. It'll hit tomorrow. All I need now is a quilt and a pillow.'

She put the glass of wine on the coffee table, held out her hand. I reached too. It felt soft and cool. She squeezed gently.

'The couch is too small. You'll sleep better in bed.'

The couch you could have rafted down the Amazon but I was too tired to argue. I let her drag me out of the armchair and up the stairs to her bedroom. She went to the bathroom, which I took as my cue to get into bed. She gave me plenty of time to do it, which was just as well, every joint in my body was locked solid. There was some blood seeping through the bandage but it was nothing to write home about, not that there was anyone at home anymore. The pain had just about subsided to a tolerable throb.

When she came back she was wearing an over-sized T-shirt, a

panda bear on the front. She got into bed, tucked me in, turned her back, staked a claim to some duvet.

'Katie?'

'Don't spoil it, Harry.'

'No disrespect, but I'm a dying man.'

'Good.'

She slept. I lay there, floating above the big empty, hearing Gonzo call my name from its gaping maw.

17

I dozed fitfully, twisting myself into a swastika, waking fast every
time I turned onto the wound. Morning was a shaft of light
angling through a chink in the curtains, right between the eyes.

I rolled a cigarette, checked the bandage. The blob of raspberry jelly had settled, hardened. Katie still had her back turned to
me, like she hadn't moved all night, even though she'd been out
to the bathroom twice. She had rucked the quilt and her hip was
exposed all the way to the white cotton of her panties, the skin
warm, downy and golden. I watched her until the outside world
grew jealous and started to punch her doorbell. I was up and
dressed before the next buzz sounded. Katie tugged the quilt tight
under her chin.

'Katie?' I tucked my T-shirt into my jeans. Both were still
damp but pneumonia was the least of my worries.

'What?' Eyes closed, pawing at her fringe.

'There's someone at the door.'

The buzzer rasped, paused, sounded again, angry this time.

Which was bad news, they weren't going away. The good news being, if they hadn't already kicked the door down, they were unlikely to do it at all.

I peered through the narrow gap between curtain and window frame. All I could see was an empty front garden, a tiny lawn that needed its grass cut, tiny drifts of sleet in the corners. It looked like we were in for a white Christmas but the prospect didn't fill me with the innocent glee it should have, mainly because there was a blue Mondeo parked in the street.

'Are you going to answer that?'

'Yeah, yeah,' she said, digging her fists into her eyes. She stumbled around the room, picking up jeans and a baggy sweater. Pulled them on over her T-shirt, hopping awkwardly when her foot got caught in one of the legs. When she was dressed she pulled her hair back off her face, tied it up with a scrunchy.

'It's the Dibble,' I warned as she padded towards the door, barefoot.

'So?'

'Exactly. And Katie? Keep it neat.'

I left the door open, listening at the crack. She opened the front door and I heard mumbling. Then the mumbling became louder and the door closed again. I crept out onto the landing. They were in the front room, the hall door open.

'I know him, yeah,' she was saying. 'What's he done?'

'He hasn't done anything.' Galway, reassuring, his tone dry. I could imagine Brady rocking on the balls of his feet, looking around for something to sneer at. He wouldn't find too much. The house was smart and bright, all polished pine floors and airy rooms with high ceilings. You could have turned a tugboat in the living room and still had room to swing a cat, so long as you were prepared to answer hard questions from the animal rights wallahs. Even Brady would have had enough room to lumber around without breaking anything. 'We just need to talk to him,' Galway added.

'You think he's here?'

'We don't know where he is. But you have been observed in his company in the past few days and we're investigating all the options open to us at this time.'

'Well, he isn't. Here, I mean.'

Brady sounded like he'd been into the whiskey again, a header into the vat followed by a couple of brisk lengths.

'Mind if we look around?' he rasped.

'Yes.' I nearly smiled – I could imagine her, half Brady's size, hands on hips, defying him.

'How come?'

'Leave it.' Galway again, sharp. Then: 'We can contact you again if we need to, Miss Donnelly?'

'Sure. Detective Brady has my number.'

'Thank you for your time. And if you do hear from Mister Rigby, please ask him to contact us as a matter of some urgency.'

'Of course.'

The front door closed again. I went back into the bedroom, peered through the gap in the curtains. Brady was driving. He turned the Mondeo in the narrow road and it rumbled off towards town. Katie trudged back upstairs.

'Contact the cops. It's a matter of some urgency. And it's your turn to put the coffee on.'

I turned at the door.

'How does it feel to be an accessory after the fact?'

'Sticks and stones, Harry. I've been called a lot worse.'

'I'm sure you have.'

'By better than you, too. So watch your mouth.'

*

I boiled the kettle, started a brew, stepped out into the back garden to air my lungs. It was mild out, and the jumble of dirty grey clouds massing out over the Atlantic meant there was snow on the way for sure. For now the morning was sharp and clear, the sun pale in a powder-blue sky. I coughed my approval, phlegmy and rich, went back inside.

I turned on the radio and listened to the news, drinking coffee and rolling a smoke. The lead story concerned a cabinet stalwart that didn't avail of a tax amnesty, mainly because he couldn't really admit to needing it, the tale nearly seventeen years old and coming of age nicely. The second story was a foiled bank robbery in Ardee. The third followed up on a story from the day before, a multiple pile-up somewhere in Cork that left three children without their father on Christmas Eve. Their mother was in intensive care, fighting for her life, and the reporter laid on the pathos like her pension depended on it, which it probably did.

There was nothing about the accident Galway reported, the one involving a kid puncturing a windscreen. That meant no one had been killed, which was good news, which was why it hadn't made the bulletin.

I tuned the radio to the local station, caught an update, but they had nothing on the Windscreen Kid either. Neither was there a mention of a shooting in the town the night before. I wasn't surprised, or maybe it was just that I didn't have the energy. I had nothing left to give, no synapses left to tingle. I was running on empty, the engine breathing fumes. All I had was the inclination to trundle on because I didn't have the strength to apply the brakes.

The coffee helped. I was onto my third mug by the time Katie came downstairs, rubbing her hair with a towel. I poured her a coffee.

'Sugar?'

'One, and milk.'

We perched on stools beside the long pine counter, sipping the coffee and not looking at one another.

'So what happens now?' she asked.

'I keep my head down until I can get to Ben and Denise. When I get there, I'll get them somewhere safer than where they are now.'

'You have somewhere in mind?'

'I'm hoping Bali is cheap off-season.'

'What about your brother?'

'What about him?'

'Won't someone have to identify the body?'

'Probably. But it can wait, he's not going anywhere.'

It came out callous but I let it carry on. She gave me a funny look, composed herself.

'Harry, if there's anything I can do . . .'

I shook my head, reached out, squeezed her hand. She didn't squeeze back.

'You've done more than enough. Most people would have screamed the house down, turned me over to the Dibble first chance they got.'

Her gaze didn't waver.

'I'm not most people.'

'True enough. How come they know where you live?'

The change of pace caught her out. She stared long enough to blink twice, which was once too often.

'How do you mean?'

'I mean, you're a reporter from out of town. How are they supposed to find you? Even know that you're still around? I presume you gave Brady your number up at Sheridan's place. You flip him the address too?'

She shook her head.

'No. Maybe they rang the magazine. I don't know.'

'They rang the magazine? On Christmas Eve? Before eight in the morning?'

She stared, stayed cool.

'Harry, if I didn't want to help I'd have turned you in when they were here. I don't know how they got my address. I own the place, it was a sweet investment, and that kind of thing is down on record. Or maybe they stuck a pin in the phone book. You want me to ring and ask them how they found you?'

'Okay, okay, I'm sorry. The way things are, I can't trust myself to take a piss standing up. No offence intended.'

'Yeah, well, offence taken.'

She went to the sink, ran the cold tap over her mug. Left it on the draining board to drip dry, stared out the window.

'Nice place,' I said, changing the topic. 'The magazine must be looking after you.'

She shot me a glance across her shoulder. Smiled, let the scene slide.

'Not as well as Tommy Finan.'

'Who he?'

'Assistant manager in the Ulster Bank, my local mole when I was buying here. He kept me posted on what bids were bullshit.' She winked. 'He's cute, too.'

'And you let him know it.'

'It was nothing he wasn't already thinking.'

She left. When she returned she had her jacket on. She stood in front of the mirror, brushed her hair out with brisk strokes.

'So,' she said, fiddling with the hairbrush. 'What's the plan now?'

I told her what I'd told her the first time she asked, giving it a different spin.

'I was going to hang here for a while, if that's okay. Chances are the Dibble are sitting around the corner waiting for me to stroll out.'

'Why would they be waiting?'

'Maybe they didn't believe you.'

'Why would I lie?'

'You did lie.'

She shrugged it off.

'Right enough. I'll swing around by your office when I get into town, let you know if I see them.'

'Sound.' I gave her Gonzo's mobile number. 'I might be gone by the time you get there, but you'll get me on this. If the signal doesn't run out.'

'Okay. Be careful.'

'That's part of the plan, yeah.'

*

I made another coffee, moved into the living room, pulled the curtains closed. Then I rang Dutchie, started rolling a smoke. He answered on the first ring.

'It's me, Dutch.'

'Harry?'

He sounded surprised. I didn't blame him. The last time I'd been up that early I'd been on my way home.

'Get you up, did I?'

'Yeah, yeah. I had a couple after . . . after that last night. You know.'

'Yeah.'

He started again, cautious: 'So how goes it?'

'Head's cabbaged, but I'm alive.'

'Yeah, yeah.'

'Shouldn't be, though.'

'How's that?'

'Last night, on the new bridge. A car pulls up out of nowhere and some fucker lets fly with a machine gun. Fucking Howitzer, he had.'

'Fuck! How—'

'I jumped.'

'Into the river?'

'No, Dutch. I went up the way, hitched a passing hang-glider.'

'Jesus Christ, Harry! Who –?'

'They didn't say; it wasn't that kind of party. But I had the Branch around this morning. Again.'

'They were around to the house?'

I realised that Galway and Brady hadn't stopped by Dutchie's. I said, slow, wondering why: 'I'm not at the house, Dutch.'

'Where are you?'

'You're better off not knowing. That way you won't have to lie when they call.'

He chewed it over.

'Think it had anything to do with Gonz?'

'I don't, no. The hang-glider bloke said it was just a coincidence.' I couldn't afford to waste any more time waiting for Dutchie to wake up. I moved on. 'I need a favour, Dutch.'

'Anything. Say the word.'

'I'll need your car. Denise took mine last night, headed for the holiday home.'

'Smart. You want to come here and pick it up?'

'Leave it at the shopping centre, the one down at the river. The third level, say. Leave the key in the usual place. And Dutch? This morning? The Dibble aren't usually that quick off the mark.'

'I hear you. I'll make some calls.'

'Okay, here's Gonzo's mobile.'

He took the number down. He said: 'Anything else I can do?'

'Yeah. Can you stow Ben's bike in the boot? It's in the keg room.'

'Yeah, yeah, no worries. And Harry?'

'What?'

He was all choked up again.

'Be cute, Harry.'

'Like Barbie, Dutch. I'll buzz you later.'

I hung up, finished the coffee, thumbed through the telephone book, made the call.

'Good morning, Ulster Bank. Mary speaking. How may I help you?'

'Hi. Can I speak to Tommy Finan, please?'

'One moment.'

'Thanks.'

Greensleeves came piping down the line. I hung up, poured another coffee. Sipped it slowly until the mobile rang.

'Harry? It's Katie.'

'What's up?'

'They're outside the office, just down the street. The girl in the coffee shop says they're investigating the break-in.'

'Break-in?'

'Yeah. Your office was trashed last night.'

'That'd be right.' Either Galway had got his search warrant, or the pros were even slicker than I'd given them credit for. Or maybe it was just a coincidence. Maybe some scumbags from The Project decided to break in and wreck the place on the very night I was running for my life. The hang-glider bloke sailed by. He was shaking his head. 'Katie?'

'What?'

'You're going to have let me buy you a coffee some time.'

'Cheap bastard.'

'Not so cheap, okay?'

I rang Herbie. The ring tone sounded strange, abrupt, not giving the phone a chance to ring. Which was bad news. There was a chance that Herbie, stoned and oblivious, had disconnected the phone the night before, but when Herbie got stoned and oblivious he generally went chasing porn on the Internet.

I rinsed out the coffee cup, shrugged into the damp Puffa. It was even heavier than I remembered. Maybe that was because I was carrying Gonzo in it now, in every pocket, in the seams of the lining, the folds of the collar, which I turned up defiantly before closing the door behind me.

18

It took me nearly an hour to get to the shopping mall, going out around by the college, doubling back through the train station. The town was mobbed, the last minute shopping only a Valium off frenzy, and the paranoia subsided only slightly when I got inside the mall. I wandered through some of the shops, backtracking, keeping an eye on my reflection, but I didn't spot anyone who shouldn't have been there. Which meant I wasn't being followed or I was being followed by pros.

Dutchie's car was parked on the third level, a tidy Fiat Bravo that could turn it up on the open road if it had to. I skulked behind a pillar and watched it for a while. Then I went back downstairs and hid out in the back of a stand-up coffee bar, gagging on a cup of coffee so bitter the ulcer gave it a standing ovation. I stocked up on a couple of bottles of Maalox in the chemist, chucked a box of painkillers in on the sale, ducked into the public toilet. When the ulcer stopped screaming I went back upstairs.

There was no one around that I recognised from the first trip. I threaded my way through the parked cars, flipped open the petrol cap guard, hooked the keys, got in. The retrieval ticket was in the glove compartment, with 'Nothing yet' scrawled on the back. I wasn't surprised. Dutchie was good and he knew a lot of people, but the kind of people Dutchie knew usually didn't surface in the a.m.

The .38 was in the glove compartment too. That did surprise me. Dutchie wasn't known for his sense of humour.

I drove out of the shopping centre, turned west on Fortfield, towards Herbie's. The lights were out on Pearse Street but Midtown wasn't any more backed up than usual, the usual heart attack of clogged arteries, the flow reduced to a stop-start trickle. Joe was directing traffic at the broken lights, waving everyone on with gusto and savagely berating anyone who ignored his directions. Which was everyone, including himself. Running his hands through his shock of white hair, lips flecked with spittle, eyes wild.

He spotted me as the car crawled through the junction. He winked, tipped a sly nod at the chaos, straightened his back and saluted. That provoked another rash of horn tooting, which only started Joe ranting again. I saluted him back and slid out onto Fortfield, grinning.

If my sanity had a shock of white hair it might have looked the way Joe did, its cogs and gears meshing, frantic, as it tried to work out the logic of walking into what was almost certainly an ambush.

*

There's no substitute for gut instinct and you can't argue a hunch with logic. My gut feeling suggested septicaemia but I also had a hunch that claimed the pros were too cute to leave themselves open to casual observation, say by staking out Herbie's place. If the pros were as good as I thought they were, and I wasn't going to underestimate anyone smart enough to squeeze a trigger, they wouldn't leave themselves open to the random vagaries of fate. They'd have something a little more professional in the pipeline, something slick and tidy that would happen at a time and place I wouldn't even dream of guessing at. My only defence was to fly below their radar, by acting even dumber than before. Which was why I was following up on the hunch about Herbie.

I cruised past the house, turned at the end of the cul-de-sac. Waited ten minutes, the car in gear, foot on the gas, in case anything moved. Nothing stirred. When I was satisfied the pros weren't around, I parked a couple of houses down from Herbie's. One thing I knew for sure, the pros weren't inside. If they were they'd have answered the phone when I rang, curious as to who might be ringing the guy they'd just turned over. Because if what Katie told me about my office was true, then Herbie had been turned over too. All that remained to be seen was how thorough the pros had been.

I rang the bell and waited. I rang again, and then started to wonder why I was ringing the bell. Traffic thrummed by out on Fortfield. Nothing moved on the avenue, no sound disturbed the chirping of the sparrows pecking at the frozen ground. It was dry, too. When it came, and the sky was already darkening, the snow was going to stick for sure. Which meant Ben was going to get his snowman. Whether or not I'd be around to help him make it was a debate I wasn't prepared to entertain.

I made my way around the side of the house, avoiding the heaped pile of refuse sacks, sidling up to the kitchen window, peering in. There was no one inside. I tried the back door, expecting it to be locked, which it was. I took a quick look around, glad that Herbie had let the back garden run riot, the hedges grow high and wild. Then, when I was sure no nosy neighbour was standing by with binoculars and Nikon at the ready, I punched my elbow against the glass pane, hard enough to crack the glass but not so hard it might shatter. When I'd pulled out the longer shards of glass, I put my hand inside and slid back the bolt.

The kitchen looked like a Delhi sewer, but that was par for the course at Herbie's. I tiptoed out into the hall. The living room door was open. I peered through the crack between door and frame. There was no one hiding behind the door. I pushed the door open. The television was on, the sound turned down, which is the only way to watch MTV. A half-eaten pizza, the size of a small wagon wheel, lay on the coffee table beside the couch. I touched the pizza. It was cold.

I picked up the poker from the fireplace, went to check the front room. Then, quietly, I climbed the stairs, poker cocked over one shoulder. If I'd thought about it I'd have reckoned, maybe, that my plan was to catch the pros napping and frighten them to death by waving the poker at them. But I didn't think about it.

I caught Herbie napping, facedown in a pillow. The pillow scarlet and sodden, hands tied behind his back with electrical cable. He groaned when I turned him over onto his side. It was a tiny sound, a grunt I wouldn't have heard if I hadn't been straining to hear it, but it told me all I needed to know. Herbie was alive.

The ginger hair was the giveaway. Everything else was pretty much unrecognisable. It looked like someone had been pulping jam with his head and pineapple jam at that. His nose was pushed to one side, lips split, the mouth an ugly red gash. His cheekbones were stove in, eyes puffed up to maybe three times their usual size. He had no teeth left that I could see, although it was possible they hadn't been able to get to the grinders right at the back. It wasn't for the want of trying if they hadn't.

I dug out Gonzo's mobile, dialled emergency.

'Herb,' I said, as I untied his hands. 'Herb? You hear me?'

'Aauugh,' he whispered. It was a guttural, primitive sound, the blood clogging up his mouth not helping. He was blind and punch-drunk but I got the impression he recognised my voice, although that was probably just wishful thinking. Maybe it was just as well. If Herbie had recognised it, he'd have known it as the voice responsible for getting him into this mess.

'Help's on the way, Herb. Hear that? I've rung for an ambulance.'

There was nothing more I could do for him, what Herbie needed was professional help and early retirement. I went across the hall and checked his computer room. The whole system was kicked asunder, hard drives mangled, screens booted in. Even the furniture had been smashed. At a rough guess, there was maybe ten grand worth of damage done. I was disappointed. I'd expected more from professionals than petty spite.

I went back to Herbie's room, opened a window and watched him while I waited for the ambulance to arrive. He was in poor shape. The pros hadn't been too worried whether he suffocated or just choked on his own blood. He'd live, I was guessing, which was good, but Herbie was never going to be the same again.

Maybe it was just as well that most of his friends lived in cyber-space.

When I heard the faint whine of the ambulance siren, the sound carrying on the clear air, I went downstairs. I found a dish-cloth in the kitchen, wiped the poker clean and put it back on the hearth. Then I left.

I parked at the bottom of the avenue, started building a smoke. Thirty seconds later an ambulance came tearing around the corner, a squad car in close attendance. When they pulled up outside Herbie's, I turned onto Fortfield and headed back towards town.

It was time the pigeon threw himself among the cats.

*

The foyer of Conway's office was bright, airy. Dust motes hung in the sunlight that angled down through the slatted wooden blinds. There was so much potted greenery I expected a pygmy to jump out and shoot off a poisoned dart.

A row of low chairs occupied the far wall. A young couple sat on two of them, her blonde, him bland, the furrowed brows sug-gesting that they were newly married and about to dive headfirst into insolvency. A balding gent in his sixties occupied a third chair. He wore a plain grey suit and his shoes were trimmed with dry mud. His face was round, ruddy and slightly anxious, the way all farmers look when walls hem them in.

The secretary was in her forties. Prim, the precise make-up job screaming inferiority complex. Her desk was so big it looked like she needed to yodel to be heard on the other side. I didn't want to be responsible for her face falling off, so I marched past.

Her expectant expression creased in confusion as I headed for the door marked 'Private'. The last thing I heard her say was, 'I said, you can't go *in* there,' but I'd heard that line from younger women than her so I just closed the door quietly behind me.

Conway's office was an amphitheatre. The plush carpet rippled away towards the horizon, where Conway sat behind a mahogany desk that could have hosted the Ziegfeld Follies. The lighting was subtle, art deco, the temperature cool. The colour scheme exuded mellow repose, pale blue walls with lime-green borders. There was more potted greenery in the corners, and the room was so quiet I guessed it was soundproofed. Given the way the property market was running, the ambience was perfect. When you're an auctioneer trying to minimise the chances of your client suffering a coronary, every little helps. Especially when you still have to tack on your own five per cent.

The woman facing Conway, cut off in mid-flow, glanced over her shoulder. She was power dressed in matching skirt and jacket, gunmetal grey with a light pinstripe. It looked like it cost an arm and a leg and she'd have looked just as good after the amputations. It took her a moment to recognise me. I slipped her the usual grubby smile.

'Excuse me for interrupting, Mrs Conway. But your husband and I have some urgent business to attend to.'

She smiled, icy.

'You're persistent, Mr Delaney, I'll grant you that. And what might you be selling today?'

I sat down in the other chair, a leather-and-tubular-steel affair that probably cost as much as all the furniture in my office put together. Started rolling a smoke. I looked at Conway and we made sheep's eyes at one another until the secretary burst through the door. Her face was livid, the skin stretched tight. If she'd been annoyed more often, maybe, she wouldn't have needed the nips and tucks that left her face looking like a map of the Burren.

'I'm sorry, Mr Conway,' she said, shooting me a venomous glance. Her cheeks were flushed beneath the layers of foundation, or maybe she'd taken time out to apply blusher before the big entrance. 'He just walked right by me.'

Conway held up a hand.

'That's okay, Martina.' If I was a surprise, I was a pleasant one. He sounded composed. There was no trace of the bluster he'd treated me to last time out. 'I believe I forgot to remind you that I had a prior appointment this morning.'

The secretary glared a couple of daggers and left.

'I don't mind if she stays,' I told Conway, nodding at the Ice Queen. 'But it's money talk.'

'Helen is privy to all my financial affairs.'

I sparked the smoke.

'This is dirty money, Frank. It's dirty because it's buried and it's buried because you can't tell anyone about it. I know about it already, but then I wouldn't recognise money if it didn't come all grimy and worn.'

The Ice Queen stood up.

'I wouldn't dream of eavesdropping, Mr Delaney.' It was an unnecessary kindness, if I ever came up with anything Helen Conway might want to hear I'd carve it in stone and shout it from the top of Mount Sinai.

'If you're interested, you can always listen to the tapes when your husband does.'

She chuckled, too deep in her throat for the humour to reach her eyes, and then she left too. Conway was sitting forward, elbows on the desk, fingers steepled and touching his lips.

'Thought you'd like a report, Frank,' I breezed. 'Everyone likes to get good news at Christmas.'

'You have good news?' Calm, collected.

'Yeah. Your wife is screwing the College football team, keeper included.'

He didn't take the bait.

'You can tell so soon? I'd have thought your investigations would be a little more rigorous than that.'

'Trust me, Frank. She's fucking with a few more people too, only now we're talking metaphors. And that includes you.'

Again he ignored the dig. I was impressed. I thought a slur on his wife's character would have been enough to get Big Frank out from behind the desk, seeing as how that'd be muscling in on Big Frank's turf. Instead he reached for the chequebook on the desk.

'That is good news.' He picked up a pen. 'What do I owe you?'

'That isn't the good news, Frank. At least, it might be good news but it's nothing you didn't know already. The good news is that you're getting a new partner.'

'Partner?'

'Not in the biblical sense. You're a good-looking cove but you're not my type. I want in.'

'In?'

'A cut, Frank. A percentage. A tidy little earner for doing sweet fuck all. And that includes not repaying the visit I had from the Dibble yesterday morning.'

He didn't flinch. Not a twitch. He really was good. I thought about what Brady told me. If Conway inspired respect in Brady, then his office was the last place I should have been sitting. Then again, Brady hadn't been shot at, or forced to put his family on the run. Not that he'd told me about anyway, Brady seemed shy that way. But I was guessing that any of those reasons would have put Brady where I was and it was unlikely Brady would have been my side of the desk.

'You want to get into the real estate business?' His tone was polite, but edgy, like he was playing to a crowd.

'The surreal-state business. Drugs, by any other name.'

'I'm a bit old for doing drugs.' He laughed, but it came up short, ending on a high note. He cleared his throat, reached for his Marlboros.

'You're never too old for a high, Frank. But I'm not talking about a few tokes. I'm talking about distribution, profit margins, the full nine yards. Word's out, Frank, you're the Candyman. I know it, the Dibble know it, and if they know it you can bet half of Christendom knows it.'

'That's libel, Rigby.'

'Slander, actually, and only if it's not true. Or is it the other way around?' I dropped him the shoulder. 'What's your favourite Bond movie, Frank?'

He bought the dummy.

'What?'

'Your favourite Bond movie, everyone has one. Mine is *Thunderball*. Connery's the main man, the only Bond. Moore's too camp and Brosnan's too posh. Anyway, there's a line in *Thunderball* where Bond reckons that once is coincidence, twice is happenstance, three times is enemy action. Know that line?'

He shook his head, licked his lips. I sat forward, grinned, waded in swinging.

'You came to me two days ago, Frank. Gave me some bullshit

about how your wife was screwing around. Which didn't scan, any time I said she was playing away you jumped like someone was into your strides with a cattle prod. Which meant you had some other reason for being there. I don't know, maybe you knew the Branch boys were keeping tabs and you were looking for a patsy.' I shrugged. 'All you had to do was ask, Frank. I don't mind being anyone's patsy, so long as they pay for the privilege.'

He didn't say anything.

'I played along, Frank. Did a little digging on the lovely Mrs Conway, not really expecting to find anything, because generally I wouldn't find water in a well, especially when the well is dry. So imagine my surprise when I discover that the lovely Mrs Conway is not only screwing someone but I manage to capture the Kodak moment.'

His lips were clamped shut but his jaws were moving.

'Choice stuff, Frank,' I needled. 'I've heard about some of those positions but I never believed them possible. Still, they say the camera never lies.'

Conway deserved a lot of things but the truth wasn't one of them. And if my instincts were right, my best bet was to push him all the way to the edge.

'Don't sweat it, there's usually something. A woman wouldn't be human if she didn't flirt a little, and your wife just happened to take it a step further.' I paused. 'Okay, so she took it about a triple jump further, but let's not split hairs. The point I'm making is, you didn't think she was screwing around at all. So that got me wondering. Why does Big Frank want me thinking his wife is screwing around? Then, yesterday morning, two Branch boys turned up in my office, asking about you. That's coincidence, Frank, in any man's book.'

He rubbed at his nose with the back of his hand.

'Dry your eyes, I didn't tell them anything. All my clients are assured of discretion, even the ones that are fucking me around. But it got me wondering, so I did a little more digging and fuck me if I didn't turn up a sweet little potato, Big Frank Conway is running party favours through Belfast. A word to the wise, Frank, and I won't charge you a penny for it. I didn't have to dig very deep. So, let's talk profit margins.'

His voice was scratched sandpaper.

'I don't know what you're talking about.'

'No? Then maybe I'm wasting my time talking to you.' I kissed the dice, let them roll. 'Do me a favour, Frank. Ring Tony Sheridan for me, I don't have his number handy. And if you don't have it, I'm sure the lovely Martina will be only too happy to oblige.'

Snake eyes. He slumped back in the chair, deflated.

'What do you want?'

'Two things. For starters I want two grand a month for keeping my trap shut. That wouldn't pay your dry cleaning bill, I know, but I'm not greedy.'

'What else?'

He was too quick, too compliant.

'Don't get smart on me now, Frank. I'll be surprised and I don't like surprises. You think I'm stupid? That I'd walk in here and start shooting my mouth off? Without taking out insurance against ending up like Gonzo?'

He'd done composed, he'd done panicked, now he was doing confused. He was wasted as an auctioneer. He should have been in Hollywood.

'Gonzo?'

'Gonzo. My brother, that enemy action I was talking about, the third coincidence. It's the other thing I want, to know why my brother was murdered last night.'

His mouth dropped open. Either he knew nothing about Gonzo or Stanislavski was officially old hat.

'Your brother was murdered?'

'Someone fed him dodgy E. His brains came out his nose in the end. When the picture's developed, I'll send you a copy. You can frame it.'

'Christ, Rigby.' He was hoarse by now. 'I didn't even know you *had* a brother.'

'He wasn't brother enough to say, but that's not the point. You mightn't have known him as my brother. Some people knew him as Gonzo. Other people knew him as Eddie. You knew him, about four years ago, as Robbie. Robbie Callaghan.'

He swallowed hard.

'Ding-ding, that rings a bell. Good old Robbie, Robbie the fall guy. Did his time without a squeak, kept your nose clean. He gets out and all of a sudden he's called Gonzo again. Or was he still calling himself Robbie? I only ask because I want to know what we should put on the headstone.'

'Robbie's dead?'

'Someone slipped him a Mickey Finn. I'm betting it was you, even though the Dibble are thinking the same.'

He gave me his best goldfish impression.

'Jesus, Rigby. I knew nothing about—'

It looked convincing, but then Big Frank was only a movie away from a nervous breakdown in the Dorothy Chandler pavilion. I stood up.

'Maybe you did and maybe you didn't and maybe you know

someone who did. If you do, tell them this. Whoever had him killed had a reason for doing it. Tell them I said the reason wasn't good enough. No matter what it was, it wasn't good enough. Which is why we're talking payback.'

He nodded, reached for the Marlboros.

'You smoke too much, Frank. Be carrying a brown envelope the next time you see me and make like I'm a TD.'

I strolled out through the foyer, slow, so my legs wouldn't give way. The secretary was still furious. She really needed to get out more, or maybe invest in a battery-powered appliance.

'You've lipstick on your teeth,' I said, and heard my second new swear word of the week.

19

I strolled up the street, settled into the window table of a café diagonally across from Conway's office. The place was clean, quiet, the tables covered with white-and-red checked plastic cloths. The smile the waitress flashed was also plastic but she didn't look anywhere near as fresh as the tablecloths. The coffee wasn't warm mud but it wanted to be.

The street was thronged but I'd have spotted Helen Conway with one eye tied behind my back. She emerged from the office with Frank in tow, disappeared around the corner. I left the waitress a tip – don't get married 'til you're thirty-five – and disappeared after them.

They crossed the street, turned another corner onto the old bridge, tripped up the steps of the Connaught Arms Hotel. I gave them a minute to get comfortable and then I tripped up the steps of the Connaught Arms Hotel too.

The foyer was warm and humid, sultry as Faulkner's socks. The gold lamé decoration tacked up over the reception desk bore the legend 'Happy Xmas'. Silver disco balls were suspended from the dusty light shades, each one boasting a sprig of mistletoe. Off to the right, an avocado three-piece suite that had seen better days in a far better place menaced a ring-marked coffee table.

The windows stretched from floor to ceiling, affording a dirt-streaked view of the river as it frothed over the weir beneath the bridge. In the distance, maybe a quarter mile away, I could see the new bridge. If I squinted I could make out the bench where I'd been sitting just before taking my header into the river, so I didn't squint. In front of the windows were long, shallow ashtrays filled with sand, cigarette butts and one or two plastic plants.

Off to the left, the doors of the hotel bar were wide open and the Christmas spirit was going down in doubles. I crossed the foyer to the reception desk, standing sideways on so I could watch the door of the bar. I tapped the bell on the desk, which was the receptionist's cue to ignore me completely. The collar of her gleaming white blouse was stiffly starched but pretty much everything else sagged. Her chins had chins and her make-up foundation was threatening to collapse under the weight of her expectations.

I coughed, polite. Still she leafed through the sheaf of papers on the desk. I coughed again, a more phlegmy effort. She pushed back the rimless spectacles that had slipped to the end of her nose and stared, imperious.

'Yes? Can I help you?'

'I'd ask for the manager, only a Hilton like this couldn't afford any other staff after meeting your demands.'

'I am the manageress.'

'Then start doing your job.'

She pushed the spectacles back again, only this time they hadn't slipped.

'Excuse me?'

'You're excused. I'd like to see a room, please.'

She looked me up and down, not liking what she saw. I didn't like what she was looking at. I hadn't shaved in two days, my clothes were still damp, and the last time I looked in the mirror a kitten had been using my face as a trampoline.

'I am sorry. We have no vacancies.'

'Last time this place was booked solid, the Black and Tans had burned out half the town. But that's not the point. I don't want a room, I want to see a room.'

She was fuming. Actually, she was a fuming ventriloquist. Her lips were clamped tight but the words clipped out, vocal chords on semi-automatic.

'I don't understand.'

'I want to know who's booked the room, the one I want to see. Show me the register.'

She made an involuntary movement towards the leather-bound register that lay open on the desk in front of her. Then she caught herself, smoothing out the wrinkles of her thought process.

'I will have to ask you to leave. If you refuse, I will call the Guards.'

'Call them. I haven't seen a cop in nearly two hours and I'm starting to get lonely.'

We stared. Her hand hovered over the telephone.

'Will you please leave?'

'No. Call the Dibble. I want to make a complaint.'

'A complaint?'

'Yeah. I'm concerned about the moral depravity of your hotel. I'm also outraged by the décor, but there's nothing the Dibble can do about that.'

'Moral depravity?'

'The words knocking and shop might ring a bell.'

'Knocking shop?'

'Knocking shop. Hammer house. Brothel. Bordello. Call it what you want, the tarts are in and out of here on roller skates. That's moral depravity. I'm offended. Blame the Christian Brothers.'

She might have been an old dragon but she was still a dragon. She nearly singed my eyebrows.

'How *dare* you?'

'Oh I dare, I dare.' I grinned. 'Look, there's nastier stuff going on in this dump than a few farmers getting their festive jollies and I don't begrudge the livestock their Christmas break. Letting me look at the register will go some way to making sure the nasty stuff doesn't happen here again. Okay?'

'What kind of—'

'Show me the register or ring the Dibble.'

She thought about it, maybe, while she was waddling away from the desk. I ran my finger down the day's entries, found nothing under the name of Frank Conway, which didn't mean a thing, even Frank Conway wasn't dumb enough to register in the Connaught Arms under his own name. There was only one entry for Christmas Eve though, and that had been booked in early.

I picked up the newspaper lying on the desk, retreated to the three-piece suite. I smoked and held the paper in front of my face, watching the front door, the double doors of the bar. The dragon came back, stood behind the desk and didn't look in my direction. I repaid the favour.

He arrived twenty minutes later, red-faced and puffing. He was wearing the same heavy tweed overcoat and flat checked cap, which he took off as he came through the door, smoothing down his wiry grey hair. Underneath the overcoat he wore a sky-blue V-necked pullover. He had a banana-yellow cravat tied loosely around his neck.

The dragon's face lit up when she recognised him but he just nodded, brusque, as he made for the bar. The dragon watched him go, crest-fallen. I sympathised. If you can't get a politician to say hello to you, then it's time to fold the tent. Tony Sheridan obviously had more on his mind than votes. I gave him a minute or two to get settled before I followed.

They were in the far corner of the bar, in wicker armchairs around a low table beside the artificial Christmas tree. Sheridan was holding forth, jabbing a stubby finger at Frank Conway. Frank was sitting forward, head bent towards Sheridan, nodding. Helen Conway was sitting upright with her back to the wall. She watched me the whole way across the bar without alerting the other two, treating me to a sardonic smile that was almost worth all the grief.

'The resourceful Mr Delaney,' she said. Sheridan turned, stared like a gutted fish. Frank Conway's eyes blazed. The Ice Queen's just twinkled merrily, as was their wont. 'Or should I call you Mr Rigby?'

'Call me whatever you want, Mrs Conway, but do call.'

'Ah yes, ever the gentleman. First you're an insurance sales-man, then you're a private detective. Now you're a gentleman extortionist. You're a man of many talents, Mr Rigby.'

'Tell it to my agent. No brown envelope, Frank?'

Conway's expression didn't change. Tony Sheridan picked a mobile phone off the table, dialled a number.

'Put the phone away, Tone.'

He ignored me. I leaned forward, plucked the phone from his hand and dunked it in the G&T at his elbow. It fizzed slightly, and then nothing happened at all. He looked at the glass, then at me, and if one were more important than the other you'd have needed callipers to measure it. He got to his feet, looked at the Conways, blank as a sleepwalker.

'If you'll just excuse me . . .'

'If you're going to the bar, get me a coffee. If you're not, sit the fuck down.'

He stayed standing, bushy eyebrows twitching. His jowls also twitched. I had the feeling that, if I squeezed them hard enough, a double G&T would leak out, ice and slice too. He said, cold, to Frank Conway: 'Who the hell is he?'

'Two fucking guesses, Tone. Now sit the fuck down.'

He wasn't used to people talking to him like that; the concept seemed to intrigue him. An acrid smile tugged at the corner of his mouth and he sat down. I pulled up a wicker armchair, smiled around at them all.

'Pray continue, Tone,' I said. 'Whatever you were saying before I arrived, it looked like fascinating stuff.'

'I'm more interested in hearing what you have to say.'

'Fine. I could pretty much guess the gist of yours anyway. Probably how best to give the boys in baseball caps their P-45s. Shoddy job last night – eh, Tone? Not that I'm complaining, mind. But it's just as well they missed, for all our sakes. You especially.'

His expression didn't change. He rubbed the back of his fingers against the faint stubble on his jaw.

'If you want me to spell it out let's go back to ABC.' I nodded at Conway. 'Fuckwit yonder is known to the Dibble, from years back, for dealing E. They haven't been able to keep tabs on him lately, and things got so quiet they were starting to think he might even have gone legit. That, as we all know, is horseshit.'

I checked Conway out, to see how he was bearing up. He was looking peaky.

'We've been through all of this earlier, Frank and me, and Frank has kindly agreed to pay me to keep my trap shut about it. Not that it'll ever cost him a penny, I wouldn't touch his money with a leper's dick, but that's the only language Frank understands. It was enough to get him on the blower to you, though, and that was enough to get you flushed out the U-bend.'

Sheridan's eyes glittered.

'See,' I said, 'something bugged me about Big Frank, when he came to see me about his wife playing away.'

Helen Conway looked sideways at her husband, amused.

'Like I told him, it didn't ring true. So when I found out she takes lakeside strolls with prominent TDs, I was pleasantly surprised. The photographs turned out lovely, by the way. I'll get you a copy of the prints when they're ready to go. Your lackeys called around too early this morning.'

Conway swung around, stared at his wife, eyes wide. She gave him a withering glance, came back to me.

'Anyway, I was even more surprised when the Dibble told me that Frank was involved with my brother a couple of years back, that my brother did time for Frank. That made sense.

That gave Frank Conway a reason for coming to see me. But it meant the Ice Queen and the TD stuck out like an arthritic thumb.'

'I'm presuming there's a point to all this.'

'Don't take the piss, Tone. The fact that you're here, and that you got here so quick, tells me two things. One, you're in this up to your oxters. Two, it's about to go off quick smart. And right now the Dibble are waiting to nab Big Frank in the act, bringing his pills in from Belfast. Happy days, maybe Gonzo's life will have been worth something after all, because it'll give the Dibble what they need to put Conway away.'

Conway's knuckles were white where they gripped the arms of the wicker armchair. It was all he could do to prevent himself from lunging across the low table. Sheridan stayed cool.

'Why are you telling me this?'

'Because Frank got me digging and what I dug up links you to his wife. Which hooks you to Frank, whose former drug courier is now dead from an overdose. None of which would make it through the door of any court in the country, but it's the kind of thing the redtops eat without salt, especially with photos to back it up. You know this already, which is why your stooges took a pop last night.'

He stared me down.

'You don't want money,' he said, deadpan. 'What do you want?'

'Nothing, Tone. Not a fucking thing. No hassle, no grief and no fuckers taking pot shots at me when I'm wandering home late at night. In return, the photos get a Christian burial and I forget where they're buried. Although I carve a tombstone, just to be on the safe side. Your tombstone.'

He mulled it over.

'It all sounds very tidy. What guarantee do I have that you won't renege?'

'I presume you won't take my word, and I'm not taking it personal, you're a politician. Your guarantee is my being alive. So long as I'm breathing you're in the clear, and I smoke sixty a day so you better start praying they find a cure for cancer.'

'I'll need some time to think about it, naturally.' He didn't even look at Conway. 'What about him?'

'He'll take his chances with the law, and the way the legal system is these days I give him a fifty-fifty chance. Besides, it'll be tough pinning Gonzo on him without me on the stand. Anyway, it sounds to me like it's time he repaid his debt to society. And I'm sure the lovely Helen will wait for him.'

She chuckled. I stood up, looked down at Tony Sheridan.

'Don't take too long thinking it over. I might grow a conscience, it's the right weather for it. And I hear the witness protection programme gets you a travel-pass on Bus Eireann.'

I turned to go, remembered something. Sheridan looked up, expectant. I balled my fist and popped him one, just under the ear, behind the chin. He pulled the wicker armchair with him going down, scattering drinks across the low table. I knelt beside him. He was too stunned to focus, not used to people punching him out, although that prospect didn't seem to intrigue him in the slightest.

'That's for the hammering the other night, I'm presuming it was you sent the pros around. If not, you deserve it for wearing a cravat.'

The barman, thin and nervy, came at me as I turned. I feinted a dig. He jumped back and I edged by him, jabbing a forefinger at his face, for show.

'I've thrown better than you out the way to get at a fight,' he sneered.

I didn't argue with him. He was probably right.

20

I tooled around town in second gear, one eye on the rear-view mirror. When I was sure I wasn't being followed I took the bypass out of town, heading north.

I dug the mobile out, checked the signal. It was still strong, Gonzo must have powered it to the hilt when he'd last charged it up. I rang Denise.

'Harry.' Her sigh of relief blew ash off my cigarette. Then, in case I might interpret it as a sign of weakness: 'Where the fuck *are* you? I've been ringing all fucking morning!'

'I should be there in an hour, tops. How's Ben?'

'He's okay. He thinks we're planning a surprise for granny and granddad.'

'Good thinking.' Denise was a smart girl, a lot smarter than I felt right about then. The thought occurred, and not for the first time, that maybe her name should be on the frosted glass and I should be the one who spent his day switching the TV channel away from Cartoon Network. 'Okay, I'll see you about twelvish.'

'Is Gonzo with you?'

'He's not, no.'

'Where is he?'

'I'll tell you everything later when I get there.'

'I'm scared, Harry.'

'Just trust me, Dee. This once, okay?'

I hung up, checked the rear-view. Caught the briefest glimpse of a blue Mondeo, maybe quarter of a mile back, a battered farmer's Range Rover and a metallic-blue Mitsubishi Galant between us. It didn't look to be in any hurry, cruising along at the same steady sixty I was motoring at. It was too far back to make out the registration, so I couldn't be sure if it was Brady or Galway, or both, but the hang-glider bloke swooped low out of the jumble of grey clouds, cocking a sardonic eyebrow. I drove on, keeping one eye on the rear-view.

Dutchie wasn't at home, or he wasn't answering the phone, so I powered down the mobile to save the battery. Turned up the stereo, sifted through the events of the last twenty-four hours, noodling the jigsaw pieces around, trying to make them fit. I was frazzled, though, too tired to concentrate, couldn't find the straight-edged pieces that framed the puzzle. And no matter how I forced the pieces together, they always segued into the same grainy black-and-white images – one of the pros sneaking up on the back door, safety catch off, Ben jumping out from the door of the shed, shouting 'Boo!' Sometimes he even got the word out, but the tape always wound off the reel on the same finale – Ben's body jerking, ripped apart by a burst from the pro's sub-machine gun. Something crawled into my stomach and curdled. I put the boot down.

Dutchie's stereo was tuned to a tired Classic Hits FM station, the presenter an All-American constipated duck. I flipped through the channels, hit something that sounded like it might have a real news bulletin. The news came and went, the lead story now the tragic tale of the multiple pile-up in Cork, the pathos intensifying as Christmas Day got closer. Then some poor bastard from Portadown, who'd had his knees blown out in the early hours of the morning. Then the foiled bank robbery in Ardee, which hadn't been foiled at all, meaning the raiders had got away with nearly quarter of a million. The tax amnesty scandal didn't even make the charts.

The weather forecast was for heavy snow, high winds. The winds hadn't kicked in yet but the snow was already coming down, thick and fast. I switched the radio off, slipped a tape into the stereo and decided that it was apt that Gonzo's overdose hadn't made the airwaves. He had contributed nothing to society in his time, so there was no reason society should mark his passing. I wondered whether that might have bothered Gonzo, acknowledged that I didn't know him well enough to tell.

The next question was whether or not I cared. I took the Fifth and checked the rear-view. The Mondeo was still there, still about a quarter mile back. I pushed the needle up past seventy. The Mondeo picked up speed. I dropped down again, took my eye off the rear-view.

There were drifts in the high mountain pass, starting to freeze over, but even so I made it just after one. Went all the way around the second roundabout and turned off into the shopping centre car park, watching for the Mondeo. It didn't show. I hauled Ben's bike out of the boot, carried it into the shopping centre. The air inside was humid, heat rising off the damp coats of the shoppers.

I bought an extra-large zip-up fleece with deep pockets, a Red

Sox baseball cap, putting them on in the public toilets. The fleece was a tight fit but I could just about swing my arms, which would come in handy if the trapeze artists ever went out on strike.

I went from the toilet to the hardware shop, then out back of the shopping centre, where I locked Ben's bike to a disused skip. I dialled one of the numbers pasted to the public phone, arranged for a taxi to pick me up at the bus station, across the car park from the Bravo. When the taxi pulled up I tugged the baseball cap low over my face and loped across the car park. I was in the back of the taxi when the driver emerged from the bus station's waiting room. He manoeuvred his huge bulk into the driver's seat and looked at me expectantly in the rear-view mirror. He had a wide face, apple-red cheeks and a flat beret of snow-white hair that had been cut with a secateurs.

'Harrison?'

'That's me.'

'Where to?'

That stumped me. We had always driven to the holiday home and I didn't know the actual address.

'Go to the bottom of the main street and turn right. Go right again up the hill. After that, I'll keep you posted.'

He dropped me about five hundred yards past the house. When he turned the car I strolled up the lane and started rolling a smoke, taking my time. Twenty minutes later I flipped the butt into the ditch. Not a single car had passed in either direction. I walked back down the hill to the house, turned into the gravelled driveway.

It was as safe a hideaway as any. I'd been turning my car up that driveway for nearly five years now and the curtains across the road still twitched. The house was set well back from the road, obscured by a row of Sycamores that ran the length of the low redbrick wall marking the boundary of the huge garden. I walked around the back, noting the tiny boot-prints in the snow. I jumped when Ben gave me his fright, threw some snowballs and let him shove snow inside my collar. When I finally shook him off I took Denise into the kitchen. She poured coffee, cocked an eye at my swollen face and waited for me to start. I let the warm kitchen soak away the tension, sensing the numbness beginning to thaw.

'Well?' Her face was pale, and she hung from her shoulders like a sail after a storm. 'What's going on?'

I swallowed half the coffee, took a deep breath.

'Gonzo's dead.'

It came easier every time I said it and I guess I could've said it easier because her face just folded. She shook her head, horrified. I nodded, grim.

'Last night. On the way home.'

'What . . . what happened? Jesus, Harry!'

'Ssshhhh. Ben's in the living room.' I got up, closed the kitchen door, went back to the table. 'We went to a club. Gonz wanted a few late ones.'

'You were drunk?'

'No more than usual, couple of pints, seven or eight. Gonz was popping E all night, though. We left and went on for a kebab.'

'There was a fight?'

'There was no fight.' I knew Dee was going to blame me, I just wanted to be blamed for the right reasons. 'We were ready to leave when Dutchie found Gonzo in the toilets, having some kind of fit. We found some dodgy E in his pockets – Flatliners, the Dibble called them – before they whisked him off to the hospital.'

'You didn't go with him?'

'Dutchie went. I was taken to the station.'

'The station?'

'The cop shop. They wanted to book me for possession with intent. I was still in the cop shop when Dutchie rang. They were pumping Gonzo out when he went into arrest.' I grinned her one I didn't feel. 'Me in the cop shop and him in arrest. Funny, isn't it?'

She laughed, a nervous giggle pitched one octave below hysteria. Her wet eyes sparkled. I gave her the second barrel.

'Then the Dibble let me go and someone shot me.'

'What?'

Her eyes bugged out like a frog on a promise.

'I was on the bridge. He hit me in the side, knocked me into the river. When I got back out I rang you. The rest you know now.'

'You're having me on. Gonzo's outside, isn't he? Having a laugh. You're a sick fucker, Harry.'

First anger, then denial – she was ploughing through the classic symptoms at a rate of knots. I pulled the fleece over my head, unbuttoned the Puffa, hauled my sweater and shirt off. The blood on the edge of the bandage was dry and crusty but there was still a dark pool of thin raspberry jelly at its centre.

She stared at me for a long time, forehead furrowed, searching my face for the tic or tremor that might suggest I was playing a bizarre joke. I shrugged.

'I'm sorry, Dee. That's the way it happened.'

Her shoulders shook, then the sobs ballooned their way to the surface and she bawled like a stubborn calf. I went around the table, put my arm around her shoulders but she shrank away, folding her arms, cradling herself. Then the shock hit, a runaway train. She put her arms on the table and cried into them until the nervous energy finally evaporated. She sat up, her face the colour of raw liver, snuffling and tugging at her sleeve for a non-existent paper tissue. I gave her a sheet of kitchen towel and she buried her face in it. Finally, nose blocked and voice muffled, she asked: 'Why?'

'That's what I don't know.'

'Well . . . who?'

'That's what I don't know as well.'

'Do you know anything?'

'I know we have to keep a cool head and dry trousers until we figure out what's going on.' I handed her a dry sheet of kitchen towel. 'No sense in us bitching at one another. We have to think of Ben.'

She took a deep breath, let it out slow, dabbed at her eyes.

'Okay, okay. Christ.' She thought for a second. 'What do the Guards say?'

'They're following a couple of leads.' I softened my tone. 'Hey, Dee?'

I reached out, took her hand. It was shaking. She didn't pull back, but she didn't respond when I squeezed it either.

'It's going to be okay,' I said. 'All we have to do is sit tight. We don't go out, we don't answer the phone. We don't even open the curtains.'

'Jesus, Harry.' She sounded helpless, the kind of lost they don't have maps for. 'Gonzo's dead.'

'We can deal with that later, Dee. Nothing we can do about it now.'

Her lip curled.

'You're a cold bastard, Harry,' she said. 'A cold and crippled bastard. You know that?'

'I do now. Can you hear Ben?'

Her eyes widened.

'Ben! Jesus!'

She went to look for Ben. I scouted out the cupboards for something edible. I settled for some soup, a sandwich and a glass of Maalox, turning the mobile on when I'd finished. It was almost three-thirty.

The phone rang before I had a chance to dial Dutchie's number, letting me know I had a message waiting. There were two. The first was from Dutchie, telling me Conway was dead. I thought about Conway for about three seconds, his cold, black piggy eyes. Then the second message arrived. It was from Katie.

'Harry—'

A northern voice, deadpan, cut in.

'The Odeon, ten bells. Play it straight and everyone walks away.'

I heard a gentle click, the sound of a giant jigsaw piece slotting neatly into place. I looked at the picture and wanted to cry, then wasted half-an-hour trying to think of people I could trust, coming up with a one-name list, but then I have high standards. I made the call and filled in the details, devised a plan. I turned the mobile off, not feeling entirely confident.

Denise came back in, red-eyed. I rolled a smoke, braced myself. Told her I was heading back to town.

'You're what?' She was angry, bewildered and scared. I could empathise. 'You said we were going to sit tight. Don't even open the curtains, you said.'

'I said you were going to sit tight,' I lied. 'I have to go back to town.'

'Why, for Christ's sake?'

'That doesn't matter.'

'Doesn't matter?' She was distraught, working herself into a frenzy. I couldn't blame her. I was pretty strung out at the prospect myself. 'Someone tried to kill you last night and the reason you're going back doesn't matter? What are you, suicidal?'

'I need to get us sorted. To get us somewhere safer than this.'

It was a bargain-basement answer and Denise wasn't buying.

'What can you do back there that you can't do from here?' She thought for a second, and her face took on a stricken expression. 'And why do we need somewhere safer? What's wrong with here?'

And suddenly I was tired again, my nervous system steeling itself for the onslaught of adrenaline.

'You wouldn't understand, Dee.'

'I wouldn't understand?'

There was menace in her voice, the implication impossible to ignore, but Katie had something I needed, something Denise couldn't give me, and you only start that kind of conversation with a woman once. You don't get to finish it, either.

'What number were you ringing this morning?' I asked.

'What?'

'The mobile number, Dee. What number did you ring?'

She told me, sullen.

'It's oh-eight-four,' I said. 'Not oh-eight-three.'

'You told me oh-eight-three.'

'Yeah well, now I'm telling you it's oh-eight-four.'

I pulled on the Puffa and the fleece. Stood there, hands in pockets, sweating in the warm kitchen. The smell of soup made me want to puke. My fingers touched something cold. I put the key of the bicycle lock on the kitchen table.

'Ben's bike is locked to a skip behind the shopping centre. Give it a while, send a taxi down to collect it.'

'Fuck Ben's bike!'

I made for the door.

'If you go,' she warned, 'I won't be here when you get back.'

'If I get back.'

I stopped at the door. She was leaning against the table, arms folded, defiant, struggling to hold back the tears. That made two of us, except I had nothing to lean on.

21

The snow was coming down hard. Visibility was almost zero, the wipers barely able to cope, and the road was glassy under two or three inches of soft snow. It was impossible to drive faster than twenty miles an hour without running the very real risk of saving the pros a bullet or two. I pushed the needle up to forty and prayed that Dutchie hadn't skimped on the radials.

I made town just after eight. The storm was blowing itself out, the streets deserted, all sound muffled under the coloured lights. Everyone was at home, wrapping presents and knocking back the mulled wine, or in the pub, hoping they wouldn't be chucked out early and already too pissed to know what time it was.

I pulled into the car park, crossed the river by the footbridge, slipped in the side door of The Cellars. The place was heaving, the punters three deep at the bar, a bloke with a fiddle giving it large just inside the front door. Dutchie was red-faced behind the ramp, taking three and four orders at a time. I shouted his name. He ignored me twice, but when he finally looked around his jaw dropped. He forced his way through the punters knotted around the hatch, leaving Marie to deal with the mob. He dragged me down to the poolroom, locked the door, gave me both barrels.

'You thick bastard! Are you looking to get killed? Get us all killed with you?'

'Easy, Dutch. I'm being cute, remember?'

'This is cute? You don't know who you're fucking with.'

'I'm not fucking with anyone, Dutch. Everyone's fucking with me.'

'The East Belfast boys want to fuck you, you bend over for the soap and wash their dicks with it when they're finished. Alright?'

'East Belfast?'

'Your party favour buddies. The ones Conway was trying to screw.'

'They issue a press release or something?'

He stared.

'Jesus, Harry, this is serious. I don't think you realise what you're into here.'

'Hey, Dutch? It was me they tried to blow off the bridge last night. Alright?'

'Alright, alright.' He puffed out his cheeks, exhaled, chewed his gum. 'These boys are hardcore, though.'

'It was them? For certs?'

He nodded.

'I heard different, Dutch. So just cut to the chase. Tell me who.'

'Who what?'

'Who bought you who.'

He stopped chewing.

'What?'

'Come on, Dutch. You sold me out. You know it, I know it,

Herbie knows it. Or he will, when he's able to hear again. I found him this morning, fucked over like you wouldn't believe. They mashed his face in, Dutch.'

'Who mashed his face in?'

'Santa's little helpers. Who do you think mashed his fucking face in?'

'Jesus, Harry—'

'Whoever put the hammer on me mashed his face in. Whoever tried to blow me off the bridge. Whoever bought you. That's who mashed his face in.'

'Fuck you.'

'Join the queue, Dutch. And you're last, because you've already blown your load.'

His face was a mask, hard set. I sympathised. He was mad at me for accusing him of selling me out, mad at himself for doing it, and mad at the world because he'd had no choice.

'It's simple, Dutch. The pros thought Herbie had compromising pictures of Tony Sheridan, and Herbie got hammered because they thought he was holding out. What I couldn't figure out was how they found out Herbie developed the pictures, and how they knew where to find him.' I shrugged. 'The answer to the first question is that I pretty much told them who developed the pictures. It was a stupid thing to do, but that's the kind of thing I do best and I'll deal with that later. But it shouldn't have mattered anyway, because even if they knew Herbie developed the shots they shouldn't have known who he was or where to find him. That's where you came in, Dutch. You put them on to Herbie. You had to. Nobody else could have.'

He denied it with his eyes, pleading.

'You called me on the mobile, Dutch. I gave you the wrong

number, like I gave it wrong to Dee and Katie, but you still called me. Who gave you the number?'

His face crumpled and his hands started to shake.

'Harry—'

I looked away.

'All I need to know is who, the who will do it. Don't tell me why, because I'm pretty sure it'll be a good enough reason and good enough is never good enough. Just tell me who.'

He took a deep breath that wobbled on the way down.

'He called himself Carroll.'

'What'd he look like?'

'Small guy, thin, well-dressed. Looked like a—'

'Galway. He's a detective, Branch. Was Brady with him?'

'Who's Brady?'

'His sidekick. Big bloke, look on his face like he wants to kick a hole in the side of his head.'

'Never seen him.'

I nodded.

'When?'

'Couple of days back. Said he'd—'

'I don't need to know, Dutch. I presume he threatened the kids, Michelle, whatever. Anyway, it's done. It's history, write it up whatever way you want. You did what you had to do. All I need to know now is if you're onside.'

'Harry—'

'I need to trust someone, Dutch, and I don't have time to make new friends. All things considered, you're still the best option I have.'

The dig hurt but he took it square on the chin.

'Anything. Just say the word.'

I told him about my visit to Conway, leaving out nothing, not even the lipstick on the secretary's teeth.

'You tapped him for two grand? Thinking he'd just had Gonz killed?' He whistled. 'You've got balls, Harry. You think with them maybe, but you've got balls.'

'I didn't tap him for anything. All I was looking for was some kind of reaction, something that linked Conway to the pros. I didn't get any. Conway's good but he's not that good. Conway had nothing to do with last night. That was Sheridan's call.'

'Sheridan?'

'Our esteemed TD. I put the spook up Big Frank and Sheridan came crawling out of the woodwork.'

'So maybe Sheridan is using the East Belfast boys.'

Dutchie didn't want to let the East Belfast boys go.

'No one uses the East Belfast boys, Dutch. Those lads aren't taking orders from anyone, least of all some Free State fucker.'

'Might do, if the money was good enough.'

'Maybe. Not that it matters either way. Thing that's bugging me is, where does Conway come into it if Sheridan already has his hook-up?'

'Maybe he was threatening to rat Sheridan out to the big boys, start a war.' He shrugged. 'You got the message? About Conway?'

'Yeah. How'd he go?'

'Not sure. Everyone's keeping their heads down, saying fuck all. It's getting out that it's a drug thing. Everyone's hiding bongs, flushing stashes.'

'Last time I saw Conway was about eleven. He was with Tony Sheridan.'

'You're saying Sheridan had Conway offed?'

'Who knows? A desperate man does desperate things.

Because whatever's going on, it's going on fast. Maybe Conway fucked up once too often.'

He didn't buy it.

'Jesus, Harry. It's a bit much.'

'Tell it to Big Frank. The way I see it, it makes perfect sense. Gonzo first, then me, then Conway.'

'How's that?'

'Gonz did time for Conway a couple of years back. That's why he was back in town, putting the squeeze on. Conway came to me, trying to work out if I was hooked up with Gonzo. Next thing Sheridan knows, I'm running around with pictures that prove he's connected to Conway. What does he do? Step one, take Gonzo out of the picture by feeding him Flatliners. Two, me, because I have the shots. Three, Conway gets his for being the prick that could've brought the house of cards down.'

'So where's Helen Conway come into it all?'

'Fuck knows. Maybe she *is* screwing Tony Sheridan. Or maybe she's running the whole show, I doubt if Helen Conway ever took a back seat to anyone in her life. Right now I'm more worried about Katie.'

He frowned.

'The journo?'

'Have to go, Dutch. Do me a favour?'

'What *about* Katie?'

'Check the street outside. See if the Dibble are still out there, watching the office.'

I was pretty sure Brady wouldn't be there. I was pretty sure Galway wouldn't be there either, but I didn't want to take any more chances than I had to. I told him about the call from Katie.

'If the Dibble are out in the street watching the office, they can't be with the pros. Basic physics, that.'

'Christ, Harry, tell me you're taking the piss. Who the fuck is Katie, some bimbo fucking journalist?'

'Right now, Dutch, she's a hostage. If it wasn't for me she'd still be a bimbo fucking journalist.'

'You're walking into an ambush, just like that? Lamb to the fucking slaughter for some bird you hardly know?'

'It's not much of an ambush. They told me where they'd be.'

He grabbed me by the shoulders, shook me hard. I let him. I needed loosening up after the long drive.

'It's a set-up, Harry! Fuck's sake, man!'

'We went through it this morning. Sheridan had a decision to make and he wants to let me know what it is. Then everyone walks away, like the man said.'

'The reason they tried to take you out last night is the reason they'll do it tonight. They think you're in with Gonz, which makes you poison.'

'Give me some credit, Dutch. It's not heat of the moment any-more. These boys are sharp. They think I want to see them taken down and all things being equal I would. The way things are, though, I couldn't give a flying fuck about them. All I give a shit about is Ben.'

'Ben?'

'I keep my trap shut about Sheridan and Helen Conway. Never saw a fucking thing, I was tucked up safe and warm in bed with Dee for the last week. Dee will back me up, no one can say differ-ent. The photos get buried. That way, nothing happens Ben and I'm happy as a pig in the proverbial.'

'You're betting on Ben?'

'I'm not betting on anyone, least of all Ben. I'm just letting them know what my priorities are.'

'What about Gonzo?'

'Fuck Gonzo.'

'Jesus, Harry. He's your brother and these boys put him to sleep. Doesn't that count for anything?'

'On its own it might count for something. Put Ben in the picture and it counts for fuck-all.'

He had a problem swallowing it but he got it down in the end.

'Alright,' he said. 'That's Plan A. What if they don't bite?'

'I'll burn that bridge when I come to it.'

'That's it?' He was incredulous.

'Pretty much.'

'Fuck. Fuckfuckfuckfuckfuck.'

'Dutch? The Dibble?'

'You're doing it?'

'It's doing me, Dutch. I'm just along for the ride.'

He left, slow and heavy. He was gone about ten minutes, and as far as he could make out no one was watching the office from the street.

He wouldn't meet my eye. I couldn't blame him. My being there was already asking too much, and he reckoned I was going to ask for more. I stood up, faked a yawn.

'Once more unto the breach, Horatio. I'm running late.'

'Yeah, yeah. Right.'

He let me out the side door, followed me into the alleyway.

'Be cute, Harry.'

'There's a first time for everything. Hey, Dutch?'

'What?'

'Did Gonzo say anything, before he died?'

'About what?'

'About anything. I don't know.'

He looked away, shook his head, no.

'He didn't get the chance, Harry.' He was choking up again. 'I told you, he never came out of the coma.'

We looked at one another for a second or two, awkward in the darkness, and then I walked away down the alleyway towards the river. Feeling lonelier, more vulnerable, than I'd ever felt in my entire life.

'Hey, Harry?'

'What?'

I didn't look back. Dutchie had sold me out and he wasn't reneging on the deal. Something perverse in me admired that, but still.

'You want me to go with you, I'll go.'

'That's why I didn't ask, Dutch.'

22

I was a tumbleweed crossing the street. Locked the door, stood in the stairwell, listening. The building was quiet, a mausoleum. I hoped that wasn't an omen, started breathing again.

I climbed the three flights of stairs. Bright yellow tape was tacked in an X across the doorway of the office. It jazzed the place up, although I'd preferred the doorway when it still had a door. I tore the tape down, balled it up and volleyed it out over the banister, wincing at the sudden dart of pain in my side. Then I stepped across what was left of the door.

Elephants had been through, tap-dancing. The filing cabinet lay on its side, contents scattered across the floor. The desk and chairs were smashed, splintered. The desk drawers had been rifled. The carpet had been ripped up, and some wallpaper had been torn off the wall. Looking for a safe. Or wanting me, or the Dibble, to think they'd been looking for a safe.

Still, it could have been worse. I might have been insured, in which case I'd be looking forward to the drip-drip torture of my claim being denied.

I found a sheet of paper, scribbled a couple of lines that didn't take any longer than a good lie took to tell. I had an insurance policy on the mortgage, which looked after Denise. What cash there was I left to Ben, to be put into a trust fund for his education. Or to be released to him when he was twenty-one, if he turned out like his father, who was genetically conditioned against learning. I knew it wasn't legally binding as a last will and testament, but I was damn sure there wouldn't be anyone contesting it either.

When I was finished I folded the sheet, slipped it into an envelope and scrawled 'Denise Gorman' on the front. I pinned the envelope to the doorframe and took one last look around. All things considered, I approved.

*

I ghosted back across the street, ducked into the alleyway. The snow had finally stopped falling, the frosty air causing the snow to harden, crunch underfoot. It was nearly as cold as the marble slab in my chest, the one someone was chiselling my name into, or maybe that was just my heart thumping. The ache in my side was a blunt knife grinding on stone. My stomach was churning eggs, and the ulcer was emitting the kind of high-pitched scream only musically inclined dogs can hear.

I dug the Maalox out of my pocket, poured the contents down a drain, threw the empty bottle into the river. I was going to need all the pain I could get, just to keep me sane. The bottle bobbed away towards the bend and the bridge, heading for the open sea.

I bade it bon voyage and told it to watch out for icebergs.

I was sweating despite the cold. The first thing I did when I lurched into the car was turn the heating up full blast. The second thing I did was freeze rigid, because that's pretty much protocol when someone grinds something cold and hard, something that feels suspiciously like the barrel of a gun, into the soft flesh just below your left ear.

'I'm halfway to shooting you already. Sit still.'

I sat still, unloading the words like they were cut glass.

'Where's the pederast?'

Wondering how he had managed to squeeze himself into the back seat without the help of a blowtorch. There isn't much room in the back seat of a Fiat Bravo and Brady needed more room than most.

'Where's what?'

'Your bum chum. Galway, the fag.'

'You tell me.' The gun ground into my neck. 'Start with Conway. Stutter once and I'll blow your head off.'

I took a gamble on how much Brady knew, started with Conway.

'Conway came to me about his wife. He reckoned she was screwing around. I got the impression he was after something else but I did what I was paid to do.'

'Nice job.'

'Pays the bills. I don't get to stick guns in strangers' ears but then you can't have everything.'

'Stick to the facts.'

'Shut the fuck up and give me a chance.'

There was a long silence, the kind that doesn't like itself. He said: 'Go on.'

'Next thing, I'm getting a hammering from some blokes who like their job. They tell me to stay away from her, they don't say who but I presume they mean Helen Conway. Next morning, you and the fag turn up. By now I know Conway's trafficking E so I presume that's what you're after. Any idea of who had him offed, by the way?'

'I'll ask the questions.'

'Say again? I get deaf when someone sticks a gun in my ear.'

There was a moment, a very tense moment, when I thought I'd pushed it too far. Then something detonated beside my ear, a safety-catch being clicked on, and he took the gun away. I rubbed at my neck. There was a circular indentation maybe a quarter of an inch deep just below my ear.

'Go on.'

'So I find out Helen Conway might be doing the dirt. Photos to prove it, too. I reckon it's a job well done in quick-smart time and that Frank Conway's in for a nasty shock that can wait until after Christmas. I'm sentimental that way. Mind if I smoke?'

'Don't try anything funny.'

I left the balloon animals in the glove compartment, rolled a twist. Sparked the smoke, watched two middle-aged men, both wearing Santa Claus hats, stagger across the footbridge, holding one another up. The man on the left detached himself, stopped and steadied, unzipped.

'I went for a few pints. It's Christmas, the job's Oxo, and my brother's home for the holidays. That's Gonzo, by the way. And Eddie. Robbie too, apparently.'

'I can cross the T's myself.'

'Gonzo ODs. On the way home a car pulls up, and some bloke

with a cannon puts me in the river. I'm presuming you know that better than I do.'

'You think it was me?'

'Come on, Brady. You and the fag come around giving me grief about Conway. Then you haul me into the station because you think I'm hooked up with Conway, because Gonzo is. Next thing I know, someone's trying to blow me away and the only fuckers using those things are the Provies and Branch. And the Provies haven't been in touch lately.'

Brady laughed, although he didn't much like the taste of it.

'For one, Rigby, Provies and Branch aren't the only ones with popguns, every half-wit with an ounce of dope has an Uzi tucked under his oxter. For two, I wasn't there. If I had been, you'd be panned out beside your brother. What next?'

'This morning I run around to my mate, Herbie. He's the bloke developed the shots of Helen Conway carrying on, and if I'd left it another hour he'd be on the slab with Gonzo. So I go to see Conway. You were looking for him and you did the shooting. I put two and two together.'

'And came up with three. Nice work, Shamus.'

I let it slide, seeing as how he was one hundred per cent right.

'So Conway gets excited and bolts from cover. Next thing I know he's chumming down with the bloke that's screwing his wife. She's there too. I figure there's more to it than wife swapping, but I don't think too well on my feet. So I tell them to leave me alone. If they don't, the negatives wind up on the front desk of every redtop in the country. Then I walk away. I haven't seen Galway since last night, and that's one of the very few things I'm happy about at this moment in time.'

I stubbed the cigarette, left out the phone-call from the pros and started to roll another twist. Brady mulled things over.

'You're lying.'

'You have a gun, Brady. You're mad as a rat. What would you do in my position?'

'I wouldn't roll over for the first fucker who put the rush on.'

'Don't flatter yourself. Conway gave up his right to confidentiality when he tried to stitch me up.'

Brady remembered something.

'You think Conway was looking for something other than proof his wife was having it away. What was he looking for?'

'I don't know. He was doing pretty well around town, developments coming up like mushrooms. Maybe he was looking to go legit, to get away from the pills, and that he was greedy.'

'Aren't we all?'

'No. Anyway, when I found out who Conway's wife was screwing, I reckoned Conway was trying to squeeze him on a re-zoning scam. The building trade will never do so well that the land can't come cheaper.'

'You said Conway didn't think she was playing away.'

'He didn't. When I asked him who was lifting her skirt he said he didn't know, which is bullshit. People think the worst even when they've no reason to think it, and the worst usually has a monogram on its pee-jays. So I reckoned Conway was setting me up with the basics, just to get me warmed up, and then he was going to come back with a name. The name would be the politico he wanted to squeeze. I'd start digging and if I turned up anything tasty Conway would use it to put the bounce on.'

'That's a bit of a long shot.'

'Maybe, but he was right. I turned up something Conway could use to bounce himself to the moon. Thing is, it was the last thing Big Frank suspected.'

'Silly bastard.' Then: 'Let me guess the politico.'

'You know?'

'Tony Sheridan.'

'Tony Sheridan, yeah.'

There was another silence. It went on so long that I thought Brady had absconded. I looked around but he was still there, the gun lying in his lap. He grinned, slow and evil.

'You're one dangerous fucker, Rigby. Know that?'

'Oh yeah, sure. People tell me that all the time. When they're sticking guns in my ear, mostly.'

'You know what we have here?'

'What I have is circumstantial evidence that Tony Sheridan is having an affair with the wife of a drug-trafficking auctioneer, who is now dead. It's going to hit the headlines, no two ways about it, his wife was murdered too, but that'll last until some Fianna Fáil back-bencher gets caught mounting the prize ram in the farmyard. Tony'll never sit in the Dáil again but all the blokes'll take one look at Helen Conway and clap him around his lap of honour, hope they're still up to no good at his age. They'll be queuing up to offer him directorships.'

'You're forgetting Conway.'

'Trying to, anyway.' Then, coming on dumb schmuck: 'What's Conway got to do with Sheridan?'

'Try this. Say Conway wasn't putting the bounce on Sheridan to re-zone some poxy site in a shit-hole town. Say maybe you're right about Conway getting greedy and wanting more. Wanting to vertically integrate his operation with Sheridan's, say.'

'Conway wanted into politics?'

'Not that bad.' He paused, relishing the moment, and said: 'Coke.'

'Coke?'

'Charlie. Snow. White. Call it what you want, Conway got a sniff that Sheridan was into it, maybe through his good wife, who knows. Either way, he wanted his cut.'

My mind had never boggled before. It was an interesting sensation.

'Sheridan's into coke? Next you'll be telling me he's into little boys.'

'If he is, we don't know about it. What we do know is that Sheridan's about to do wonders for the sale of Kleenex in the northwest. At the moment the market is in the region of nine million a year. That's expected to treble in the next two years, and that's a conservative estimate. If it sounds like a lot of money, think about the potential clientele. Doctors, solicitors, dentists, accountants – all those fuckers can pay top dollar and keep on paying it.'

'Christ. Tony Sheridan though?'

'Man's looking to the future. A Dáil seat isn't worth its varnish since they started poking into offshore accounts and Legal Aid isn't going to pay for the villa in Marbella.'

I digested that, thinking about Gonzo dying on a toilet floor. Herbie with his face mashed in. Remembering the glutinous mud at the bottom of the river. Thinking about the grainy, slow-mo images of a pro's sub-machine gun ripping Ben apart.

'If you know all this, how come you haven't put him away already?'

'We need proof.' The last word came coated in salt. 'We

need to connect Sheridan with his supply.'

'And you don't know who his suppliers are.'

'We know who his supplier is. It's a small-time operation, relatively speaking.'

'Relative to what? Microsoft?'

'But he's going big. He's waiting on the delivery to come down, we thought maybe yesterday. Nothing doing. So we thought maybe today. There was always the possibility you were off on a wee errand this afternoon, bringing a taster in.'

I twisted around, so I was looking straight at him. His gaze didn't waver.

'You're kidding. Me, with a kid to look after, moving coke around the countryside?'

'There's good money in it.'

'Fuck you and your money. Fuck all you sick bastards and your money.'

'That's pretty high-minded for a man with a kid to look after.'

'Look, Brady, all I was doing was my job. I did it, did it well and then someone poisoned my brother and now they're trying to kill me. Alright? I'm not involved in coke or smack or dope. No one I know is involved either.'

'Relax. I searched the car while you were playing snowballs with the kid. Nothing. I searched it again while you were yakking in the pub. Still nothing. You didn't have time to take a piss in between, never mind salt away a stash of coke.'

I forgot about the gun. I jabbed a forefinger in his face.

'Stay the fuck away from the kid. Don't drag him into this.'

'He's already in it, Rigby. You're in it, your wife's in it, the kid's in it.' I didn't quibble over my marital status. 'Eddie dragged you all into it.'

'Gonzo? What the fuck has he to do with it?'

The question was out before I remembered that I didn't want to know. Brady laughed, enjoying himself.

'Eddie had everything to do with it.'

'The coke? Gonz was into pills, a couple of tokes. Where would he get that much coke?'

He grinned.

'Galway.'

'There's that much coke in Galway?'

'There's that much coke in any two-horse burg you want to mention. But I'm not talking about the town. I'm talking about . . .' He grinned again, that slow and evil grin. 'What did you call him?'

The penny dropped like the first lemming.

'The pederast?'

'The very man. There's a cop that's bent all ways up.'

Something crawled up my back, leaving a trail. The gun lay in Brady's lap, forgotten, but a gun isn't the kind of thing you forget for long.

'Jesus fucking Christ.'

'Relax, Rigby. Galway's no friend of mine. We've been watching him for the last year but we've never been able to finger him properly. Something like this, you want to get your facts right. Put him away for the full stretch.'

I nodded, dumb.

'Galway's been creaming off the top for a long time now. The coke comes into the country, every now and again we stop some and most of that gets destroyed. What isn't destroyed, the cheap crap, goes back on the streets. Depending on the streets, a blind eye can be turned. If it's going into Ballymun, say, no one says fuck all. Keeps the natives from getting restless.' He shrugged. 'They call it passive policing. Got it from New York, the time they brought in zero tolerance. Works a treat, too. If it starts filtering out anywhere else, though, anywhere outside Dublin, or Cork or Limerick, bells start ringing. Galway's tripped a couple of alarms already.'

'So what was all the Tyson bullshit about yesterday?'

'Jesus, Rigby.' Brady ran a hand through his hair, took a deep breath. 'We're down here to keep an eye on Conway, the Flatliners. That's what Galway thinks. Then Imelda Sheridan gets her throat cut and we get pulled onto that, it's too much of a coincidence. Meanwhile, Galway is trying to keep me out of Conway's face, because they're both tight with Sheridan. Which suits me, because I'm keeping tabs on Galway.'

'And Galway's moving coke onto Sheridan.'

Brady picked at his teeth with a dirty fingernail.

'Yes and no.'

'Yes and no?'

'Fact is, there is no coke. As far as Sheridan knows, he's reeling in a deal with Galway. We're not sure how much to kick off with, but we think it's in the region of half a million. That's what Sheridan thinks. We know Galway doesn't have a half million in coke, because no one could turn a blind eye to that much gear going missing.'

I wasn't surprised. I had all the blind eyes going.

'So Galway hears that some bloke wants to exploit a niche in the market. He throws out some hooks and Sheridan bites, they set up a deal.'

'But there's no coke.'

'But there's no coke. That's where Eddie comes in. Eddie puts the bounce on Sheridan, tells him he won't go public about the coke if everything's kept sweet. Sheridan does his sums and reckons it's still worth it. Eddie takes the money and runs, splits it down the middle with Galway, they're laughing. Sheridan's left twisting in the wind and not a dry fucking eye in the house. Who's he going to call, Ghostbusters?'

My stomach turned over.

'Except Sheridan doesn't play ball.'

'Which is when Eddie pays his wife a visit, and she winds up with a hole in her throat.'

I noodled that around, trying to work out how I should feel. Nothing suggested itself.

'I still don't see where I come into it.'

'Wake up, Rigby. You were the fall guy. Galway put Conway onto you so you'd start digging on his wife. When Imelda Sheridan gets investigated, you're the man with the blackmail motive, the negatives to prove it.'

'And Gonzo put Galway wise about me.'

'Correct.'

I was going to vomit. Three nights running, it was a record.

'So how come they turned on Gonzo?'

'No one turned on him. Eddie took too many pills. Shit happens.'

'Convenient. Who took the pop at me?'

'Galway.'

'Galway?'

'Not Galway himself, he wouldn't get his hands dirty. But it was his call.'

Something in his tone gave it away.

'You knew? Brady? You fucking *knew* he was going to take a

pop? You sat back and let him try to fucking *kill* me?'

'Relax, Rigby. Jesus.'

'Relax? You cunt, I'll fucking—'

I was halfway across the seat, not knowing what I was going to do when I got all the way there, when he bounced the butt against my temple. I slumped back in the seat, shaking.

'Yeah I knew, of course I fucking knew, I jarked the fucking gun myself. Only for me you'd be slabbed out. So get fucking grateful and do it fast.'

My voice sounded hollow.

'There's no way you could have done that without clearance from upstairs.'

There was another pause. When he spoke he sounded slightly robotic.

'We are encouraged to show initiative in the field.'

'Bullshit.'

He abandoned the pretence.

'Believe what you want, Rigby, I give a fuck. You're alive, stop whinging.'

I rolled another smoke, trying to think.

'So what happens now?'

'What happens now is we find Galway. Sheridan took Conway out, so Galway's next, which is why Galway is running scared. We figure he'll lie low for a couple of days, bail out of the country with the rush after New Year's. We need to get to him before he gets out. Once we have him, we'll have Sheridan testify that Galway was in cahoots with Conway. Galway won't squeak about Sheridan and the coke, because we'll cop him a plea that gets him off the Imelda Sheridan beef, which Gonzo wears.'

'And Sheridan?'

'He gets an amnesty for testifying.'

'And for knowing the right people to testify to.'

'Something like that, yeah.' He sucked his teeth. 'You still have that number I gave you?'

'Engraved on my heart. You know they're trying to kill me and you're not going to do anything about it?'

'You had your chance. Yesterday morning, you had all the chances in the world. Now the gig's fucked you're coming crying to me? When I can nail Galway?'

'Jesus.' I felt sick, deflated. 'You want his job that bad?'

Brady checked his watch.

'You're a smart fucker, Rigby, work this one out. Eight years ago I'm called out to this gig in Darndale. There's been a shooting, non-fatal as far as we know. I'm two years on the job, looking to get on, so I'm first through the door. This junkie is lying on the floor in the front room, blood pumping. I'm on my knees with a cushion stuck against the hole and my hands covered in blood before I even think about the AIDS thing.' He shrugged. 'I got lucky. Ten months later the junkie's in some granny's window and she wakes up long enough for her ticker to give out. He got fourteen quid from her purse, she got a few hymns and a thank fuck from her kids, who've better things to be doing than listen to her gripe. The junkie gets eighteen months, aggravated assault, and he's back on the streets before the granny's stiff. So fuck you and your junkies and rapists and scumbags.'

'They're not mine, Brady.'

'Yeah, and they're not mine either. That's what's wrong with this fucking hole of a country, no one gives a fuck, someone else'll take care of it. Then the shit comes down and you come looking to me, expect me to give a fuck. Well, I give a fuck, Rigby. Fuck you, that's the fuck I give. I'm ten years in this gig, haven't moved up since the junkie offed the granny. Galway's job'll pay the bills and a whole lot more besides. All you give me is a pain in the hole. Besides, you're smart, maybe too smart for your own good. You'll lie low until this has blown over.'

He gave me one last blast of his evil smile.

'You hear from Galway,' he said, winking, 'give me a bell. Regards to the wife and kid.'

Then he was gone. I threw open the car door and vomited something thin and stringy. Dragged myself back into the car, slumped in the seat, wasted some time trying to square what I knew with Brady's revelations. Then I gave up, mainly because I was too smart for my own good. Too smart not to meet with the pros at any rate.

23

I drove through the deserted streets, stereo on full blast, the Pixies threatening to blow out the windows. Adrenaline, the cleanest drug of them all, charged through my veins. By the time I pulled in opposite The Odeon I was ready. Ready for what, I wasn't so sure. But I was as ready as I was ever going to be.

The Odeon loomed into the night sky, four storeys, glowering down, as if I was mocking it by turning up at its doors. It had been an imposing building once, its foyer boasting a vaulted ceiling, gothic fittings decorated in gold flake. The auditorium sat two hundred, most of whom came to see a movie that didn't necessarily involve helicopter chases and exploding buildings, as was generally the choice on the six screens of the Omniplex on the other side of town. Its main claim to fame, though, was that when the lights went up the double seats in the rear section under the balcony had to be swabbed down.

The health authority had closed the Odeon about ten years back. The official reason was, people wouldn't get value for money watching a movie while rats scampered across the back of the worn velvet seats. The real reason was, the secretary of the health authority was a trustee on the board of the Omniplex.

It was only when I got to the door that I realised I didn't know what the etiquette was. Knocking seemed a bit twee, and standing out in the snow wasn't going to achieve anything except maybe get Katie killed. I stood there for what felt like an aeon, feeling useless, stupid and bone-deep tired. But stupid, mostly.

The bells of The Friary at the top of the street rang ten o'clock. The sound had shivered away on the frosty air before the door swung open, hinges creaking. I couldn't see anything in the darkness beyond but I took a deep breath, slipped through the gap. An iron hand gripped the scruff of my neck, pushed me against the wall, grinding my face into the mildewed, mushy wallpaper. Something cold and hard touched the base of my skull.

'Move and I'll kill you.'

There was no menace in his voice. He was matter-of-fact, like the last time, when he'd been when talking about Ben.

'Hands against the wall.'

He ran a practised hand up both inside legs, inside the fleece top and Puffa, around my waist, under the shoulders.

'Turn around.'

I turned, keeping my hands high on the off chance that he might think I'd try anything insane, like resistance. He didn't look at my face. I didn't look at his. I looked down the barrel of the cannon in his hand. Looked at the hand, which had been grafted on from the wrist of a corpse. He patted the pockets of the Puffa with the other hand, reached inside, came up holding Gonzo's mobile.

'Want a go?' I asked. 'Dial 999. Shortest number there is.'

He smiled, turned the phone off, slipped it back inside my pocket. Stepped back, clicked the safety catch on, cuffed me above the ear. When I was able to stand up again, he clicked the safety off and pushed me ahead of him across the vast foyer.

'Shut the fuck up,' he said.

I shut the fuck up. He pushed me through a swing door on the far side of the foyer, ignoring the worn sign that said Staff Only. Beyond the door was a rusting spiral staircase. The dust on the floor was thick enough for footprints, and there was a musty smell that made me want to gag, a thick aroma that suggested the disgruntled staff hadn't swabbed down the night The Odeon finally closed its doors.

The staircase led to a tiny landing, a door marked Projection Room. He prodded me between the shoulders with the gun; I pushed through the swing door, blinking at the bright light. A huge, moth-eaten tarpaulin half-covered the old projector against the far wall. There were some tea chests behind the door, markings obliterated, a couple of spindly stools. Old movie posters hung in tatters on the walls. I recognised *True Romance* and *Wild at Heart* but the rest were too badly rotted to make out. Cobwebs swayed in the breeze caused by the swinging door. I wouldn't have been surprised if Miss Havisham had stood up, brushed down her wedding dress and come forward to greet me.

Helen Conway did, which didn't surprise me at all. Wearing a three-quarters length coat, black with white fur trim on the cuffs and collar, a high-necked ivory-tinted blouse in material that shimmered as she moved. Tastefully understated they most certainly were, widow's weeds they were not. She smiled, eyes sparkling. Her voice was dry, husky.

'It's a small world, Mr Rigby.'

'Yeah, but I'd hate to have to hoover it. My condolences on your husband, by the way.'

The smile snapped in two. She stepped up, slapped me hard across the face. It sounded like a pistol-shot in the enclosed space, which was just about when I realised the projector room would have been soundproofed back in the good old days. I took my hat off to her. There are better places to deal with reluctant interviewees than a soundproofed room four storeys up in a deserted building. But if your finances don't stretch to chartering a jet to a Siberian gulag, the projector room of an abandoned cinema will do just as well. The pro growled.

'I told you to shut the fuck up.'

'It's manners to speak when you're spoken to. You alright?' This last to Katie, hunched on a tea chest opposite Tony Sheridan, who was sitting beside the projector. She didn't look all right, not by a long shot, not unless you consider abject desolation an acceptable mental state. Her hands were tied behind her back, face flushed, eyes raw and bloodshot. She'd looked up hopefully when I entered the room but now her head hung low, the peek-a-boo bob obscuring her face, her faith in my ability to rescue her matched by everyone else in the room, myself included. The bob didn't obscure her neck and throat, though, or the ugly red welts that disfigured both. 'Katie? You okay?'

'She's okay,' the Ice Queen purred. 'She's young and healthy. She'll live.'

She turned on her heel, walked back to the projector, footsteps echoing. Sat down on the tea chest beside Tony Sheridan, dusting it off first, lit a cigarette. Katie jumped at the clink-flick of her lighter, eyes bulging, staring at the smouldering end of the cigarette. Tony Sheridan was hunched over, hands jammed in the pockets of his overcoat, glum.

'Bad night for canvassing, Tone.'

He looked up, not at me but at the pro, and nodded. This time the pro cuffed me properly. I stayed down for the full count but even so I had double vision when he dragged me back to my feet. That made two Tony Sheridans, two pros, two Helen Conways and two Katies, which was bad news. Plan A was based on getting one Katie out of there, and I was pretty sure Plan A wasn't going to cut the mustard. I went into my spiel anyway.

'This is the way I see it.' The words sounded thick in my mouth. 'Galway is fucking me as much as he's fucking you. Whatever problem you have is with him, not me. And not her, either.'

The indifference was Homeric.

'What I said this morning still plays. No one fucks with me and that camera stays buried. Everything else that's happened, I won't even remember it in the morning. Kids do that, play havoc with your memory. Things happen and then I talk to Ben after, I can't remember what happened before. Not a fucking thing.'

Tony Sheridan examined his fingernails. The Ice Queen stared at Katie. Katie stared at the floor. I might as well have been saying grace before meals. Finally Helen Conway spoke.

'That's an interesting story, Mr Rigby. Unfortunately, we don't have time for fairy tales.'

'I'm not—'

'We know we can't trust you.' She picked her words carefully. 'We also know that you offered a deal this morning that you have since welched on. I didn't agree with the deal at the time but—'

'I haven't welched on *any* deal. What the fuck are you talking about?'

'Francis told me about your phone call, Mr Rigby. We know how much you want. We're simply not prepared to pay it.' She made a throwaway gesture with her hand that could have meant anything and nothing at all. 'The fact remains that you cannot be trusted. So, this time, we do things my way.'

'It must have been Galway made that call. *He's* fucking with you.'

She wasn't listening. She dropped her cigarette, stubbed it out with a delicate size three.

'Where is it?'

'Where's what?'

'The camera, Mr Rigby. The camera.'

'I don't have it.'

'Who has it?'

'No one has it.'

'You won't give us the camera?'

'I don't have it.'

She stood up, moved across to Katie, untied her hands. Katie rubbed at her wrists, trying to get the circulation back into her fingers. The Ice Queen helped her, taking Katie's left wrist, rubbing the back of the hand.

'Nice hands,' she said, thoughtful. 'I used to have hands like that. Soft and smooth.' She picked out a finger, the second smallest on Katie's left hand. 'There should be a ring on that finger,' she said. Then she snapped it.

The piercing scream went through me for a shortcut. I started forward but a blow from behind brought me to my senses, eventually, face down in the dust. The pro dragged me to my feet again, quicker this time, getting better with practice. He touched the gun against the back of my thigh.

'Next time, I'll blow your fucking knee out.'

The bone in Katie's finger was sticking out at a ninety-degree angle to the second joint. She was sobbing hard, moaning some word I couldn't understand, pawing at Helen Conway's arm. The Ice Queen stroked the back of Katie's hand, making it impossible for her to pull it away without causing herself unimaginable pain.

'I'm not accustomed to torture, Mr Rigby,' she said. I could hardly hear her over the drone of Katie's sobbing. 'But I do know this is not torture. Every time I break a bone, the agony subsides to a level that can be tolerated. Even now, Katie's body has forgotten the intensity of the pain, because our bodies have no physical recollection process. All that is left is the fear that it will happen again, and fear can be conquered.'

'I've told you—'

'Ideally, torture should involve the gradual increase of pain, to the point that the victim will do anything to be released. This isn't ideal, but . . .'

She checked her watch.

'We've been here five minutes already. For each minute we are here from now, I will break another finger. Every time I hear a wrong answer, I will break another finger. Now – where is it?'

'I don't—'

Crack.

'Jesus Christ!'

Crack. Tony Sheridan studied the floor.

'I don't fucking have—'

Crack.

Katie's howls were coming in waves, from somewhere deep inside, somewhere where her survival instincts still held sway.

'You stupid bitch!' I was raving, waving my arms like a loon. The pro's gun bored into the back of my thigh. 'I don't fucking have it *here!*'

She finally got the message. By then Katie's hand was a swollen, shapeless lump. The fingers stuck out at odd angles. Her sobs were the dry heaves of an agony I couldn't begin to imagine. Helen Conway said: 'Where is it?'

'It's in the car! Jesus Christ . . .'

She stared, cool.

'I do believe,' she said, 'that we have over-estimated Mr Rigby.' Tony Sheridan looked up for the first time, his glum expression giving way to grim satisfaction, a look that made me sick to my stomach. Machiavelli wasn't a patch on Tony Sheridan. 'And where is the car?'

'Outside. It's outside.'

'It's outside,' she repeated. 'The camera is in the car, which is outside, and you didn't bring it with you? My God, we have been guilty of over-estimating you. You're not very bright at all, Mr Rigby, are you? Are you sure Eddie is your brother?'

She nodded at the pro. He marched me out the door, down the stairs across the foyer. When we got to the front door he said: 'Where's the car?'

'Across the street.'

He grunted.

'You got that much right, anyway.'

Then he turned me around to face him. He held up the gun, in case I'd forgotten about it, then he slipped his hand into his pocket. The barrel bulged against the fabric. He looked like Bogie spoofing on Edward G. Robinson. I didn't laugh.

'Don't try anything stupid.'

'No worries. I'm all out of stupid.'

'Says you.'

*

We crossed the deserted street to the car, crunching snow. I slid in behind the steering wheel, leaned across the handbrake, pulling down the door of the glove compartment. Cursing myself as I pawed through the envelopes, sweet wrappers and empty water bottles. Plan A couldn't have fallen apart quicker if I'd poured battery acid on it, and I was under no illusions that Helen Conway was letting us walk away from the projection room. We weren't walking away, we weren't crawling away and we weren't going be carried out on stretchers. The only way we were leaving the projection room was in body bags.

The Ice Queen had overestimated me, and I'd returned the favour by underestimating her and Tony Sheridan. Even after the machine gun on the bridge, I still thought they'd have played by the rules. They were playing by one rule, though, and that rule was, there were no rules. I should have listened to Dutchie. Even knowing that Dutchie had sold me out – especially knowing that Dutchie had sold me out – I should have listened to him, heard what he was trying to say. 'What's Plan B?' Dutchie wanted to know.

'Come on, for fucks sakes,' the pro growled. He bent down to see what the delay was and my hand closed on the worn butt of a stubby Plan B.

I didn't stop to think. The last thirty-six hours I'd tried to plan, working it out step by step. Getting Denise and Ben to safety, confronting Big Frank, leading Brady a merry dance while he chased me the length and breadth of the country. And all that planning had walked me into a death trap, because the only issue in doubt if I handed over the camera was who would put the bullet in the back of my head.

I started to back out of the car. The pro took a step back to let me out and he should have taken two, because by then I was in his face, inside his reach, the .38 grinding into his throat, my arm around his neck, pulling him onto the barrel.

'I'll kill you, you cunt. I'll fucking *kill* you!' I was snarling, grinding teeth, eyes wild. We were forehead-to-forehead, close enough to kiss, and I couldn't give him time to think. His first instinct had to be that I'd lost it, that I was willing to do whatever it took, and that he was first in line for whatevering. 'Drop it or I *will* blow your fucking head off.'

There was a dull clunk, his gun hitting snow. I didn't breathe. I ground my forehead into his, in case he tried to butt me.

'Put your hands behind your head. Real fucking slow.'

He did it, fear in his eyes. He'd been in this situation before, from the other side of the gun, knew the procedure.

'On your knees. Real slow.'

He started to dip, bending his knees. When his forehead reached the level of my nose, I swung my knee full force into his groin. He went down squealing, sprawled out on the snow, face down. Buckled as he was, he still reached for his gun; I didn't make a game of it. I drew a boot on the side of his head, connected so well he ricocheted off the car door. He curled into a ball, groaning. I flicked his gun away with the side of my foot and booted him again, this time full in the face, crunching bone. He scrabbled to one side, a giant roach as he tried to crawl under the car. I moved away, picked up his gun, checked the safety catch. It was off. I put the .38 into my pocket. His gun was heavier, but not so heavy I couldn't carry the extra weight.

'Get up. On your knees.'

He tried, blood pumping from his face, a pink stain seeping into the snow. I thought of Gonzo in the toilets of the kebab house.

'Get the fuck *up*! Now.'

He pushed himself to his knees, leaning back against the car door, whimpering. I moved in, inching it, hooked an arm around his throat, dug the gun into the side of his neck. He lurched to his feet, staggered forward. I went with him, then jerked my arm tight around his throat.

'You know, I've never done this before. And that's not good news, because it means I could do anything, anything at all. The smallest twitch, a trip or a stumble, and the gun'll go off and your head'll come off with it.' I tightened the chokehold again. 'Hear me?'

He grunted.

'One step at a time. Go.'

He went. I pushed him through the cinema doors, across the foyer, holding him close. We went up the rickety stairs side-by-side, which was awkward, but we managed. I pulled him up short on the tiny landing outside the projection room.

'Move and I'll do it. And I want to do it. You know I want to do it. Yeah?'

He nodded.

'If everyone plays ball we're out of here. Nothing stupid and everyone walks away. Hear me?'

Again he nodded.

'Okay. Let's go.'

We pushed through the projection room door. The Ice Queen turned to greet us and her smile died so fast it went happy. Tony Sheridan started up off the tea chest. Katie looked up, still sobbing, a bewildered expression creasing her face. No one spoke. I realised they were waiting on me.

'Get up, Katie. Over here.'

She stood, tottering, made to move towards the door. Without looking, Helen Conway put out a hand to bar her way.

'I'll kill him,' I said, tightening my chokehold on the pro. 'Don't doubt it.'

Katie made to brush past Helen Conway's arm, cradling her warped hand, but the Ice Queen was made of sterner stuff. So was her voice. The husky chuckle was gone, replaced with a monotone you could have knocked sparks off.

'I wouldn't, honey,' she warned Katie. 'He's the one we want. Don't pick the wrong side now.'

Katie hesitated, looked at me. I looked at Helen Conway. My plan, if that was the right word for it, had been to get Katie out and then back myself out of the room. Now that the bluff had failed, I had no idea of what happened next. The Ice Queen was first to speak.

'It would seem,' she said, moving to her right, behind Katie, 'that we didn't underestimate you after all.'

'You've seen too many Bond films. Move again and I'll blow his fucking head off.'

She was gliding towards the far wall.

'I believe you, Mr Rigby. Really, I do.' She reached the wall, holding Katie by the elbow. I watched her from the corner of my eye, keeping the other on Tony Sheridan. He hadn't moved. 'In fact, I'm willing to offer you a deal. We'll pay your price for the camera.'

I didn't believe a word. I'd seen it too often in the movies, where the bad guy talks you into a corner and then, just when you're least expecting it, he whips out a knife and takes an ear off. Or maybe it's a gun, and you're blown into the emergency ward, or the morgue. The Ice Queen was still moving, though, and there was nothing I could do about it. Either she reckoned I was bluffing about pulling the trigger on the pro, or she didn't care about him either way. She was wrong about the first – I wasn't sure when, but I'd crossed some line I hadn't even known existed.

I was right about the second.

'How much?' I asked, buying time, still watching Tony Sheridan. Helen Conway I could deal with, even if she was now out of my field of vision, against the far wall. 'That camera was worth a neat pile a couple of hours ago and inflation's a bitch. Right now I'd say it's worth—'

I've never been kicked in the ribs by a rogue elephant but I won't have to go on safari to know how it feels. I took off like a burst balloon and hit the ground two seconds short of the land speed record, the pro sprawled across me.

I hadn't bargained on Helen Conway carrying a gun. If I'd thought about it, maybe, I'd have considered it a possibility, but I hadn't even thought about it, mainly because I need keyhole surgery to get ideas into my head. But she had a gun. Once she had a clear shot, a position where the danger to the pro was minimised, she'd let fly. Minimised, but not entirely neutralised. He'd taken the bullet. I'd taken everything it had left over, which was enough to save my life. The impact pitched us both across the room into the middle of the tea chests.

As soon as I hit the ground, the Ice Queen started snapping off shots. I scrabbled around, desperately trying to manoeuvre myself under the dead man. Splinters of wood, metal and celluloid flew as I tried to bury myself in the floor. The noise was deafening, so loud I couldn't even hear myself scream. I was a dead man, as dead as the pro on my chest. I knew it – *felt* it – it was only a matter of time before a bullet finally found me.

Time comes in split seconds, infinitesimal moments. Somewhere, sometime, in a parallel universe, that split second arrived; the bullet found me and the cosmos ceased to be. Back on planet Rigby, another split second arrived. One of the tea chests toppled over, giving me a clear view of the Ice Queen along the barrel of the pro's gun, her head suspended above the sight like a coconut at a shy. Never mind your Grand Canyons, your newborn babies or your tropical sunsets – the sight of the Ice Queen's grim features resting on the barrel of the gun was the most beautiful thing I'd ever seen.

I squeezed the trigger. Nothing happened. I realised that I hadn't flipped the safety catch off. Then I heard a twenty-one-gun salute and the Ice Queen buckled sideways, disappeared from sight.

I rolled to one side, aiming to get as far under the tea chests as possible. I had no idea where Helen Conway was or what she was doing, but I had a fair idea she wasn't ringing out for wreaths. And then I heard, dimly, through the pealing bells, the voice of God.

'Son? You alright, son?'

I peered over the tea chest. Baluba Joe was standing in the doorway, taller than I remembered him. Shoulders back, still wearing the grimy great coat, the soiled pants, the black beret. His right arm was extended, the old Colt .45 at the end of it pointed at the Ice Queen's face. She didn't seem offended, too busy trying to push her guts back into the hole in her side.

Katie was hunched in a corner, face to the wall, holding her crippled hand by the wrist. I pushed the tea chest away, staggered to my feet, legs shaking, breathing hard. My eyes were streaming from the stench of cordite, which was good, because it meant I couldn't focus on the dead pro as I stepped over him. Tony Sheridan had jammed himself between the projector and far wall, hands over his ears. I prodded him with the gun.

'Get up, you bastard.'

He looked at me, fearful, not fully comprehending. Or maybe he didn't hear me properly, my ears were ringing so badly I hardly heard myself. I jerked the gun at him. Still he didn't move, so I cracked him one with the butt of the gun. I hit maybe harder than I had hit anything before in my life, the adrenaline coursing. He slumped, didn't move. Blood ebbed from his temple. I cracked him another one, for luck.

Katie's face was blank and white, all colour drained. She looked to be in shock. I hunkered down beside her.

'Katie? You okay? Katie?'

She didn't answer, gaze riveted on the Ice Queen. I stood up, wiggled the pro's gun at her.

'Kick it over here.'

She didn't hear me. She too looked to be in shock, still trying to hold in the spaghetti of guts that overflowed her hands. I walked across, picked her gun up, slipped it deep into the pocket of the fleece. Then I went to the doorway. The Colt .45 must have weighed a ton but his arm didn't waver. He said, soft: 'How you doing, son?'

'Fine, Joe. Now the cavalry is here.'

His eyes were still wide, blue and wild but at least he'd made an attempt to comb his hair. He said: 'What happens now?'

'What happens now is you go home. I'll look after it from here.'

'There's more?'

'It's only getting started, Joe. But I'm getting the hang of it, fast.'

'Don't kid yourself, son. You never get the hang of it.' He gestured at Helen Conway and Tony Sheridan. 'But whatever it is, you don't need these catching up with you at the wrong time.'

'No thanks, Joe. It's bad enough, me getting you caught up in it. From now on it's my rap.'

'You'll do what you're told, son. And I'm telling you to fuck off and do whatever you have to do. I'll just sit here and have a smoke, wait'll I hear the all clear.'

'Your call, Joe.'

'My call, son.'

I helped Katie up, put an arm around her shoulders, which were shaking almost as hard as my own.

'We're going to get you to a hospital, Katie. Okay?'

She didn't respond. She didn't seem to be aware of my presence, still staring at Helen Conway. When I tried to move her towards the door she resisted, reached for the gun in my hand. I held it away, out of her reach. The Ice Queen was slipping fast, shaking hard, pain eating into the shock, blood ebbing out into the kind of pool that has a deep end. She glared, baleful. I looked away, more important things to do than be turned to stone.

I checked on Tony Sheridan. He was still panned out. I cracked him another one, in case he was playing possum. Then I led Katie out of the room, patted Joe on the shoulder in passing.

He didn't acknowledge me. Helen Conway watched us go, face ugly with loathing. I winked at her.

'Sorry about the hole. A good girl like you, Santa's bound to bring bandages.'

She spat something, through bubbles of blood. I made a wish. It was my third new expletive in as many days.

24

The bells of The Friary were ringing for midnight mass, the sound coming sharp in the clear night air. The cold air started me coughing, which brought up blood, but then that's a sixty-a-day hazard.

I helped Katie into the car and got in, tugged up the jacket, checked the wound. The bullet hitting the pro had opened the hole again; blood was leaking from under the bandage, weak and thin. I watched it ooze, not feeling any pain. It was just the way things were, something else to deal with it, to get past.

I eased the car down the street, leaving it in second gear, letting gravity do the work. The snow was slick with frost, thick enough to keep all but the most dedicated penitents from venturing out, which meant The Friary would have a higher ratio of drunks to God-fearing Catholics than usual. It was a good time to get Katie to emergency, before the winos started shuffling up the Mall, looking for a warm bed for the night that was in it. I met no traffic on the drive through town.

Katie stared straight ahead, seeing nothing. Cradling her swollen fist, whimpering when her hand moved. Her complexion was cream cheese, the orange mop of hair in shocking contrast to the pale below. She seemed oblivious.

In the hospital car park, I leaned across and touched her cheek. She didn't flinch. I was tempted to touch the ugly welts on her throat but I got out the car, locked it, crunched through the snow to the hospital. I knew it was a callous thing to do, leaving her alone. I knew that. I didn't feel it.

The antiseptic smell washed over me when the automatic doors slid back, the blast of heat giving me goose bumps. The girl behind the reception desk was mid-twenties, homely, eyeing me over a pair of half-moon glasses as I made for the desk, begrudging the effort of sliding the window back. I didn't hold it against her. No one wants to be in hospital on Christmas Eve, least of all the staff.

'Hi,' I breezed, digging deep. 'I'd like to check on a friend of mine?'

'I'm sorry.' Her tone that let me know that, whatever she was apologising for, it was my fault. 'Visiting hours finished two hours ago.'

'That's okay. I just want to know how he's doing. He came in this morning. Hit and run. His name is Herbie O'Malley.'

'I'm sorry,' she said, a mechanical tone, 'but we could only release that information to a family member.'

'I'm a family member.'

She frowned.

'You just said you were his friend.'

'He's a cousin, actually. But we're good mates too.'

'I'm sorry, only immediate family members are privy to that kind of information.'

'His family are away for Christmas. I'm the only one around. I'm going to be ringing them later, and I'd like to let them know how he is.'

'You're not going to go away until you find out, are you?'

I smiled, apologetic.

'Alright,' she sighed. 'Wait a minute.'

She pulled the window closed, so I couldn't hear what she was saying, made a couple of calls. Pulled the window open again, holding the phone against her none too impressive embonpoint.

'Herbie O'Malley?'

'That's right.'

'And you are?'

'Frankie Byrne. His cousin.'

'Hold on.'

Back went the glass door. She finished the call. Again with the window.

'Herbie O'Malley wasn't involved in a hit and run.'

'No? I heard he was, in the pub. The boys said he'd been mangled.'

'Well, he's badly hurt alright. He's still in intensive care. He's going to need extensive surgery but the ECTs showed up positive. There's no serious tissue damage and he's in a stable condition.'

'Thanks a million. You've been a great help.'

She said: 'Don't you want to see him?'

'I thought visiting hours were finished.'

'They are. But in your case . . .'

Some people are born spoofers. Other people die every time they lie. She knew it sounded wrong and looked away, refusing to meet my eyes. I scoped the foyer for a night porter or security guard but we were alone in the vast hall. I reckoned I had about five minutes, if that, before the Dibble arrived.

'That's decent, cheers. Where's intensive care?'

'Fourth floor. Take a right when you get out of the lift.'

I turned away from the desk, hesitated, turned back. She had the window half-closed. I played the hunch.

'I don't suppose you could let me know how Robbie Callaghan is?'

'Who?'

'Robbie Callaghan.' I figured that Galway would have booked Gonzo into the morgue under that name. 'It's either Robbie Callaghan or Eddie Rigby.'

'You don't know what his name is?'

'He uses a pseudonym. Does some writing for the paper.'

'Oh, right. And is he family?'

I grinned and she smiled, co-conspirators.

'No, he's just a mate. He overdid it on the pints last night. They brought him in to have his stomach pumped.'

'I really shouldn't tell you, but . . .'

'You're a star.'

She checked through the list of in-patients on the desk, taking her time. Twice she looked down the hall to the double doors, looking up at me both times, and both times I smiled, counting the seconds. When she finally told me that there was no record of a Robbie Callaghan or an Eddie Rigby, I reckoned I had maybe two minutes grace.

'There's nothing?'

'Nothing for the emergency ward, and that's where they'd have taken him. I'd have known, it was my shift.'

'Maybe they wrote it up wrong. He was on E as well. A Detective-Inspector Galway brought him in.'

She checked again.

'Nothing like that. There was no Detective-Inspector Galway here last night.'

It didn't make sense but then there was no reason it should have made sense, if it made sense it'd have been the first time in three days I'd have understood what was going on.

'Cheers,' I said, made for the exit.

'What about your cousin?'

She'd leaned forward, pulled the window all the way back.

'Thanks all the same, but I'll see him tomorrow.'

From the bed beside him, probably, and the way things were going intensive care sounded like an attractive proposition. There's not an awful lot more they can do to you once they put you in intensive care.

*

I drove out of the car park to a lay-by, a quarter mile away. Katie was shaking hard.

'Katie? Can you hear me?'

It took her a couple of seconds to turn her head and when she did her eyes were dead. She needed a lorry-load of morphine and a good therapist, and I hoped she got them. What I needed were answers, which was why I took her good hand.

'Katie,' I said, stroking it gently, 'there's something I need to know. I think you know what I'm talking about.'

She stayed blank.

'Last night, when I stayed at your place?'

Still no response. She was a million miles away, or maybe just half a mile, back in the projection room.

'It was comfortable, comfortable and easy. Call me cynical, but it was a little too easy.'

Recognition finally flickered in her eyes. She edged away from me, as far as she could go, which brought her up against the passenger door. Her mouth opened slightly, and she mouthed a word. No.

'They used your neck for an ashtray tonight, Katie.' It was probably the most superfluous thing I've ever said. 'Why would they do that? Not for kicks, these people are pros, that kind of buzz they keep for Saturday nights. They were burning you for a reason, they wanted to know something you know. And I want to know it too. Difference is, this time there's no cavalry on the way. No one knows you're here. So – where is he?'

There was nothing in her eyes by then. No fear, no revulsion, no flicker of recognition. There was, if I looked hard enough, still a semblance of humanity, but it was fading fast. Her eyes were nothing more than opaque marbles, seeing nothing, inside or out.

'Where is he, Katie?' Harsher this time, squeezing her hand. I concentrated on the self-loathing, feeding off it. If I'd thought for a second about what Katie was enduring, I'd never had the strength to do what I was going to have to do. I reminded myself that, even though Dutchie had sold me out to Galway, the only person who knew Herbie had the pictures was Katie. I'd told her, she'd told Galway, and Galway had put the squeeze on Dutchie. I thought it only right that I should put the squeeze on Katie.

The pressure of my hand finally filtered through. She started to cry, quietly, fat tears rolling down her cheeks. I couldn't blame her, she'd had a rough day, but my day hadn't been what you might call a Sunday at Butlins and my day was far from over. She tried to pull her hand away. I tightened my grip.

'Where is he, Katie? That's all I want to know. Where's Galway?'

It took maybe ten minutes, and a few more broken fingers, but in the end she told me what I wanted to know. I dropped her at the driveway of the hospital. She could hardly stand up, fainting from pain, but I had other things on my mind. One was how to keep down the rising gorge of bile and self-disgust.

The other was also a nauseous sensation, this one driven by fear, a primal instinct I had never experienced before, even when the Ice Queen was churning the tea chests to splinters. This was a fear for someone else, a sleepy-eyed kid who wouldn't even know he was in danger until it was too late, for whom it was maybe already too late. I hit the road, put the boot to the floor, dug out the mobile and dialled. He didn't answer until the tenth or eleventh ring.

'Who's this?' Voice thick with sleep and one too many double Jameson's.

'Happy Christmas, big man. Santa's arrived and he's heard you've been a good boy.'

'Rigby?'

'Just about. You still in town?'

'Yeah. What—'

'You know The Odeon?'

'What?'

'There's an old cinema on Connolly Street, it was closed down years ago. Get there and get to the top floor. The projection room.'

'What's going on, Rigby?'

'Nothing. It's gone on. Sheridan should still be there, and Helen Conway. She'll have a hole in her side, if she's still alive, and he'll have a lump on his head. You'll need stretchers.'

'Rigby?'

'You'll need a body bag too. A gunnie, I'm thinking maybe ex-Provie.'

'Jesus fucking Christ, Rigby! Slow down. Start at the start.'

'No time, Brady. It's all over and the ending is getting happier by the minute. Here's what you're going to do. You're going to get to The Odeon with a couple of your Dibble mates, and you're going to arrest those two and put them away for as long as possible. Understand?'

'You're giving me orders, Rigby?'

Still a yard off the pace.

'There'll be an old bloke there too, doing your job for you. And you're going to do whatever it takes to keep him and me out of it. Alright?'

'No it's not fucking alright.' He did his best to impose himself on the proceedings. 'What did you do to get into it?'

'Nothing, Brady. I was there as an impartial observer, a UN gig.'

I could hear heavy breathing, Brady weighing up his options. I couldn't wait for him to work it out, a species could evolve from the slime and be hunted to extinction before Brady got the knots out of his shoelaces.

'Brady?'

'What were you observing, Rigby?'

'Jesus, Brady!' I took a deep breath. 'Helen Conway convened her fan club. When we turned up she ran amok and shot at us all, including herself, except she missed me. Can't understand why, she was such a good shot with the Provie.'

'Helen Conway? The flaky tart?'

'She was running the show, Brady. Sheridan's just a front, a poster boy. The Ice Queen's the one you want.'

'What are you, clairvoyant?'

'Just a shamus doing his sums, Brady. I'm guessing that's what Frank Conway was looking for me to dig up when he came to me first. Not that it matters a fuck now.' I paused. 'Whenever you want the murder weapon I'll turn it over. A magic gun it is, too, fires different kinds of bullets, some of them at the same time. But you've dealt with that kind of shit before, right?'

He said, slow, measuring the words: 'Right now, Rigby, I'm wondering why I shouldn't put you out on the air, have you hauled in on suspicion of murder. I'm wondering, too, why you're giving me orders. And I'm wondering why you should be kept out of whatever the fuck happened in that cinema when you're going to be the star turn at the trial, as defendant or witness.'

It was the $64,000 question. Actually, it was three $64,000 dollar questions.

'Because you're like me, Brady. You're a selfish bastard who'll do whatever it takes to get what he wants. And I'm going to give you what you want on a plate.'

'What I want? *What* do I want?'

I let him dangle. Then: 'Galway.'

There was another silence, but I could hear it tingling. He said, cautious: 'You know where Galway is?'

'I know where Galway is.'

'Where?'

'I was never at The Odeon?'

There was the briefest of pauses. Then he said, cold: 'Who are you? Who the fuck am I talking to?'

I sighed some relief, not enough, but some. Then I gave him explicit instructions, hung up before he had time to argue. The road was clear, the perfect white of the snow scarred by the tracks of traffic that had gone before me. I put the boot down. I had a long way to go and the trip got longer every time.

25

It was almost four when I crawled off the main road, taking the back lane. I cut the headlights halfway down the hill, parked up. Slipped and slid through the pitch black on foot.

The house was dark, no light showing from the road, no tyre-tracks in the driveway, which meant nothing. The snow had obliterated everything that wasn't moving. I jumped the wall, made my way up the garden behind the rhododendron bushes, so I wouldn't trip the spotlights, emerging behind the woodshed.

The kitchen was dark. The snow between the shed and kitchen door was unmarked, the white van's bonnet cold, which meant its driver had been inside long enough to get warm and maybe a little too comfortable. It wasn't much of an advantage, but it was something.

I slipped the safety off the Ice Queen's gun, trying not to breathe, my breath pluming, a dead give-away if anybody was lurking in the shadows. Crossed the open yard, every pore attuned for the slightest hint of impending oblivion, knowing full well I wouldn't even hear it coming.

The back door was unlocked. I eased it open, crept through the kitchen on tiptoe, opened the kitchen door a crack. The hall ran the full length of the house, all the rooms opening off it, and once I started walking I was a sitting duck. A murmur came from the living room at the end of the hall, voices confident enough not to be whispering. Voices that belonged to people not disposed to jumping out of doorways and blasting everything in sight. When I finally convinced myself of this fact, I slipped through the door and began inching down the hall. It took me a good ten minutes to traverse the sixty feet or so to the living room. Threw back my shoulders, pushed the door in.

The conversation stopped. By the looks of things, it had been a little one-sided anyway. Denise, sitting forward on the end of the couch, looked even less enchanted by small talk than usual. Hugging herself like she was trying to stay warm, dressed in a pair of her father's outrageous tartan pyjamas, feet bare, face haggard. She looked up quickly when I walked in; from the expression in her eyes, a quick blaze of hope, gratitude and irrational expectation, I could have been Saint Nick himself.

Galway wasn't a believer. He snorted, derisive, casual on the other end of the couch. What looked like a Smith and Wesson 9MM, standard Branch issue, appeared in his hand. Ben, lying in front of the couch, playing trucks, swung around. His face lit up and he struggled into a sitting position.

'Dad!' he shouted, pointing at the bike in the corner of the room beside the Christmas tree. 'Santa brought a bicycle. Look!'

'It's lovely, Ben.'

'And a dumper truck, Dad!' He trotted across the room to

show me the truck, a red-and-yellow plastic tractor with a shov-el on the front that tipped up and down. I ruffled his hair. Chocolate had dried on his cheeks.

'That's lovely too.' I swallowed hard but the lump in my throat stuck to its guns. 'Now go sit with your mum.'

He pouted.

'But Dad—'

'Ben!'

Denise's voice was harsh enough to make him jump; he mooched back to the couch. Denise took the truck from him, folded him in her arms.

'Take him to the bedroom,' I said. She started to get up, strug-gling to lift Ben from a sitting position, but she didn't even make it off the couch.

'Nice try, Harry,' Gonzo said, laconic. His sleepy eyes looked me up and down, lazy. He was sprawled out on the armchair opposite the TV, in good shape for a corpse, relaxed, a can of beer at his elbow. All he needed was a pipe and a pair of slippers. 'Sit down, Dee,' he said. 'It's too late to start listening to Harry now.'

'Whatever it is, Gonz, it's between you and me. She has noth-ing to do with it.'

He laughed, crooked a lazy finger.

'Come on in. Sit down. Have a beer. And put that down before you do yourself a damage.'

I put the Ice Queen's gun on the coffee table, sat in the arm-chair beside the TV, facing Gonzo. Galway didn't take his eyes off me. I stuffed my hands deep into the pockets of the zip-up fleece, shivering. Gonzo picked up the gun, sniffed the barrel. He looked at me, intrigued.

'You been practising, Harry?'

I shrugged him off, looked at Galway.

'You know what they do to Dibble inside?' A prim smile twitched at the corner of his mouth. 'No lubricant, either. Payback's a bitch. But then you're the expert when it comes to bitches.'

His confidence was rock-solid but he didn't like the dig. He sat forward, backhanded me across the face.

'Grow up. Jesus.' Gonzo sounded tired. 'Time's a-wasting, Harry. Where's the camera?'

'What's the hurry, Gonz? The party's only starting. Galway's mates are on their way and they'll be looking for their coke. Not that there is any, but you know what I mean.'

Galway shot me a quick one. Gonzo cocked his head to one side.

'Say again?'

'They know about Galway. They've known all along. Brady has you nailed.'

Galway looked at Gonzo, Gonzo at me.

'They know?' It wasn't a question.

Galway licked his lips, said, a little too fast: 'He's bluffing.'

Gonzo put a finger to his lips, nodded at me.

'Talk me through it.'

'What the fuck's going on, Eddie?'

'You're a liability is what's going on,' I needled. 'Like I say, payback's a bitch.'

Galway surged forward; a click stopped him dead. Denise screamed, turned away, pulling Ben into her breasts, pushing him between her and the sofa cushions. His surprised squawk came muffled. Galway didn't have to turn to know that Gonzo was pointing the Ice Queen's gun at him but maybe he needed the exercise because he turned anyway.

'Sit still,' Gonzo said. His voice was silky. 'And drop the rod.'

Galway looked frantic, thumb trembling over the safety of the Smith & Wesson.

'Do it now or I'll do it for you.'

Galway dropped the gun.

'Now slide it over here.'

He did it. Gonzo didn't take his eyes off him. He said: 'Go on, Harry.'

Denise was staring at me, bewildered. I held her gaze, kept my voice calm.

'The way Brady tells it,' I said, jerking a thumb at Galway, 'the fairy here is public enemy number one. Brady reckons the boys in the back room don't like their own running rings around them, especially when they're not getting their cut. Galway got greedy and didn't look after the lads. Now the lads are going to look after him.'

Denise clutching Ben so tight he was in grievous danger of smothering.

'The way it was supposed to happen was, Galway sets up a deal with Sheridan. Coke, like. Sheridan bites. Once Sheridan is on the hook, Gonzo hits him on the bounce. The boys walk away, quids in. It's so sweet it's rotting my teeth just talking about it.'

Gonzo said nothing. Galway twitched.

'Only thing is, there's no coke. Only other thing is, Tony Sheridan isn't playing ball. So Galway's getting nervous, because there's only so many times you can pull the scam he's pulling, and that's once. So Galway goes for the Big Kahuna and Imelda Sheridan winds up dead. Now the pressure is back on Tony, but

Galway needs a fall guy. He tells Sheridan that I've been snooping around with a camera. The timing couldn't have been any worse. Tony is nailing a drug dealer's wife, they're waiting on Galway to bring a shipment through, and all of a sudden Gonzo is squeezing them on the coke front. Then they find out there are compromising photos doing the rounds. All that coke sloshing around, and there's the possibility that Sheridan is going to have the tabloids crawling up his crevices.'

Denise was staring at me across the top of Ben's head, who had nodded off to sleep. The excitement had finally sapped his energy.

'So Galway and Sheridan cook up a way to take Gonz out of the picture, feeding him dodgy pills. Nice plan, except Galway and Gonz are best buds. Gonz pulled a choker in the toilets and Galway whisked him away. Then Galway rang Brady and told him to let me go. On the way home I get mown down and Gonzo comes out of the woodwork, putting the bounce on Sheridan again, this time for murder, aka The Big Kahuna.'

I looked at Gonzo.

'That was the idea, yeah? You wanted them to nail me so you could sit back and milk them. Except I fucked it all up by staying alive. Then I really queered the pitch by playing hardball with Sheridan and Conway. So you tried to set me up again, tonight, by putting Katie in the frame.'

He didn't even have the decency to look embarrassed. Denise transferred her wide-eyed gaze from me to Gonzo. He should have shrivelled up and died. He didn't.

'They could have killed me, Gonz. They tried, Christ knows they tried.'

'Don't take it personal, Harry.'

'Just business, Gonz. You set me up to take a bullet for a few lousy quid?'

'You're smart, Harry. I had faith in you.'

'I'm touched. I'd imagine Katie is too. Touched in the head, she looked pretty fried when I dropped her off at the hospital. I presume you were going to ask how she was doing, seeing as how you were knocking her off?'

'Katie can look after herself.'

'Maybe. She looked after me pretty well.' I ignored the affronted look Denise shot me. 'See, she looked after me too well, someone she hardly knew, some lunatic who turned up at that hour of the morning telling her that his brother had been murdered. I was grateful, don't get me wrong, and it's nice to see that Irish hospitality is still alive and well. But still.'

Galway was shifting in his seat, edgy. His breath was coming short and I could almost hear him sweat. I knew, and Gonzo knew, that he was going to do something desperate.

'Get Dee out of here, Gonz. For Ben's sake.'

He shook his head, motioned with the gun, which was still pointed at Galway.

'On the floor. Now. Face down, hands out. Do it slow.'

Galway eased himself off the couch, spread-eagled himself on the shag-pile. Gonzo looked at me.

'Katie's a friendly girl. So she's friendly to you. So what?'

'So she thinks I'm mixed up in a murder attempt. That's the kind of friendly you buy and the last time I checked my stock was rock bottom. Friendly to some stranger who won't go to the Dibble about being shot? Who's that friendly? No one, that's who. Not unless they know there's no murder.'

'You knew I wasn't dead.'

'Not until tonight.'

'What can I say, Holmes?' he drawled. 'You're a fucking genius.'

I ignored him. While I was talking I was still alive, and Ben was still alive, and Denise was still alive. Gonzo had to be alive too, to do the listening, but then you can't have everything.

'So I'm supposed to think you're dead, which was fine and dandy by me. People die every day, even brothers. Galway and Brady even turned up the next morning to keep the show on the road. The only person who knew I was at Katie's was Katie, she had to let them know. Had to let you know, rather, and you told Galway. They could have looked around while they were there but they didn't, because they would have found me. And that wouldn't have done at all. So off they toddled, job done, waiting for me to make my next stupid move. It was only a matter of waiting.'

I looked back at Denise.

'Anyway, Gonzo's dead. Sad but true. I was more worried about the living, which was why I got Ben and you out of town. Once I knew you were safe I started worrying about Herbie, who wasn't answering the phone. So I take a stroll around to Herbie's and the boy's in bad shape, because someone told Sheridan that Herbie had the photos of him and Helen Conway. How did they know Herbie had the camera? Katie knew, because I told her. So Galway gets on the blower to Sheridan, tells him this could wreck the deal, and Herbie gets the shitty end of the stick. They don't find the camera, because I have it, but what I couldn't work out was how they managed to find Herbie. Who knew where Herbie was? Dutch.'

Gonzo looked away from Galway, stared at me, eyes hooded,

lips pursed. Then he went back to Galway.

'I don't blame Dutch, he did what he had to do. But once I knew he was offside he was offside for good. And Dutchie would have worked out where Denise and Ben were, which meant Gonz could find you if he looked hard enough. That was okay, though, because you were safe until the shit hit the fan, which it did tonight in The Odeon. As far as Gonzo was concerned, I'd get a bullet and he could nail Sheridan for murder. Worse case scenario, I'd walk away with the camera and Gonzo would take it off me. Either way, Gonz was quids in.'

I shrugged.

'It didn't happen that way and now the gig's fucked. Brady wants Galway, there's no coke, and there are no ATMs where Helen Conway and Tony Sheridan are going.'

Gonzo nodded, satisfied, as if his plan was working out perfectly.

'They'll keep. They'll be out soon enough, if they ever go in.'

'Besides,' I said, 'the money was only ever a bonus.'

The temperature dropped a couple of degrees. Galway twisted to stare at Gonzo.

'What the fuck is he talking about?'

I grinned a cold one.

'Jesus, Galway, get with the programme. Gonz didn't have to come home to sting some sleazebag politico for beer money. He could have done that anywhere in the country, and in any country you care to mention.'

Gonzo looked suddenly tired, his eyes even more sleepy than usual.

'Gonzo's home for something money can't buy. Kill two birds with one stone while he's at it.'

They were a rapt audience, Denise especially. I said, to Gonzo: 'I always thought the best thing you ever did for me was screw Celine because if you hadn't I'd never have met Dee. But that wasn't the best thing you did. The best thing you did was not turn up for the christening. How could you? Godfather and father of the same child? Even you're not that sick.'

Denise goggled. Gonzo just stared, cool and hard.

'Think I didn't know, Gonz?' I laughed, but not for long, because the branding iron slipped back into my side. 'Jesus, just look at him. The eyes are the giveaway.'

Denise was shaking her head, a fruitless denial. Gonzo didn't react. Galway stared at Ben, still snuggled asleep in Denise's arms. Then he looked at Gonzo.

'It's yours?'

'Gonzo did the easy part, but Ben's mine.' Gonzo was still staring at me. 'Think again, Gonz. If you're planning on leaving here with Ben, make a new plan. I'll kill you first. Believe me, I'll do time before I let you take him away. Because bad as I am, you're poison, and I'll be damned if I'll let you touch him again.'

He sat forward, lazy and slow.

'Nice speech, Harry,' he drawled. 'But you're forgetting one thing.' He changed the angle of the gun, so it was pointing at me instead of Galway. 'Don't make promises you can't keep.'

'I'm only making the one.'

'Don't push it.'

'You're taking him?'

'I'm taking him.'

'You'd better be better than you think you are.'

'Whatever,' he said, lifting the gun and firing in one smooth, practised movement. It clicked. Then it clicked again. Then he

275

went for the floor, for Galway's gun, and as he went there was a confused expression of admiration and fear on his face.

He didn't get far. The pro's gun was already cocked, safety off, deep in the pocket of the zip-up fleece. All I had to do was squeeze. I squeezed. It caught him high in the chest, the impact slamming him back against the cushion. He rebounded, flopping, useless.

'Harry!'

Denise screamed. Galway lunged up off the carpet, going for his gun, a scrumhalf in a loose maul, but he was too late, by then it was too late for anything but a prayer before bedtime. Brady was kicking in the door, two Emergency Response Unit wallahs behind him, machine-pistols to the fore, all three screaming conflicting instructions to freeze, lie down, put our hands behind our heads. Galway froze. I froze. Ben screamed, Denise huddling over him, also screaming. One of the ERU wallahs dragged Galway's arms behind his back to handcuff him. Then he started to read him his rights.

Brady prised the gun from Gonzo's grip, pulled his head back, Gonzo's breathing coming in gurgles. Denise lurched to her feet, a hand to her mouth, retching, making for the door. The second ERU wallah threw out an arm to block her way. Brady nodded her past, and I heard the sound of her bare feet padding up the hallway as the din from the gunshot faded.

Brady looked at me, the burn mark on the pocket of the fleece, then looked at Gonzo. He had fallen to one side, a hole the size of a boxing glove punched through his back, a pool of blood seeping between his legs.

'Sibling rivalry,' he sneered.

I didn't answer. I was suddenly tired, so tired I hadn't the strength to close my eyes. Brady held his hand out, snapped his fingers. I handed him the pro's gun. He gave it a quick once over, removed the clip, dropped to one knee in front of Galway.

'Alright, boss?' he asked, the evil smile on full wattage. 'How goes it?'

Galway said nothing. Brady clapped him lightly on the shoulder, moved around behind him. Then he slipped the butt of the pro's gun into Galway's hand, closing Galway's fingers around it. The ERU wallah watched, impassive. When Brady finished he stood again, holding the gun by the trigger-guard.

'Take him out. Put him in the van and don't drop him too often. There's a lot of people want to see Detective-Inspector Galway and I want him in good nick for receiving visitors.' He jerked a thumb at Gonzo. 'And get someone in here to look after that.'

They hauled Galway to his feet. He glared at me, a look of pure hatred.

'Remember what I said, chief,' I reminded him. 'No lubrication.'

He spat, a filthy gob that landed squarely on my cheek, and then they were gone. A third ERU wallah came and stood in the doorway, nervous, machine-gun clutched to his chest. I could hear voices outside, orders being barked, doors slamming. Two medics appeared, began tending to Gonzo. They covered his face with an oxygen mask, stuck a needle in his arm, but even I could see it was a lost cause. Gonzo's head was lolling, the pool of blood widening by the second. Brady stood over me as I rubbed at Galway's spittle, plastering it all over the side of my face, unable to take my eyes off Gonzo.

'You'll make Commissioner for this,' I said.

'Aye. And you'll do time.'

'All things considered, I'll take prison any day. You find what you wanted at The Odeon?'

'Pretty much.' He nodded at the Ice Queen's gun. 'That the magic gun?'

'Yeah. Rub the barrel and a genie pops out.'

Gonzo went into a spasm of coughing, spattering the medics with a spray of blood.

'She'd lost a lot of blood, Rigby. Another twenty minutes, maybe, she'd have bled to death.'

'Stop teasing. What about Sheridan?'

'Made a full confession on the spot. Named you as the leader of a gang of dissident Republicans that had kidnapped him and Helen Conway for ransom.'

'Obviously in shock, poor lad.'

'Obviously. The fractured skull wasn't doing him any favours.'

'That confession goes on the record?'

'Has to.'

'So I'm getting a day out in my Sunday best?'

'Let you into court with a mouth like that? Fuck no. The way my report reads, Galway ran the show and plugged his own side when they double-crossed him. Then he came looking for you. When Eddie there bravely tried to protect his brother and sister-in-law, Galway nailed him too. Extortion, drugs, murder . . . Fuck me, Galway won't get out until the anti-Christ arrives.' He paused. 'Whether they'll believe the report is another matter, of course.'

'Of course. What about Joe?'

'The old bloke? Ascended into heaven in a fiery chariot just as we arrived.' He looked at Gonzo. Then: 'You alright, Rigby?'

'Why wouldn't I be?'

He laughed, gruff.

'I'm ten years on the force and I've shot a gun in anger twice. Never came near hitting the target either time and you better believe I'm twice as happy as they were that I didn't.'

'Next time open your eyes.'

'You've just shot your brother, Rigby. You're telling me you can deal with that?'

I looked across at Gonzo. I had an impulse to say something to him before he died, because nothing was surer than Gonzo's dying, this time for real. Nothing came to mind.

'Who's going to deal with it for me if I don't?'

'You're some cold bastard.'

'What do you want, poetry?'

'You killed him, Rigby, your own brother. The papers are going to love that.'

I shrugged. He said: 'Got a brief? If they don't run with my report?'

'No.'

'Get one. If you're stuck, I know some people. They'll tell you what I'm telling you now. Self-defence, he was going for the gun. Better still, he had the gun and you took it off him. You'll get manslaughter at worst, be out in five. Plus, you've apprehended a bent copper while you were at it, saved your wife and child. You'll be a fucking hero.'

I needed a shower, sleep and a smoke, maybe a coffee.

'It's done, Brady. I did it. End of story. I'll take my chances with the way it happened.'

'Big-balls Rigby.'

'Someone had to, Brady. I didn't see you in the queue.'

'You were looking in the wrong queue.' He came to a decision. 'Alright. Forensics will be in so don't touch anything. And I'd get out of here before the press Johnnies get here. For her sake, and the kid.'

'Jesus, Brady. It's Christmas day.'

'Parasites don't take holidays. Which reminds me. Take a holiday yourself.'

'Can't afford it. Conway's a bust, and I haven't had a gig in two months.'

'I'm not talking about the sun. I'm talking about the job. I'd pack it in for a while. There's going to be a lot of pissed-off suits up at the station tomorrow morning.'

'Any ideas what I should do for money?'

'Try politics. You've the smart mouth for it and there's a by-election due.'

He left. I rolled a smoke, hands shaking, watching the medics working on Gonzo until they finally gave up, recorded a time of death. When I was sure he was dead I left.

26

I found Denise on her parents' bed, lights off, crying, cuddling Ben, who was still snuffling. I sat on the edge of the bed, not knowing what to say, smoothing the wrinkled duvet with the palm of my hand.

'You okay?'

She didn't speak.

'Is Ben okay?'

'He's okay.' Her nose sounded blocked. 'I told him you were playing cops and robbers with the big boys. The noise gave him a fright.'

'Me and him both. C'mon, we have to get out of here.'

'What am I going to tell Mam and Dad?'

'That you heard about it on the news, same way as everyone else. That some mad bastards broke in on Christmas Eve, started shooting one another. I don't know, we'll have to make it up as we go along. Worst case scenario, I'm guessing Brendan'll pay for your ticket to Dallas next time.'

She giggled through the tears, took a deep breath, wiping her cheeks with the back of her hand.

'And . . . Gonz?'

I nodded.

'This time for good.'

'He was doing everything you said?'

'That's as far as I know. That's the last couple of days. Fuck knows what he was at for the last four years.'

'When I saw him . . . earlier, when they arrived. Harry, I nearly died.'

'I know the feeling.' I stood up. 'Come on. Get your stuff packed. And for Christ's sake leave those pyjamas behind.'

'Harry?'

'What?'

'I'm sorry, Harry . . .'

'Don't be. If you apologise you'll want to explain and I don't need the gory details. Get packed.'

I sat in the living room until they were ready to go, smoking, looking at Gonzo. The medics were gone, leaving the corpse behind, that and a thick wad of padded cotton wool they'd been using to staunch the flow of blood. The bleeding had stopped by then, and he sat in a black pool that was maybe a couple of inches deep. I felt no remorse for killing him, no regret that he was dead. I felt nothing, numb. All I knew was that the world was one sociopath fewer. He had been my brother but from where I was sitting that wasn't a hanging offence.

The only thing that bothered me was, his screwing Denise was now out in the open, which meant that Ben would probably find out when he was old enough to understand. When that might be I didn't know. I had thirty years on Ben and I still didn't get it.

And then I remembered something. I stubbed the smoke, got up and walked across to Gonzo. Ruffled his hair, bent down, kissed his forehead.

'You play the player, Gonz,' I whispered. 'Not the cards.'

*

Brady stopped me as we left.

'You'll be around? I don't have to take you in?'

'I'll be asleep, Brady. Just don't wake me when you throw me in the wagon.'

'Alright. I'll ring those people.'

'Cheers.'

Dawn was breaking dull beyond the mountains by the time we got away. We drove for home, Ben strapped into the back seat, asleep before we even hit the main road, Denise driving. I rolled a smoke, told her what Brady had said about packing in the job, on the off chance that she might want to fill the silence with something more important.

'And will you?'

'I don't know.'

'But what else can you do?'

'I don't know, something'll come up.' I thought of the feeding frenzy the photos would cause, once the murders hit the air-waves. Even when I subtracted Herbie's cut, the money would still take up a lot of room in the deposit box of whatever bank I decided to favour with my custom. 'I'll worry about it next week. If I wake up.'

She smiled at that, looked across. I didn't have the energy to smile back. Her expression grew serious.

'Harry?'

'Don't, Dee.'

'What you said, Monday night?'

'Jesus, Dee. I'm trying to forget what I did an hour ago.'

'About me having an affair? That you'd kill him and cripple me?'

I didn't look at her.

'Don't read too much into it, Dee. He was going to kill me and take Ben.' I looked out the window, watching the thaw charge down the hillsides, coursing through the ditches. I wasn't sure if she could hear me. I wasn't even sure who it was I was supposed to be talking to. 'Anyway, you're already a cripple,' I said. 'Me too. You're my crutch. I think that's the whole idea.'

She didn't say anything to that. I switched on the stereo, turned away, tried to make myself comfortable, the wound starting to burn again. Closed my eyes but couldn't stop thinking, about Gonzo, panned out on the pool table and holding the eight ball over the pocket because what else can you do when they want you to play with a crooked cue. I thought about Dutchie, sitting at home, hoping I was dead and hoping I wasn't and realising, way too late, that you only ever have a choice in hindsight. I thought about Ben, how he'd have to wait another year for his snowman, wondering about who might help him build it. I thought about Denise, and how she might fare out getting someone to take her on with another man's kid in tow. And I thought too about a dumb blonde answering the door in the middle of the night, shivering, not knowing that the cold was the last thing she would ever feel.

I knew Denise was watching, waiting. I liked that. Not enough to stay, but still.